Unrelenting Love

Banished Saga, Book 5

Ramona Flightner

Grizzly Damsel Publishing
Missoula, Montana

Ramona Flightner/Grizzly Damsel Publishing
P.O. Box 1795
Missoula, MT 59806
www.ramonaflightner.com

Publisher's Note: This is a work of fiction. Names, characters, places, and incidents are a product of the author's imagination. Locales and public names are sometimes used for atmospheric purposes. Any resemblance to actual people, living or dead, or to businesses, companies, events, institutions, or locales is completely coincidental.

Cover Design: Jennifer Quinlan

Book Layout ©2013 BookDesignTemplates.com

Ordering Information:
Quantity sales. Special discounts are available on quantity purchases by corporations, associations, and others. For details, contact the "Special Sales Department" at the address above.

Unrelenting Love/ Ramona Flightner. -- 1st ed.
ISBN 978-1-945609-02-2

DB,

Your insight, your enthusiasm,
And your unwavering belief
In my writing are priceless.
Thank you.

CAST OF CHARACTERS

BOSTON:

Zylphia McLeod- daughter to Delia and Aidan, suffragist and painter,

Aidan McLeod-uncle to the McLeod boys, married to Delia, father to Zylphia, excellent businessman.

Delia McLeod- married to Aidan, mother to Zylphia, still aids the orphanage

Parthena Tyler- Zylphia's friend; excellent pianist, fellow suffragist

Genevieve Tyler- Parthena's second sister, plays the violin

Eudora Tyler- Parthena's third sister

Isabel Tyler- Parthena's youngest sister

Morgan Wheeler- Parthena's nemesis, successful Boston businessman.

Lucas Russell: world-renowned pianist, brother to Savannah, cousin to Clarissa and Colin

Matilda Russell: mother to Lucas and Savannah, aunt to Clarissa, interested in social appearances

Martin Russell: Lucas and Savannah's father, married to Matilda, owns a fine linen shop, *Russell's* in the South End.

Richard McLeod- brother to Gabriel, married to Florence, blacksmith

Florence Butler – married to Richard, used to teach with Clarissa

Sophronia Chickering- suffragist, mentor to the McLeod women

Theodore Goff- Zylphia's beloved, missing in the Great War

Rowena Clement- Zylphia's friend, helps teach her social norms. Suffragist

Owen Hubbard: successful Boston businessman; Zylphia's nemesis since she spurned him

Eugenie Abingdon- Teddy's cousin, a suffragette in England

MONTANA:

Gabriel McLeod- cabinetmaker, married to Clarissa

Clarissa Sullivan McLeod- married to Gabriel, used to work as a teacher and a librarian, suffragist

Jeremy McLeod- cabinetmaker, works with his brother Gabriel at his shop, married to Savannah

Savannah Russell McLeod- married to Jeremy,

Melinda Sullivan McLeod- Savannah and Jeremy's adopted daughter, Colin/ Clarissa/ Patrick's much younger sister

Colin Sullivan-Clarissa and Patrick's brother, blacksmith

Araminta- friend to the McLeods, helps care for their children and clean their homes

Hester Loken- new librarian in town, championed by Mr. Pickens

CHAPTER ONE

Boston, May 1915

The teacups rattled, and the silverware jumped as his fist slammed the tabletop. "Dammit, I forbid you to travel there."

"What makes you think I have to listen to you? I'm an adult. I have free will. I can do as I please."

"When you have your own money, you can do as you please."

"I can't believe you'd hold your fortune over my head, forcing me to remain here against my will."

"Zylphia, Aidan, enough," Delia hissed as she entered the dining room, closing the door behind her to prevent the servants from listening further. "You're only speaking to harm each other, not to communicate."

"I have to try to find him. I can't keep waiting," Zylphia said, her voice faltering as she fought tears.

"Do you think your Teddy would exult at you traversing the perils of the Atlantic, the very Atlantic where ships are sunk weekly by the Germans?" Aidan held up the morning newspaper with its headlines of war and mayhem in France and shook it in Zylphia's direction. "Do you think he'd then relish the thought of you traveling across the channel to France, traipsing from one makeshift hospital to the next, looking for him?" her father demanded, his deep voice filled with desperation.

"I have to do something," Zylphia said, her voice stronger as she thought of her alternate plan.

"So you think to travel from one field hospital to the next, examining each soldier who's unknown, to determine if he's your Teddy? Don't you realize, if he's still alive, what helps him face each day is the knowledge you're far away from the destruction being wrought in those trenches in France? That he doesn't have to worry about you suffering the same fate as those poor wretches on the Lusitania?" Aidan demanded. He slammed his hand down again, shaking off Delia's soothing caress of his shoulder.

Zylphia stiffened, her brilliant blue eyes defiant and angry, shrouding her agony. "Fine. If you won't allow me to travel to Europe, I'm still leaving. I'm going to Washington, DC. To work with Alice Paul."

"That's a fine way to show loyalty to the women of Massachusetts," Aidan snapped. "Abandon them when they're in the throes of their campaign for the vote."

Zylphia glared at him. "I hate you," she yelled before she rose, storming from the room.

Aidan slumped into his chair, resting his head in his palms for a moment. His broad shoulders heaved as he took a deep breath, and he ran a hand over his head, disheveling his salt-and-pepper hair, before reaching back to rub at a sore spot on his shoulder.

"That was well done," Delia said as she fixed herself a cup of tea, having settled in a chair to Aidan's right.

"Don't start."

"I'm not. You're the one who engaged her in this battle of wills. You know as well as I do that she wouldn't travel to Europe." Delia buttered a piece of cold toast, setting it aside as she reached for Aidan's hand.

After a long moment, he clasped her fingers. "The problem is, I don't know that. She's desperate enough right now, engulfed in her grief over her Teddy, that she's unpredictable. I can't say with any certainty what she'd do." Aidan released Delia's hand and scrubbed at his face. "And it terrifies me."

"She'd never sail to Europe," Delia said with a wry smile. "She doesn't have a passport."

"If you think that's what's preventing her from traveling, you're delusional. She's intrepid enough to find a way." Aidan frowned. "Nearly 1,200 died when the Lusitania sank last week, including over 100 Americans. I can't let the same happen to Zee."

"She doesn't really hate you," Delia murmured.

"I know. But it hurts all the same to have her scream that at me." He rubbed at his chest. "I can't bear the thought of any harm coming to her."

"Every day she doesn't know what's happened to Theodore Goff is one where she's being harmed. A part of her exuberance dies." Delia blinked away tears, and Aidan brushed his fingers over her cheek. "There's nothing worse than to see her this sad and to know I can do nothing to help her."

"I feel the same," Aidan whispered. "All I seem to do is make her angrier."

Delia smiled at him. "I'm not sure that's such an awful thing. If she's angry, at least she's still feeling. I'd hate for our Zee to become an emotionless woman."

Aidan's shoulders slumped. "If she doesn't hear anything about Goff soon, I fear what will happen to her."

***

Zylphia sat on a comfortable camelback settee in her friend Parthena Tyler's private sitting room. Bright light shone through two tall windows, and the cream-colored curtains rippled occasionally with the day's gentle breeze. She waited for Parthena to finish playing the piece by Mozart, barely clapping when she finished. Zylphia rose, wandering the room as her agitation mounted.

"Zee, why are you here today?" Parthena asked as she continued to tinker at the piano.

"I had another argument with my father." She stood in front of a painting of a river valley lit at dawn. She calmed as she lost herself in the brilliant colors and strong brushstrokes, imagining how the artist created such a work.

"You know he only acts as he does because he cares for you," Parthena said, interrupting Zylphia's reverie as she studied the painting.

"He's forbidden me to travel to Europe."

"Thank God. You know it was a crack-brained idea. I'd hate for harm to befall you. Or for you to become stranded over there until the end of this wretched conflict." Parthena began to play a soothing song, much like a lullaby.

Zylphia approached the piano bench and sat on a chair next to it. "I can't handle doing nothing. I have to do something. Teddy's somewhere over there, missing. Most likely wounded. Why can't my father understand that I must ..."

Parthena waited a moment, pausing in playing the piano for a moment, widening her eyes as though coaxing Zee to say more. As only silence ensued, Parthena said, "Even you can't finish that sentence because it's ludicrous. You won't find him if the British Army hasn't. You'll only bring yourself more grief." She reached forward and clasped Zylphia's hand. "Now, what we can do is focus on how to ensure that the women of Massachusetts have success in their goal for enfranchisement, just like the women of Montana last year."

Zylphia half smiled. "If there's one thing I learned in Montana, it was that the women canvassed every household. No distance was too great."

"Can you imagine visiting every home in Boston?"

Zylphia groaned as she collapsed against the back of her chair. "No, I can't. But that's what we must do to win. We must show all women that they are important, that their voices matter. And we need to show their husbands the same."

"The next meeting is a few weeks from now. We should discuss this plan with the members of the committee."

Zylphia shook her head in frustration. "I've already spoken with many of them privately, and they think it's not necessary." She stared at the painting on the wall again. "When I asked them why they'd sent me to Montana to learn how to be successful if they wouldn't listen to my advice, they admitted it was simply to keep Sophronia happy."

"Do you mean that they never intended to heed your suggestions?" Parthena slammed her hands onto the piano keys, making a jarring noise.

"Yes. One member even said nothing was to be learned from such a backwater state and that I insulted her and the committee in thinking I could teach them anything."

Parthena gasped.

"When I confronted Sophie, she admitted she knew it would be a struggle to have them listen to my suggestions, but she'd hoped they'd change their opinion." Zylphia sighed. "I'd always thought I was tricking the NAWSA members here in Massachusetts by being in Montana when I really supported Alice Paul and her nonviolent tactics. I guess the joke was on me because they never wanted my input." Zylphia's shoulders slumped as she thought about the National American Woman Suffrage Association.

Parthena squinted. "And I'm sure they were only too glad when your father footed the bill."

Zylphia nodded her head in agreement. "He considered it a worthwhile donation and he was delighted I could visit my family there." She sobered further. "I hurt him, P.T." She paused as she thought through her conversation with her father. "I told him that I hated him."

"Zee, you never did." Parthena turned to face Zylphia.

She nodded. "I wanted to hurt him as much as I was hurting. I'm so accustomed to him granting me my every wish that, when he doesn't, I act like a petulant child."

"Even though he's protecting you from yourself."

"Oh, P.T., what am I going to do? There are no words for how I ache to see Teddy again. I dream of him speaking to me. I hear his voice in my dreams, and I don't want to wake because I know, when I do, he'll be gone." She shared a forlorn smile with her friend. "Thank you for listening. I can't imagine it's been much fun, hearing me moan about Teddy these last months."

"I look forward to the day when you can rejoice over him. I refuse to give up hope until we know for certain what's happened."

Zylphia nodded. "I try to remain hopeful, but it's difficult with all the horrible news coming from France."

"I'd tell you not to read the papers, but I know you wouldn't listen to me." P.T. sobered. "Are you attending the Wheeler soiree tomorrow?"

Zylphia frowned. "I'd thought to send my regrets. Why?"

"I need you there, Zee." Parthena's hazel eyes clouded with trepidation. "There's to be some sort of announcement, and I'm nervous."

***

Zylphia crept into her father's study. Bookcases lined two walls, and the third held a painting of the Boston Harbor at dawn she'd painted for him a few years ago. A large clipper ship, partially obscured by the dawn's mist, approached its dock, while smaller vessels floated on the calm waters. Her throat tightened as she recalled how he always showed her painting to all guests to his library, as though she were a great master of the craft.

She paused, watching her father. He sat behind his large mahogany desk with his shoulders stooped and his head in his hands. After a moment, he slammed his hand onto his desk and reared his head back to stare at the ceiling.

"I'm sorry, Father," Zylphia whispered.

His head whipped toward her voice, his face filled with anguish.

She eased the heavy door shut behind her.

"What are you sorry for, Zee?"

"I don't hate you. I could never hate you." Her whispered voice was tinged with embarrassment.

He held out a hand to her as he rose. She approached him, and he pulled her into his strong arms, cradling her against his shoulder as she fought her battle against her rising sobs. "I know you don't, my darling daughter. But thank you."

"I hurt, more than I knew I could hurt," Zee stuttered out around her sobs. "I wanted you to hurt too."

"I know." He kissed her head. "I've done the same." He sighed. "I'm sorry to be at odds with you, but I can't support you traveling to Europe. Not now."

Zylphia eased away, moving toward one of the comfortable chairs in front of his desk, but not sitting. Aidan followed her and leaned against his desk, watching her with concern. "I know. I realized how foolish I was being when I spoke with P.T. today."

Aidan smiled, relief shining in his blue eyes. "Thank God she was able to help you see sense where I failed."

"I wouldn't have been so angry with you if I hadn't known you were right."

Aidan chuckled. "I'm a McLeod too. I know how hard it can be to admit when I'm wrong." He sobered. "I know you miss your Teddy. That you are worried about him. I would do anything to ease you of this torment, Zee."

She nodded, brushing at her cheeks as a few more tears escaped. "Thank you." She took a deep breath. "For now I realize you are correct. I must focus on the battle for the vote here in Massachusetts. It is a worthwhile cause and will aid in distracting me."

"You also have your marvelous painting talent," he said with pride shining in his eyes.

Zylphia flushed. "I'm finding it difficult to paint anything right now. It's as though all my artistic inclination has disappeared."

"I know it will return. You're too talented to never paint again. Be patient, and be willing to spend hours in your studio when your muse returns."

She leaned into his embrace a moment. "Thank you, Father. Thank you for supporting me in all I do, especially my suffragist pursuits."

"I hope it will provide some sort of solace as your work intensifies while you struggle toward your goal here." He clasped her hand. "I know what it is to be separated from the one I love, Zee. I pray you will be reunited soon."

CHAPTER TWO

Dear Miss McLeod,

I pray this letter finds you well and send my warm regards to you across the Atlantic. I learned from my aunt, dear Theodore's mother, that you were a particular friend of his. I wanted to write to offer what support I could as we await news of our dear Teddy.

When Teddy was with us last summer, he seemed out of sorts. He's always been a favorite of mine, most likely because he's forever insisted on doing what he desires. His defiance in returning to Boston after university showed me that I could also act in an equally independent manner. Although my parents have been disheartened and surprised by my decisions, I took comfort in knowing Theodore also refused to bow to his parents' expectations, as well as Grandfather's.

Teddy never bent to my grandparents' will until he agreed to join the army. I'm uncertain why he did so. I do know I've never seen my grandparents as proud as they were that day. It was as though, by seeing my cousin in his uniform, my grandfather had a miraculous recovery after having suffered so severely from his apoplexy.

Keep faith, Miss McLeod, that dear Teddy will return to us. Stories of miraculous reunions are recounted every day in England. I pray our family will soon experience such a miracle.

Yours Sincerely,

Eugenie Abingdon

Zylphia stared at the postmark, dated before the Lusitania sank. She set aside the letter and curled onto the tufted red settee in her studio. She recalled her conversations with Teddy, remembering he had mentioned an English suffragette cousin who'd been imprisoned the year before and had lived through a hunger strike. "Eugenie," she murmured.

Galvanized, she rose and approached a blank canvas. She picked up a fresh palette, and—rather than the gray, black, and dark greens she'd painted with in recent months—she placed splotches of bright colors the palette instead. A street scene soon took shape, the colors of the buildings melding with the large maple trees granting shade. Flowers in window boxes and along the sidewalk's path formed a riotous kaleidoscope of color. She frowned as she studied the painting, belatedly recognizing it from her life.

She set down her palette, picking up a cloth to swipe at her hands. A harried knock interrupted her reverie, and she called out, "Come in."

Delia poked her head in, dressed formally after making calls that afternoon. "May I?" she asked.

"Of course, Mother. But be careful with that beautiful dress. I never know where I've accidentally splattered paint."

Delia moved toward Zylphia's largely completed painting, her gaze roving over it with wonder. "Oh, Zee. This is tremendous." She reached forward, uncaring of Zylphia's dirty hands, and gripped one. "It's such a relief to see you painting in color again."

"In Paris—"

"I couldn't give a hoot what they are painting in Paris now. You need to paint what calls to you. Not what some other artist is painting and calling art. This is beautiful."

"Teddy and I walked a street like this, the fall we knew each other," Zylphia whispered.

"Then you must keep it." She glanced around Zee's studio, at the stacks of finished paintings leaning against a wall. "I still believe you should have a showing. Your art shouldn't remain hidden."

Zylphia took a deep breath. "I think you are correct. I want more than to have my paintings piled on top of each other here." She bit her lip. "Do you think Father would help me?"

Delia beamed. "He'd only be too happy. I'm sure, with all the people he knows, he has a contact in the art world."

"Thank you, Mother," Zylphia whispered as she leaned forward and embraced her mother, careful to only lean against her and not place her dirty hands against her mother's fine dress. "What brought you to my studio?"

"Are you planning to attend the Wheeler soiree tonight?"

Zylphia's eyes bulged as she glanced outside, noting the long shadows. "Oh, no. I have to change. I promised P.T. that I wouldn't miss it."

Delia smiled wryly. "I thought that might be the case. Let the painting settle for the night, and return to it tomorrow, darling. You must hurry if we are to arrive within a reasonable hour."

Zylphia set her paintbrushes in turpentine and departed from the room.

***

Delia remained in Zylphia's studio, battling tears as she reached forward to trace the vibrant brushstrokes on the drying canvas. "You're coming back to us," she whispered.

***

Zylphia entered the Wheeler mansion on Commonwealth Avenue and attempted to act aloof to the grandeur of her surroundings, left largely as they were when the elder Wheeler, a widower, still lived. The mansion was an homage to a French chateau in cream-colored granite with two black slate-covered turrets, large bow-fronted windows on either side of the immense entryway and small gargoylelike statues along the drainpipes.

She left her light wrap with a maid, accepted a glass of champagne from a passing servant and moved through the rooms on the lower floor, looking for her friends. As she rounded a corner, she bumped into Owen Hubbard, sloshing champagne onto his pristine tuxedo. "I beg your pardon," she murmured.

He laughed. "I'd expect no better from you, Miss McLeod."

"Why is that?" she asked. She cringed as those nearby were alerted to her distress by his booming voice. As rapacious as vultures, their inquisitive gazes delighted in her discomfort and fed on her disquiet.

"You've never learned how to move in polite society."

"Although you've moved in society for years, Hubbard," a man said, his deep voice sounding behind her, "you've never mastered the art of accepting defeat."

A firm hand gripped her elbow, and she met the supportive gaze of the evening's host, Morgan Wheeler.

"If you would do me the honor, Miss McLeod?" He motioned toward the dance floor where the musicians played the first strains of a waltz.

She nodded, raising her head as she walked past Owen without further word or notice on her part. She placed her champagne coupe on the tray of a passing servant and turned to face Morgan on the dance floor.

"I'm surprised he still harbors such resentment against you, Miss McLeod," Morgan murmured as he drew her to him. He smiled as she moved with increasing fluidity and focused on their conversation.

"I think he hates being thwarted." She gasped an apology as she tripped on his feet.

He stifled a chuckle as his tight hold prevented her from falling and steered her in the right direction. "He also dislikes how you chose another man over him." Morgan nodded toward someone standing on the side of the ballroom. "And he hated losing your father's influence."

"I'm worth more than my father's influence," Zylphia scoffed.

Morgan watched her with a flare of respect in his gaze. The waltz ended, and he escorted her to the side of the ballroom far from Owen Hubbard and his friends. "Thank you, Miss McLeod."

She nodded and smiled. As he faded into the crowd, Zylphia backed away from the dance floor.

"Why are you trying to disappear into the masses?" a man with a familiar voice asked behind her.

An inquisitive frown already on her face, she spun to face him. She beamed as she barely stifled her squeal of delight. "Lucas!" She gripped his arm, remembering at the last minute how she should not hug a male not truly related to her at a ball. "How long have you been in Boston? What are you doing here?"

"I was invited, in a roundabout way, and thought it sounded interesting." His amber eyes shone with amusement to find himself in a fancy Boston ballroom. He ran a hand through his brown hair, cut slightly longer than fashionable, before he tugged on the bottom of his tux's coat.

"I've been back here for a few weeks. Settling in as I can't travel to Europe right now."

"I'm amazed you'd willingly come to one of these events. Savannah always wrote about how much you hate these things." Zylphia swatted him on his arm. "I can't believe you've been here so long and never notified us. You'll have to come to dinner soon."

He flushed. "If you must know, I need to be seen among the elite of society with the hopes that they continue to support my music. And I'd love to come to dinner and see your family."

"I'd think your music would speak for itself," Zylphia said as she squeezed his hand.

"Well, rumors abound about how my penchant for composing and sequestering myself away are my manner of masking my increasing battle against lunacy."

Zylphia gasped. "Who would say such a thing?"

"Oh, I have my ideas," Lucas murmured as he smiled impersonally to the woman joining their group. He nodded as though he were to leave them, but Zylphia gripped his hand and shook her head.

"Zee, what were you doing dancing with that impossible man?" Parthena demanded.

"He's not impossible. Mr. Wheeler saved me from an uncomfortable situation with Mr. Hubbard. P.T., I want—"

"I tell you, Zee, he's up to something, acting agreeable when we know he's onerous." Parthena scanned the room as though searching him out.

"P.T., quit worrying about him. I want you to meet my cousin, of sorts." Zylphia winked at Lucas. "Parthena Tyler, this is Lucas Russell."

Parthena stilled, mouth slightly agape as she beheld Lucas. "You're Lucas Russell?"

Lucas nodded, a humorous smile flitting across his lips. "Yes."

Parthena's expression was lit with a transcendent joy. "I've dreamed of meeting you. I collect all your sheet music."

Lucas nodded with understanding. "You're a pianist too."

"Of sorts. I'd never compare myself to your grand talent."

"I'm sure you're too modest," Lucas said with a wry smile.

"She is. She's a wonderful pianist," Zylphia said, looping her arm through Parthena's in a show of solidarity.

"Perhaps we could meet some day and I could hear you play," Lucas said. "If my cousin wouldn't mind also attending to act as chaperone."

"No, I think it's a marvelous idea," Zylphia said. She stifled a shriek as Parthena's mother approached, wrenching the two of them apart.

Parthena obeyed her mother's silent command and followed her toward the central part of the ballroom where the majority of attendees now mingled. Zylphia belatedly realized the music had stopped.

"I like your friend," Lucas murmured as he watched Parthena's retreat.

"She's independent and willful, like me," Zylphia whispered.

"Like Clarissa and Sav," Lucas said with a warm smile.

Zylphia studied him for a moment as she watched his gaze track Parthena's movements. "Why would you be interested in her? You hate society events."

"Marrying into society would only help me and my career. Marrying someone who has an appreciation for music, and who would understand when I disappear for hours and days on end when I compose ..." He shook his head a few times. "That would be wholly unexpected and priceless."

"I doubt her parents would countenance such a match." Zylphia turned to see her friend standing between her parents, Parthena's expression remote as though her body were present but her spirit elsewhere.

"Nothing is impossible," Lucas whispered, quieting when Parthena's father raised his arms to garner the full attention of the room.

"My dear friends." He held up his hands as the room quieted. "It is wonderful to be among such esteemed friends this evening. I would like to thank Mr. Wheeler for granting me the opportunity to speak for a few moments tonight." Parthena's father beamed. "This is a wondrous occasion, and I'm sure many of you are curious as to the promised announcement." He puffed out his chest with pride to the point the buttons on his gaudy puce waistcoat almost burst. He glanced around the room, no doubt relishing being the center of attention.

"Oh, no," Zylphia whispered. She gripped Lucas's arm in her distress.

"It is my greatest pleasure to announce that, one month hence, my dear daughter Miss Parthena Tyler will marry our close friend Mr. Morgan Wheeler."

Morgan appeared next to Parthena as the announcement was made, Parthena's mother moving aside at the last moment to prevent Parthena from bolting. He lifted Parthena's stiff hand, kissing it. Parthena stood stock-still, her eyes rounded with shock.

"Damn," Lucas muttered. He gripped Zylphia's arm, preventing her from rushing to her friend. "Don't make any more of a scene," he breathed into her ear.

As the crowd applauded, and a few men catcalled, Zylphia met her friend's horrified gaze.

***

"Relax, dammit," Morgan hissed as he leaned forward to kiss her cheek.

Parthena remained as stiff as a board.

"When I back away, smile."

Parthena blinked rapidly, forcing a smile as well-wishers surrounded them. Morgan fended off questions about their courtship, downplaying their previous tumultuous interactions, including the New Year's Ball where Parthena had pushed him into a fountain.

He maintained a firm grip on her arm, bolstering her as her trembling became more pronounced. He glared toward a group of women gossiping loudly about the couple's haste to marry and said, "We've always planned to marry. We decided we'd waited long enough."

Zylphia approached with Rowena, and they enfolded Parthena in warm embraces. Parthena shook almost violently now. Zylphia backed up and whispered to Morgan. "She must leave with us. You don't want to cause a scene where she faints and exposes the two of you to even more undesirable gossip."

He frowned but nodded. Morgan called to a friend, moving away from Parthena and granting her two friends the opportunity to usher Parthena into a small alcove hidden by a screen, away from prying eyes. Parthena collapsed onto a wooden bench, tears coursing down her cheeks as she gasped for air. Rowena stroked a hand down her arm while Zylphia rubbed her friend's back and shoulders.

Zylphia stiffened while she listened to the women chattering on the other side of the screen.

"You know the only reason he'd marry her is because she's in some sort of difficult situation, and her father is paying him handsomely to act the gentleman," a woman with a nasal voice intoned.

"Well, if it's not for that, her father certainly paid him. How else was he to rid himself of such a troublesome daughter?" her friend responded with a snicker.

"Zee," Rowena whispered, grabbing Zylphia's hand and holding her in place. Rowena shook her head silently, her gaze entreating Zylphia to hold her temper.

The gossiping females grew silent, the sound of their heels indicating they'd moved away. Muted voices permeated the space behind the screen, with those conversations indistinct and free of any further barbs.

"You can't fight my battles for me, Zee. I can't even fight them for myself," Parthena said on a stuttering sigh as her tears abated.

Rowena and Zylphia huddled around Parthena, kneeling on the floor in front of her. The trio of friends spoke barely above a whisper, allowing them to remain undetected in the alcove. "Had you no idea what your father had planned to announce this evening?" Rowena asked.

"He said he had an important announcement," Parthena said. "I thought he would announce a business merger. Numerous lawyers have been in and out of the house this week, like always when he's in an acquisitive mood." She closed her eyes and fought a shudder. "I never realized he was intent on disposing of his problematic daughter."

"You're not being sent to your death," Zylphia whispered.

"You don't understand. Morgan's not like the men in your family," Parthena said, her usual glow and vitality dimmed in her gaze.

"Refuse to marry him," Zylphia said with a defiant tilt to her chin.

Rowena gaped at Zylphia a moment before reluctantly nodding her head in agreement.

"You know I can't," Parthena said, an air of resignation shrouding her. "I must honor my father and my family."

"No, P.T. You must honor yourself first," Zylphia argued, clasping P.T.'s hand.

"Give her time to think about what just happened," Rowena soothed. "Besides, no matter what she does decide later, she should now reappear to forestall any further gossip."

The sound of a throat clearing on the other side of the screen brought Parthena out of her momentary stupor. She rose, swiping a hand over her skirts before she brushed at her cheeks and then pinched them to give them color.

"You look beautiful, as always," Zylphia soothed. She poked her head around the screen to see Lucas lounging against the nearby pillar, acting as a sentry.

He winked at her and then moved toward a group of women glancing in the alcove's direction. While he distracted them, Zylphia and her friends returned to the ballroom.

Parthena approached Morgan, quelling a shudder as she reached out a hand to touch his arm. She gripped it and smiled at those who approached to wish them well. She bantered with a few of the gentlemen and evaded intrusive questions from the women. Morgan nodded his head in encouragement before leading her to the dance floor.

As Parthena continued to smile while he spun her around the room, she whispered into his ear, "Why are you doing this?"

"There is no reason to worry yourself at this time about my intentions, except to know they are honorable."

She fought a glower, her smile becoming more brittle the longer they danced. At the last strain of the waltz, she stepped away as though to bolt from the dance floor. He gripped her around her waist to prevent any sudden movement. "No, Parthena. I refuse to allow you to make a scene or humiliate me in any way."

"Of course. Social respectability must always be maintained," Parthena rasped. She felt Morgan stiffen as he glared at a person watching them from the side of the ballroom. "What has you so incensed?"

"I'm surprised Lucas Russell was invited tonight. I don't remember including him on the guest list."

"Why should you be upset that the preeminent pianist of our city decided to favor us with his presence tonight?"

Morgan scoffed at Parthena. "I doubt he's as talented as they say. Besides, if he were as gifted as you declare he is, I'm surprised he doesn't wish to speak with you. After all, you proclaim to be proficient at the same instrument."

Parthena stiffened further under his hold as he tucked her arm in his, his hand like a manacle over hers, preventing any freedom of movement. Parthena grimaced, no longer able to maintain the fiction of joy or ease at being in his arms. "I am more than proficient, although I cannot pretend that I have near his talent." She glared at Morgan. "As for why he hasn't approached me, I assume it is because he has good manners, unlike many here, and does not wish to intrude after our announcement."

"Offering us congratulations is not intruding," Morgan said as he nodded at an acquaintance and shared a few moments of polite conversation with a prominent banker.

Parthena stood next to Morgan, smiling in a vapid manner and nodding her head when she thought it appropriate, willing the evening to end.

***

Lucas paced his small living quarters, the lights from the low lamps casting shadows on the walls and failing to brighten the room. The open window allowed a hint of a breeze to enter as the evening slowly cooled after a warm, humid day in late May. At the nearly inaudible knock at his door, he strode to it and flung it open. "Finally," he murmured, as the woman slipped inside. The door *clicked* shut behind her, and he flipped the lock.

She lowered the cloak concealing her face and shook her head at Lucas as he reached for her. "No, we have to talk."

"Dammit, did you know they would make that announcement tonight? It took all my ability to act as though I were happy." He traced a hand down her cloak until he grasped her hand and gave it a gentle squeeze. "As though I were meeting you for the first time."

"I don't know what to do, Lucas."

"You'll marry me, Parthena," he said, moving forward to clasp her face with both his hands, pushing tendrils of hair off her face and forehead. "You can't marry Wheeler. He's not your equal."

"In that, I'm afraid you're wrong. He's my equal in every way that matters." She bit her trembling lip as her eyes filled.

"Not in the ways that are truly important. Not in your spirit, your passions." He traced a thumb over her eyebrow.

"Why didn't you tell Zee that you already knew me?" Parthena whispered.

"I promised you that I wouldn't." He continued to stroke a thumb over her cheek, the stiffness leaving his shoulders as he saw her relax with his gentle caress. "I would never break a promise to you."

"Everyone breaks promises, Lucas. You will one day." She gently broke away from him and moved farther into his living space. "Do you think Zee believed that we weren't acquainted?"

"She's so focused on her worries for Teddy that she has little to spare for those around her. If it had been the old Zee, we wouldn't have stood a chance. As it was, I think I fooled her." He closed his eyes. "I hate lying to those I love."

Parthena nodded, tears finally escaping and pouring down her cheeks. "I'm sorry. I should never have sought you out."

"Never regret the time we've had together. The past few weeks—" Lucas broke off and shook his head. "I want you in my life, Thena."

"I don't know what to do."

"He won't want you. Not when he realizes you aren't ..." He broke off at her entreating gaze. Lucas ran a hand through his hair. "I'm sorry, Thena. I never meant for us to become so entangled."

She half smiled, sniffling as she fought more tears. "I know. I'm the one who barged in here, demanding to meet you and learn from you. I was desperate not to miss my opportunity for your tutelage."

Lucas dropped his hands and moved into his small living room, leaning one hip against the edge of his piano that took up over half the space. "If I remember correctly, little musical tutoring occurred."

Parthena blushed, and her mournful partial smile transformed into one of mischief and pleasure. "Of course you remember correctly. Although I believe you fail to recall that I seduced you, so you have little to apologize for." She wandered to the piano bench and sat on it, her gaze unfocused. "It seems long ago, yet it was only recently when I forced myself into your rooms. Although I wouldn't say you never gave me piano lessons."

Lucas's smile faded. "It's all I should have done." He sighed, pinching the bridge of his nose. "I must speak with your father, explain to him that you will marry me."

"Don't approach him, not yet," she pleaded. "I must determine why he's intent on my marrying Mr. Wheeler."

Lucas stiffened at her rejection of his marriage proposal, although it had been oblique. "I agree to a few days' delay. Nothing more."

"Promise me that you won't speak with him without my approval." Her hazel eyes shone with desperation.

He frowned before shaking his head ruefully. "As I just swore, I'd never break a promise to you. You drive a hard bargain, Thena. But, yes, I promise. I hope you know what you're asking of me." He paused. "Of us."

She rose and pushed herself into his embrace. He sighed with momentary contentment to feel her in his arms again. After he kissed her softly on the top of her head, he murmured, "This won't be enough, Thena." He contented himself with holding her as she succumbed to her tears in his arms.

***

Zylphia roamed the sitting room, tracing the edge of a cream-colored curtain that fluttered in the early June breeze. A piano sat to one side of the room, while two chairs and a small settee upholstered in red velvet were nearer to the two open windows. She glanced toward Lucas who stared at Parthena's collection of sheet music. He approached the small piano, his fingers stroking the tops of the keys without pressing down. His gaze distant, a smile of contentment lit his expression.

"Play something while we wait," Zylphia urged.

"It's not polite to play on another's piano without the owner's invitation." He continued his caress of the keys.

"Not everyone feels as you do about pianos, Lucas. Play something if you're moved to." Zylphia sat in a chair in expectation as he settled on the bench in front of the piano.

Parthena burst into the room, flushed and slightly disheveled. The door shut behind her with a resounding *click*, and she rushed into her sitting room. "You came." She shared a long look with Lucas.

"Of course we came," Zylphia said, her gaze puzzled at her friend's surprised tone. She stilled as she watched the silent communication between Parthena and Lucas.

"I'm greatly interested in hearing you play," Lucas said, rising from the seat in front of the piano. He motioned for Parthena to take the bench and dragged an ottoman from a far corner of the room.

"What should I play?" Parthena asked.

"Your favorite piece," Lucas said. "Whatever brings you joy."

Parthena smiled, her first real smile since she had entered the sitting room and since her father's announcement. She began to play a slow, lilting piece.

Lucas settled on the ottoman and closed his eyes as he listened. In certain places he frowned or squinted his eyes, but his expression was always one of delight.

Parthena ceased playing, and Lucas sighed with contentment. "That was beautiful."

"I'm certain you would have played it in a different manner," Parthena said.

"I would have failed to evoke the sensitivity and subtlety of the piece," Lucas said. "You have a gift, Miss Tyler." He rose, and she scooted over on the bench.

He played the same song, and Zylphia heard subtle differences in his performance. Whereas Parthena rushed notes together, when Lucas played, the notes were distinct, yet lyrical. Zylphia closed her eyes, beginning to understand the difference between an expert player and a master.

She heard Lucas murmuring to Parthena as he played and her quiet words of agreement. He responded to her questions, and they moved from one piece to the next. Zylphia leaned back in her chair, lost to the music.

The parlor door crashed open. Fingers stumbled on the keys, forming a discordant racket rather than lyrical harmony as Parthena's father roared, "Get away from my daughter!"

"Father!" Parthena exclaimed, rising from her seat next to Lucas.

"I thought you understood all your piano nonsense was forbidden now you are to marry Mr. Wheeler," her father said, his eyes flashing with ire.

"I'm sorry to have caused any discord between you and your daughter, sir," Lucas said, rising and moving from the piano. "However, I believe she has a true talent that should not be wasted."

"You will not entice her from the man she is to marry."

"Of course not," Lucas said with a wry smile. "I can see what joy her upcoming nuptials bring."

Parthena and Zylphia flinched as her father slammed shut the door to prevent the servants from hearing anything further to share as gossip.

He stalked into the room. "Do you think I don't know who you are? What you've already attempted to do?" Mr. Tyler asked. "Do you think you will wreak havoc on my family as is your family's propensity?"

"I believe you are mistaken, sir. My family members are all respectable."

Mr. Tyler snapped his finger at his daughter and pointed at his side.

Parthena rose, walking to him.

"She isn't some animal, trained to follow your commands," Zylphia hissed as she rose.

"No, she is a daughter, here to do as I say for as long as she is unmarried and a horrific expense."

"You have no right to disregard her desires. She has rights, like any man," Zylphia said, fisting her hands with futile rage as she saw her friend's momentary joy leach away.

"You are Zylphia McLeod. The woman so unnatural you caused the most important financier of this town to flee from you." He laughed with malicious glee when he saw Zylphia pale. "It seems a war was preferable to remaining in your company."

"How dare you speak about Te—Mr. Goff—in such a manner." Zylphia instinctively moved toward Lucas.

"I wonder if Parthena would want to remain your friend if she realized it's your fault she has to marry Mr. Wheeler?" When Zylphia shared a confused look with Parthena, Mr. Tyler laughed again. "Yes, I lost thousands when Goff left town, and now I must look to those such as Mr. Wheeler to replenish the family coffers."

"I'd hardly call your ineptitude with your own finances my fault," Zylphia scoffed.

"As for you, Mr. Russell, I'd thank you for keeping your distance from my daughter. She has no need of your influence."

"My influence would be to encourage her talent as a wonderful pianist," Lucas said, his voice soft but underlaid with steel.

"How do I know you won't warp her sensibilities? That you won't encourage her to act in as shameless and criminal way as your sister?" He smiled with gleeful maliciousness. "You might like to believe her infamous actions have been forgotten, but they never will be."

Lucas stiffened with Mr. Tyler's effrontery. "My sister defended herself from a man who treated her in a brutal manner."

"That is what your family has claimed. However, I know that whenever that Chickering woman is involved, things are not always as they appear."

"Would you like to see the scar from where he shot me?" Lucas asked. "For not only did he almost kill my sister before she escaped the violence of her daily life with him, he shot my father and me the night he died."

Lucas began to unbutton his waistcoat, his cheeks flushed with his agitation.

"You will cease disrobing this instant in my home, sir!"

Zylphia giggled at Lucas's impudence and Mr. Tyler's discomfort. Lucas stilled his movements before settling his gaze on a detached Parthena. "Is that what you wish on your daughter? A marriage where her spirit is eroded from her? Maybe not with fists or violence but with a quiet condemnation of all she values?"

Parthena's bottom lip quivered as she fought tears.

"She deserves better than that, sir. No matter how much money you've lost." Lucas watched Mr. Tyler with abject scorn in his gaze. "Nothing is worth losing your daughter's happiness." Lucas nodded at Mr. Tyler, gripped Zylphia's hand, and pushed past Parthena and her father as he flung open the sitting room door, his boot heels clicking on the marble floor.

***

Lucas stormed from the Tyler mansion, Zylphia's long legs allowing her to keep up with his rapid pace. They strode down Commonwealth Avenue and crossed into the Public Garden. He slowed his pace as others strolling through the garden noted their frenetic movement. "Damn that man," Lucas muttered.

"I don't know what can be done for P.T.," Zylphia murmured. She smiled at a passing matron, a woman who habitually frowned at Zylphia at balls. She nodded at another, a woman vaguely familiar from a recent suffragist gathering.

Zylphia grabbed his arm before he stormed down a shady side path in the garden. She then prevented him from plowing into a woman pushing a bassinette. "Lucas, why are you this upset? I have the sense you aren't telling me something." Her hold on his arm tightened as her gaze raced over the occupants in the garden but was distant, as though reexamining recent scenes. "You already knew Parthena. All of this was for show."

Lucas flinched at the accusation in her voice. "Not now, Zee."

"Tell me, Lucas. Did you really think me so stupid that I wouldn't figure it out?"

"No, I had hoped you would remain so focused on Teddy and your suffragist activities that you'd continue to ignore the more clandestine activities of your friends." He shared a desperate look with her. "Please, leave it be."

"No, not when you're as miserable as she is." Her grip on his arm lessened and became soothing. "Why don't you proclaim your intentions for her?"

Lucas ignored her question. "Are you still friends with Mrs. Chickering?"

"Of course."

"Come then," Lucas said, wending his way through the garden paths toward Beacon Street.

"We can't call now," Zylphia protested.

"Of course we can. I'll charm her with some music," Lucas said with a smile and a wink. "Besides, if she's the same as I remember from years ago, she'll be worried about your Miss Tyler." He approached Sophronia's front door and rapped on it.

He nodded at the butler who opened the door, smiling his understanding as they were ushered into the front hall while the butler determined if Mrs. Chickering was at home to receive them.

After a few moments, they were led upstairs to Sophie, relaxing in her informal parlor at the back of the house. "Had I realized you meant to call, I would have had the staff prepare tea," Sophie said.

Lucas beamed at her, bending to kiss her on her cheek, his informality belying a close relationship with her.

"How are you, my dear boy?" she asked as she tapped him on his cheek.

"Well enough."

"Although your transition home hasn't been as smooth as you'd hoped," Sophie said in her characteristic scratchy voice, her aquamarine eyes shining with perceptiveness.

He smiled with fondness at her. "You always know the gossip before it's even happened." He sobered. "No, it hasn't gone as I'd expected, but I'm hopeful it will all resolve soon."

"You know what you must do," Sophie said. She shared a long look with Lucas, who nodded reluctantly. "However, I am curious as to what could bring you and my Zylphia here today." Sophie frowned as she beheld Zylphia's worried expression. "It's that Tyler girl, isn't it?"

"Of course. We had a horrible run-in with her father today," Zylphia said, collapsing on a chair beside Sophie.

Lucas paced in front of the dormant fireplace. "He heard Miss Tyler and me playing the piano and became irate," Lucas said.

"I should think that would be one of life's greatest pleasures, to hear the two of you play together," Sophie said. She harrumphed when Zylphia nodded her agreement.

"He was horrible, Sophie," Zylphia said. "Bringing up Savannah's scandal, saying that Lucas was a terrible influence for Parthena. He also said it was my fault P.T. has to marry Mr. Wheeler because I forced Teddy to flee."

"I always knew that man was pea-brained, and this proves it. He thinks to shackle his eldest daughter, the only one with any real gumption, to that ill-suited Morgan for money."

"It is the way in your class," Lucas said.

Sophie slammed down her hand on the edge of her chair. "When the girl has no sense and no desire for anything different, maybe. However, I refuse to believe that a woman must marry a man solely because her father is forcing her to do so."

"What can she do, Sophie?" Zylphia asked. "Without her father's support, she'll have no money, nothing."

"She knows she could come to me, but she never would because she wouldn't want to cause a rift in the family." Sophronia raised a speculative gaze at Lucas. "You should marry her."

Lucas shook his head. "No, I'm afraid I can't."

"Why not? It's perfect. You both love the piano, and you said yourself how she reminds you of Sav and Rissa," Zylphia said.

Lucas sat in a chair and shook his head. He met Sophronia's too-knowing gaze. "I'd love to marry her. It would be an honor to marry her. But she doesn't want to marry me."

"What?" Zylphia gasped, her mouth opening and closing as she attempted to form words and then decided to remain silent as she waited to hear what more he had to say.

"I thought you said you needed a wife who didn't bring scandal. Absconding with Parthena after that ghastly announcement would bring a notoriety not often seen in Boston," Sophie said, alluding to a private conversation they'd recently had.

"I know. I don't care. She sees me, not the famous pianist. However, she doesn't want me, and I have to accept that." Lucas ran a hand through his hair, looking away from them as though to hide his internal anguish.

"Lucas ..."

"Listen, Zee, she doesn't want me. She forbade me from speaking with her father without her permission, and, after today's confrontation with that man, we know that would be a pointless endeavor." Lucas sighed. "It's obvious he needs money and lots of it. He's clinging to his respectability as the only thing worth bartering." He tapped his legs in agitation.

"An astute assessment of her father and his desperation," Sophie said.

"I hate that she could suffer a fate similar to Sav's, but I can do nothing about that now. I refuse to march into the church on her wedding day and cause any more scandal," Lucas said. "She needs to want to change the dictates of her life, and she doesn't."

Sophronia watched him with understanding and sympathy. "Of course you can't march into the church," she said before she chuckled. "Although it would be the most entertaining wedding I'd been to in years if you acted in such a manner." She shared a long glance with Lucas.

"How will we help Parthena then?" Zylphia asked.

"I don't know. Her father is foolish but influential." Sophie gripped the handle of her cane as she frowned. "As the girl herself has agreed to this match, I'm afraid Lucas is correct. There is nothing for us to do, except support her afterward."

"Will you tell me more about this Morgan fellow? What is he like? Who are his friends? What are his passions?" Lucas asked Sophie.

Sophie sighed. "Not all men are like you, dearest. Not all men have a great abiding passion. I fear Morgan's passion is maintaining control of his world and of his business. Parthena will soon be a part of that world."

"And thus under his control. Is Morgan an evil man? Will he treat Parthena poorly?" Lucas asked.

"He doesn't support her beliefs," Zylphia said. "He mocks her skills at the piano. Everyday her joy will be drained from her until she becomes a woman who I no longer recognize."

"Like Sav," Lucas whispered. "I stood by and watched my sister slowly turn into a ghost of her former self."

"You've known Parthena a few weeks, Lucas. Why are you determined to care for her?" Zylphia asked.

Lucas flushed. "She began to write me about a year ago—when I was in Montana and staying with Savannah, composing new music. Her letters were refreshing because her words were truly interested in the music, in my compositions, in me, not just the fame and trappings that come with success."

He gazed at Zee and then Sophie, a bemused smile flitting across his face. "I met her for a moment last fall when I played a concert here in Boston. We continued to write each other, and, when I returned to Boston in late April, she somehow found out where I lived. Demanded I tutor her."

Sophie shared a wry smile with Zylphia. "It seems you tutored her in more aspects than the piano."

Lucas flushed but didn't disagree with Sophie. "We agreed to act as though we'd never met on the night of the Wheeler gathering to forestall any gossip. I'd never harm her." Lucas paused. "I'd known, since I'd received her first letter, that she was a woman who could understand me, my passion for music. And never find me wanting because I became lost in a composition for hours on end."

"Oh, Lucas, I'm so sorry," Zylphia whispered as she reached forward and gripped his hand. "I can only imagine how difficult this is for you."

"We all have our dreams, Zee, and not all of them come true," Lucas whispered. "She will always be one of my greatest joys. I can never regret having had her in my life."

CHAPTER THREE

Lucas sat in his rented rooms at a desk lit by a small lamp. One corner of the sitting area was filled by a grand piano, while a chair, settee, and ottoman were pushed into a corner. A pencil and sheets of torn and used paper were strewn on the floor around him. He sighed at the knock on the door and rose. "Coming."

He stilled from opening the door farther when he beheld his visitor. "What are you doing here?"

"Isn't it proper for a mother to visit her son?" She stood with slightly stooped shoulders, making her five-foot-one frame seem even smaller. Her honey-blond hair was pulled back in a severe bun, while her light-blue eyes flashed with disapproval as she beheld her son dressed in worn pants and a cream-colored shirt with the sleeves rolled up to his elbows.

"Not my mother." Lucas stepped forward, ushering his mother into the hallway before shutting the door behind him. "What do you want?"

"Merely to ensure you are well. We haven't seen you at the store more than two or three times since you returned to Boston." Matilda's gaze roved over Lucas, from his disheveled hair to his untucked shirt to his stockinged feet. "You don't look well."

"And why would that be, Mother?" The muscles along his unshaven jaw flexed as he clamped it shut.

"I would not presume to know." She sniffed with displeasure as the sounds of neighbors arguing seeped through a nearby door.

Lucas sighed and reluctantly opened the door to his small home. "I'm only allowing you in here because I don't care to share our gossip with others."

"There is no gossip."

"Of course there is. Wherever you are concerned, there always is." He refrained from slamming the door behind her, his fist clenched on the handle a moment before he moved into his sitting room.

"Lucas, may I remind you that I am your mother and I am deserving of your respect?" Matilda Russell looked around the small room, unable to hide her disdain at the used furniture and shabby furnishings.

"I will never forget you are my mother." He watched her with a dispassionate loathing. "However, you will never merit my respect after what occurred with Jonas."

"I did what any mother, desiring respectability, would do." She tapped her finger with displeasure on the wooden arm of her chair. "Besides, the sordid incident occurred over ten years ago. It is best to forget such things."

Lucas sat on one of the chairs, sinking into the well-worn cushions. "Do you expect me to believe that most mothers would be willing to sacrifice the happiness and well-being of their only daughter to a maniacal, violent man for the sake of a worthless reputation? That any amount of time would make what occurred acceptable?"

He glared at his mother's indifference. "I've lied over the years. Telling Clarissa and Savannah I've seen you. That I've forgiven you for what you did. For what you failed to do. But you and I know the truth."

"Yes, that you are an ungrateful son, who refuses to answer my letters and visit me when you are in Boston. I merit more consideration from you."

"You lost any reason for me to grant you respect when you failed to demonstrate an ounce of remorse at inviting Jonas to the house that night. Were you happy he shot me? That I nearly died?" Lucas's eyes flashed with anger, the hurt at her betrayal nearly hidden by his ire. "Did you think to be rid of your bothersome son who was fascinated by music?"

"That was an unfortunate event," Matilda said, waving her hand in the air as though little of consequence had occurred that evening.

"Jonas was intent on controlling Savannah's fate, and he would have killed her had Colin not interrupted." He let out a huff of air in exasperation. "He attempted to kill father and me too."

"Lucas, there is no reason for you to live in such a hovel," Matilda said, ignoring any further attempts to discuss the events that led to Jonas's death. "You must come home and live with us."

"So you can claim you are curing your lunatic son?" Lucas asked. "Yes, Mother, I've heard the rumors, and I know they could only have come from you or the grandparents."

Matilda clamped her jaw shut, her cheeks flushing red with her agitation.

"You have an extraordinary manner for showing your motherly devotion. First, your abandonment of Savannah. Now your denouncement of me. Is it your dream that, if you make my life too uncomfortable, I'll give up the piano?" He shook his head at his mother's foolish hope shining in her eyes. "I'm never coming back to the store. I will never work with Father again selling linen. I'll play the piano until my hands are arthritic and unable to touch the keys. And then I'll hum tunes. I'll teach. I'll have soirees where I discuss the joys of playing the piano. It's the one thing in this world that has ever brought me joy."

She flinched as she saw the contempt in his gaze as it raked over her, perfectly attired. "Do you really believe one such as Miss Tyler would want anything to do with you? Look how you live. How you dress. You are barely acceptable."

"Acceptable or respectable?" Lucas challenged. "I shouldn't think she would pay much attention to one such as I, Mother. Even if she is an excellent pianist."

"No woman of decent birth will ever want a man like you as long as you continue to eschew a proper profession. I fear you will spend the rest of your life alone, with nothing but your piano to love."

"You may be correct, Mother, but at least I will have known joy. I will have known passion."

"Don't speak to me of passion. If there is one thing in this family that we need less of, it's passion. It has been our downfall."

Lucas watched his mother with a mixture of scorn and pity. "Only because you didn't have the courage to embrace it. Aunt Agnes and Aunt Betsy knew better than you." His head jerked backward as his mother slapped him.

"You'll never understand what I sacrificed due to giving into my passion. What I lost. You stupid boy." She rose, quivering with her agitation. She snapped her fingers at him, and he frowned at her. "Come along. I expect you to come home with me now."

Lucas laughed, but it was filled with rancor rather than humor. "I'm not some dog that will jump to your bidding. I'm not returning home with you now, Mother. I'm never returning home with you. I'll visit Father soon, hopefully on a day you are out."

She bristled with indignation as her son continued to sit even while she stood. She opened her mouth as though to spew further vitriol, but then spun on her heel and stormed out the door.

Lucas heaved a sigh and rose, locking the door behind her.

***

Dear Miss McLeod,

Thank you for your recent letter. It is wonderful to correspond with Teddy's dear friend who is also a suffragette. In your next letter, you must write more about your suffragist activities. I'm eager to resume my work for the cause here, but I find I remain quite weakened after the last hunger strike from my most recent imprisonment. I am only capable of stuffing envelopes at our main headquarters.

I can imagine you are quite curious about Teddy when he was younger. He and Lawrence were always my favorite cousins because they never minded a girl joining their antics. My mother blames them for giving me the notion I could do anything a boy could do and thus demanding more in the way of suffragism. She may be correct.

Teddy had a tendency toward seriousness. Lawrence was the only person who could fully lighten his mood. His death was a blow to all of us but to Teddy most of all. The rambunctious antics ceased overnight, and he buried himself in science and math. I worried, until my dear aunt wrote about you, that he would remain immersed in scientific endeavors for the remainder of his life.

If you don't mind me asking, what occurred to force Teddy to return to England? I'd thought he'd never return until he had a wife. Our grandmother has always insisted he marry a lady of noble blood, something Teddy has resisted. However, upon his arrival, that resistance seemed to have weakened. As had his desire to avoid our grandfather's dictate that he fulfill a grand and noble act in his life and thus enlist for duty in the Great War.

Please forgive me my impertinence. As you are curious about Teddy's life in England, I am curious about his in Boston.

Yours Sincerely,

Eugenie Abingdon

***

"I heard you played the piano recently with Lucas Russell," Morgan Wheeler said as he sat in the formal parlor at the Tyler residence. Parthena sat in a settee across from him. They were alone, her parents deeming that, as an engaged couple, they did not need a formal chaperone. The door to the parlor remained open, their nod to propriety. The deep blue wallpaper made the large room feel small, as did the dark mahogany furniture.

"He visited with Miss McLeod," Parthena said, her voice without inflection. The tea sat in front of them, unpoured and cooling.

He looked from the tea to Parthena, then at the tea again. Parthena's gaze remained fixed on the carpet. "Parthena, I know we haven't always been on the friendliest of terms, but I believe we can have a successful union."

"I'm certain, if you repeat that to yourself enough times, you might come to believe it."

"Do you believe I'd offer to marry you and make myself miserable in the process?"

"Yes, because that's what you've done to me." She raised a defiant gaze to him, her hands fisting on her lap as she saw his jaw clench.

"What is it you want from me, Parthena?" When she remained mutinously quiet, he glared at her. "Do you want me to go to your father and say I won't marry you? If so, your family, rather than continuing to live in the splendor of your Back Bay mansion, will be forced to sell it and move to a tenement. Do you think I want to see you working at a back-breaking job, rather than tinkering at your piano and your social causes? I couldn't countenance that scenario." When she remained stubbornly silent, he demanded, "Is that what you'd prefer?"

Parthena clamped her mouth shut, her jaw trembling. She glared at him before she finally spoke. "I will never forgive you for forcing me to marry you."

Morgan slapped his hand on the edge of his chair and rose, slamming the door to the parlor shut on the two of them. "When did your father start complaining about the expense of his four daughters?" His intense stare forced an answer.

"A little over two years ago."

"Why do you think he, all of a sudden, thought having daughters was bothersome?"

"'Daughters are an expense with no hope for a return on the expenditures outlaid in their upbringing.'"

"You parrot your father quite well," Morgan said with a half smile.

"I've had years of listening to him say a variation on the same theme."

"When did he become desperate for you to marry?"

Parthena's gaze became unfocused as she thought about his question. "Last fall."

"Exactly. Mr. Goff, who'd been helping your father extract himself from his financial nightmare, left town precipitously the previous spring. Thus, your father, who remained without the financial sense or fiscal fortitude to extricate himself from total ruin, became desperate to marry you off."

"I have nothing of value. Only a fool would pay to marry me." Parthena looked at Morgan mockingly.

"I'm certain you would have been delighted then to know your father was on the verge of announcing your engagement to Mr. Carlisle."

Parthena gasped, paling. "He wouldn't have."

"Yes, he would. It seems aging Mr. Carlisle wanted a young wife of the highest social standing to provide him with a son."

"But he's—he's—"

Morgan nodded at her horror. "Old enough to be your father and also takes great pleasure in provoking pain."

Parthena shuddered. "We know what happened to his last wife," she whispered.

"We suspect." Morgan watched his fiancée with concern. They were silent a moment as they recalled Mr. Carlisle's wife, Andrea, who was rumored to have committed suicide rather than continue to live with Mr. Carlisle.

"One way or another, you were to marry. Lucas Russell, no matter how successful a pianist he has become, doesn't have the resources needed to salvage your father's finances."

"Why must I be the one to pay for his ineptitude?" Parthena wailed, a tear leaking out.

"I'd like to think I'm a better option than Mr. Carlisle," Morgan snapped.

Parthena closed her eyes in silent agreement.

"If you refuse to marry me, your father will have Genevieve marry that old letch Carlisle."

Parthena gasped at the thought of her next youngest sister bound to Mr. Carlisle. She stared vacantly at the spot on the carpet again. "I'd like to say he wouldn't, but I know I'd be lying to myself. He's been a different father these past few years."

Morgan approached Parthena's settee and sat next to her. "I know I'm not the man you envisioned marrying." He reached forward and placed one of his large hands over her clasped hands on her lap. "However, we've known each other since childhood. I know we can make each other happy."

Parthena raised hazel eyes to meet his gaze. "How do you know this?"

He raised a hesitant hand, stretching his fingers to lightly trace her cheek. "Because I've always wanted to do this," he whispered, leaning forward to kiss her. His kiss began as a gentle coaxing of his lips against hers but he soon deepened the kiss, pulling her against him in a tight embrace.

When he attempted to bring her even more fully against him, Parthena pushed him away. "No, no, I shouldn't," she whispered, touching first her lips, then his a moment, as she scooted farther from him. Her hazel eyes were rounded, filled with confusion.

"Shouldn't kiss me in your mother's parlor? Or shouldn't enjoy it?" His eyes flashed with frustration, while his cheeks were flushed with the remnants of desire.

Parthena flinched at his comment. "Both. Neither. I don't know." She covered her face with her hands.

"Parthena, we are to be married. I want you to feel joy at my touch." He ran a hand over her hair to her shoulder. He leaned forward, kissing the top of her head before standing. "I will leave you now. Thank you for inviting me for tea."

Parthena smiled weakly at his subtle criticism, as no tea had been poured from the full teapot. She looked at him as he strode toward the door, exchanging an intense glance with him before he opened it and departed.

***

Rowena sat in Zylphia's conservatory, the windows opened to allow in a breeze on a hot June day. A pitcher of lemonade sat on the small table, forming a puddle of condensation as the ice melted. The diaphanous drapes obscured most of the bright afternoon light, although they barely moved with the weak breeze. Wicker furniture was scattered throughout the room, while ferns gave the room a tropical feel.

"I thought you said she would meet us," Rowena said from a settee near the open window. The pale yellow of her dress accented her auburn hair, pulled back in a delicate chignon.

"She accepted the invitation," Zylphia responded. She paced the room, tracing fern fronds. She came to a stop and settled one hip against a window frame, fanning herself.

"The heat came early this year," Rowena remarked, wiping daintily at her brow before fanning herself too. She watched Zylphia closely. "Have you had any word of Mr. Goff?"

"Not directly, no. I'm corresponding with his cousin in England. He's still missing, but I comfort myself with the knowledge that they remain hopeful of good news." Zylphia's gaze became distant.

"How did you come to write her?"

"She wrote me." Zylphia's expression lightened as she thought of Eugenie's letters. "She's a suffragette in England. Teddy had told me about her. I believe she's met the Pankhursts."

"Wow," Rowena murmured.

"She's been imprisoned and lived through hunger strikes." Zylphia shared a long look with Rowena. "Just like Miss Paul and Miss Burns."

"Speaking of Miss Paul, have you seen the latest copy of the Suffragist?" Rowena asked, pulling the weekly newspaper from her purse. Zylphia shook her head as she plucked it from Rowena's fingers. "Isn't the latest cartoon by Miss Allender divine?"

Zylphia studied the drawing titled "Changing Fashions: She Used to Be Satisfied with So Little" on the front page, and her smile bloomed. "It's brilliant. I wish I could create this type of art."

"You have a different talent." Rowena stood so that she and Zylphia studied the drawing of a woman wearing a ball gown with the words National Constitutional Amendment along the hem. In her elaborate hat and ribbons, the state names of Massachusetts, New Jersey, New York, and Pennsylvania were noted. To one side a congressman looked on, shaking his head in consternation; while, in a corner, a woman stood in a plain dress with Montana and Nevada written on her hem, indicating 1914.

The door thrust open, which startled Zylphia, her glance darting there.

Rowena turned around and smiled her welcome to Parthena. "P.T.!" Rowena exclaimed, rising. "You've come!" She refrained from embracing her friend as Parthena looked brittle, as though she'd break apart with any contact. Rowena sat again on her settee.

Zylphia frowned. "You look like hell."

"Thanks, Zee," P.T. said as she sat on a chair by Rowena. She reached forward and helped herself to a glass of lemonade. "What was so important that we needed to meet?"

Zylphia's frown deepened. "Besides the fact you're being forced to marry in a week and your friends are concerned about you?"

"And the fact that you've avoided us for the better part of two weeks?" Rowena said with a raised eyebrow.

Parthena let out a low groan, leaning against the back of her chair. "I knew it would serve no purpose to speak with you." She stared pointedly at Zylphia. "You'd insist I find a way out of this marriage to Morgan."

"Of course," Zylphia said, bristling with indignation as she envisioned her friend entering an arranged, loveless marriage.

"Zee, please don't," Parthena whispered. "This is what I must do, and I will fulfill my duty. To my father and to my family. I refuse to be seen as someone who runs away from her problems."

Zylphia moved toward her and reached forward, clasping her hand. "Of course you're not, but you don't have to do this. I know we can find another solution."

"Like marry Mr. Carlisle?" Parthena asked, a mirthless laugh sounding at her friend's horrified expressions. "My father confirmed what Morgan had told me earlier. That's my option. I either marry Morgan or I marry Mr. Carlisle."

"Not if you're already married to someone else," Zylphia said as Rowena nodded her agreement.

"I'm not you, Zylphia. I won't stand up to my father, not when I would then consign one of my sisters to marry such a man as Mr. Carlisle. And I can't countenance forcing my family into penury. This is what I must do." Her gaze was haunted and desperate with resignation.

"But you loathe Morgan," Zylphia said, a deep frown marring her expression as she attempted to understand her friend's decision.

"We'll have a conventional marriage. He'll busy himself with his work and I with my causes. And we'll be perfectly contented."

"You should want more," Zylphia whispered, earning a hiss from P.T. and a swat of the fan from Rowena.

"You've always protected your sisters, P.T," Rowena said. "Do they realize all you're sacrificing for them?"

Parthena shook her head. "Genevieve has always thought Morgan dashing and wonders at the animosity I've felt toward him."

"Then she should marry him," Zylphia said, earning a frown from Parthena and a stifled giggle from Rowena. Zylphia studied her friend in confusion.

"Has he kissed you?" Rowena asked.

Parthena blushed. "Yes." She shared a confused gaze with her friends. "How can I enjoy his kiss when I loathe him?" She met Zylphia's near glare and sat even taller. "I know you have lost respect for me, and I'm sorry."

"I'm merely trying to understand how you can act as you do. Purport to feel as you do about Morgan's kisses after ..." She shook her head, flushing when she noticed Rowena watching them in confusion.

Parthena glared at Zylphia. "I wouldn't expect you to understand as you have always been so noble. However, I suspect some day you will find yourself challenged, and I hope you don't disappoint yourself." Parthena rose. "If you will excuse me, I must return home. My mother is most desirous to discuss wedding plans with me."

Zylphia sighed as Parthena stormed out, the slamming door echoing through the room and, Zylphia also suspected, the first floor. She thwacked her fan on her chair's arm in annoyance.

"What was that all about?" Rowena asked.

"I think you'd have to ask Parthena. It's not my story to tell." Zylphia sighed with frustration.

"It seems more than Parthena is miserable," Rowena murmured.

Zylphia laughed. "I always forget how perceptive you are. I hate when those I care about are miserable, and more than Parthena are upset. That's all I can say."

Rowena settled into her chair, curling a foot underneath. "Well, if you can't tell me anything further about Parthena, tell me all you can about Teddy, your art, anything of interest."

Zylphia smiled, stretching out her legs in front of her as she caught up on her latest news with a close friend.

***

"Parthena, quit acting as though you are being led to that awful French contraption," her mother snapped, referring to the guillotine. "You are making the seamstresses' job much more difficult than it needs to be."

Parthena attempted to cease fidgeting and stood motionless as the pair of seamstresses muttered about hem lengths and the unrealistic desire to have a wedding gown completed in a matter of weeks. Parthena flinched as a needle jabbed her in the ankle, scowling at her mother when she reprimanded Parthena again for her movements. She tuned out her mother's harping and thought about a piano piece she was having difficulty with. Finally, the seamstresses gathered their belongings, motioned for Parthena to step out of the pinned-together dress, and departed with a promise of another visit the following day.

Parthena sighed and collapsed onto the chaise longue in her bedroom in only her underclothes.

Her mother glowered at her as she tossed a robe at her.

"Mother, no one is going to bother me here. I might as well be somewhat comfortable on a hot day."

"That is your problem, Parthena. You've always thought of your comfort and desires before those of your family. It's what's led us to this point."

Parthena gaped at her mother, who stood in front of her in an elaborate rose-colored afternoon dress. Her brown and gray hair was pulled back with pearl-encrusted combs. "How can you say such a thing to me?"

"If you had married earlier, we would have been spared the expense of you all these years."

Parthena gripped the robe in her hands, nearly ripping the fine silk material in her agitation. "You'd dare blame Father's incompetence with finances on me? That I'm the reason we are in financial difficulties?"

Her mother's blue eyes became as ice chips as she stared at Parthena. "If you had made an advantageous marriage years ago, we could have been spared your father's inabilities. Instead, there was no one to rein him in." She took a deep breath. "If you had made acceptable friends, rather than that horrid McLeod girl, who's filled your head with nonsensical ideas about women, then you'd have already done your duty."

"Zylphia is a loyal and wonderful friend. In fact, even today, she had hope that I'd find my way free of this marriage. She had hope when I had none." Parthena's shoulders stooped before glaring again at her mother. "Zylphia would never be forced into such a travesty by her parents."

"We will never agree that she is a good influence. I will continue to pray that you cease all association with her, and I will hope Mr. Wheeler has some influence over you in that regard." She frowned at Parthena. "If you had been sensible and married Mr. Wheeler of your own accord—years ago as I had hoped you would—we would never have come to such a point. He has the business acumen and the strength of character to aid your father as few can."

Parthena stared at her mother. "Yes, it must be such an embarrassing time for you, Mother."

Her mother ignored her sarcasm and paced around Parthena's large room. "Do you know what it is like to have one's acquaintances know that one's daughter is being bought like a prized camel so as to replenish the family coffers?" She smiled when she saw Parthena squirm and blush. "I only hope Morgan doesn't regret his part of the bargain as I do not want my brothers to feel they need to interfere in any way."

Parthena gaped at her mother. "Do you mean you haven't asked my uncles for help?" At her mother's frosty silence, Parthena scrubbed at her temple. "You know they would be delighted to aid you, especially if it would prevent me from marrying a man I do not love."

Mrs. Tyler's eyes shone with derision, the icy disdain disappearing with her anger. "Do you have any idea how many times I have already sought their aid? How many times they have donated to the coffers of this family to keep us out of the tenements?" At Parthena's shocked gaze, her mother spoke in a soft, yet vehement voice. "I refuse to ask them for another dollar. They have proffered enough to sustain my family. It is time the members of this family were willing to make some sort of sacrifice to ensure our continued well-being."

Parthena blinked away tears. "You don't know what you are asking."

Her mother laughed scornfully. "Of course I do. You must do as I did, as all the women in our family who came before you did. You must give up your infatuation with an unacceptable man and marry the man chosen for you by your father. Neither your father nor I would ever have agreed to such a socially disastrous liaison for one of our daughters."

Parthena sat for a moment in silence. "Which is why you don't want your brothers, my uncles, to understand what is truly occurring." She watched her mother with disappointment. "How can you do this to me?"

Her mother shook her head. "You are doing this to yourself. You have made a decision that you would rather marry Mr. Wheeler, our dear friend Morgan, rather than marry Mr. Carlisle. Or have your sister, Genevieve, marry Mr. Carlisle." She willed her daughter into silence for a moment with her rigid countenance. "Morgan will marry only you. He doesn't want to marry any of your sisters."

"I'll speak with the uncles. They'll help me. They always do," Parthena said, unable to hide the excitement from her voice.

"Feel free to speak with them. All you will do is ensure that one of your sisters must marry Mr. Carlisle. No amount of monetary infusion from your uncles or anyone else will change your father's mind."

Parthena slumped onto the chaise, attempting to hide her tears from her mother. "Why?"

A momentary sadness flickered through her mother's gaze but was gone in an instant. "Your father is determined that his daughters marry—and marry well. He wants to start with you but will begin with Genevieve if necessary."

"How can you possibly stand by, as our mother, and countenance him marrying us off to a man such as Mr. Carlisle? Do you have no motherly instinct in you?" Parthena asked, her chest heaving with her barely repressed emotions.

"I believe your father knows best in this regard. He would never wittingly align himself with a man who would harm any of you. And, no, I do not believe the rumors about Mr. Carlisle."

Parthena shook her head in defeat and fisted her hands on her lap. "He would never have treated us like this if we were his sons. He would have wanted us then. He would have cherished us." She faced her mother, her expression determined. "Promise me that you will protect Genevieve, Eudora, and Isabel from any of his schemes when I'm not here."

Her mother shook her head. "You know I am incapable of making any such promises." She smiled at her eldest daughter. "As for you, Parthena, you have made a brilliant match, and I expect you shall be very happy. You young ones have such odd notions about love, but I am certain you shall be quite content with Morgan."

Parthena groaned as she flopped against the back of the chaise. "Content. That's such a horrid word." She glared at her mother. "And I didn't make this match."

"Sometimes it is better to accept one's fate than to constantly battle against it." Mrs. Tyler raised her eyebrows as she waited for Parthena's rejoinder. When none came, she left her daughter in deep contemplation.

CHAPTER FOUR

Zylphia climbed the stairs to the triple decker, panting as she came to a stop at the third-floor home. She attempted to take a deep breath but had to make do with short inhalations due to her corset. She paused a moment, checked that her hat was in place, and squared her shoulders before she knocked on the door.

She pasted on a friendly smile as the door was held ajar by a woman wearing an apron. "Good afternoon, ma'am. I'm here to speak with you about the referendum in November which would grant women the right to vote in Massachusetts."

"My husband isn't home, and he's the one you should speak with. He votes. Not me." She moved to shut the door, but Zylphia jammed her foot in the doorway.

"Are you for suffrage? Would you like to vote?"

"I don't know why I should need the vote. My husband treats me fairly. I shouldn't have the vote forced on me if I don't want it." She shook her head as she kicked Zylphia's foot out of the way and slammed the door shut.

Zylphia clambered down the stairs, sputtering to herself until she saw Florence waiting for her on the sidewalk. "How did it go?" Zylphia called out with a bright smile.

"Not well. The first floor occupant wasn't home, and the second floor resident wasn't inclined to listen to anything I had to say." Florence stopped at the street corner and fanned herself with one of the pamphlets. "We've been walking up and down tenements for hours. Let's stop and have a rest." She nodded to a café across the street.

"I agree," Zylphia said, entering the café and sitting with Florence in a booth. After ordering glasses of lemonade, they sat in silence. "I don't know what to make of our efforts," Zylphia whispered as she leaned toward Florence. "Few of the women we've spoken with seem inclined to want the vote."

Florence sighed. "I fear that film, Your Girl and Mine, isn't helping the cause here. When I saw it last week, even I was uncomfortable with the portrayal of men. Today many of the women I spoke with were offended by how men were shown as evildoers with women at their mercy."

"Aren't they smart enough to realize it's a parable?" Zylphia hissed.

"I think they're smart enough to be put off by the representation of all men as villains, just as I was, and I'm a suffragist! They also don't see how suffrage will lead to anything but a loss of male chivalry and an increase in social chaos."

"One woman I spoke with said she didn't want to have the vote forced on her. As though by being granted the right to vote means she has to vote." Zylphia smiled at the waiter who brought them their drinks. "What irony. We want to ensure she and her daughters have a better life, and she's too shortsighted to acknowledge the struggle's merit."

After taking a sip of her drink, Florence pulled a quarterly paper from her bag. She handed it to Zylphia with raised eyebrows. "This is what the Antis are saying."

Zylphia unfolded the latest copy of The Remonstrance against Woman Suffrage. She glanced at the articles and shook her head. "Most of the women I'm meeting are parroting their arguments." She shared a frustrated look with Florence. "How did you get a copy?"

"I sent them money as Florence Butler. If I'd used my married name, I think they would have realized I was related to you. Also the fact I live in Dorchester helps." She pulled the paper closer to her and tapped at one part. "This section to the men of Massachusetts is damning. They are making the men feel as though they are betraying their chivalric duty to protect women and children if they vote for universal suffrage."

"Chivalry, my foot. They will stoop to nothing to get their way," Zylphia said, pushing the publication back toward Florence.

"I'd think the same could be said of you," Florence teased. "The larger problem than this paper is that we have no backing from the mayor or the governor. As Democrats, they are against universal suffrage. Add in the influence of the Catholic church ..." Florence shook her head in dismay. "They are forceful voices in this state, and I don't know how we would countermand their censure."

Zylphia drummed her fingers on the table. "Sophie knows everyone and seems to be due a favor from almost as many. Even she doesn't know how to sway them to her way of thinking. If only President Wilson would make a more forceful statement for suffrage. Then his party members would follow his lead."

Florence leaned forward and whispered, "Are we doomed as we just begin?"

Zylphia shook her head emphatically. "I refuse to concede defeat when it is only late June. Much can change between now and November. However, I think canvassing at this point is not a worthwhile endeavor. We need to put our energies into other activities that will have a greater impact."

"Even though going door to door in Montana was essential for success?"

"It is essential, but I think it's too early right now. We need to focus our energies on other things at this time." Zylphia tapped the copy of the Remonstrance. "We must have a greater argument for women voting than the Antis have against us. And we must be more eloquent and more persuasive. Our newspapers must have better distribution." She continued to tap the paper as she thought through a new approach.

"Well, as to that, I must be home soon. Richard has his hands full with the children." She smiled fondly as though imagining the scene at home. "I can only envision the chaos that is occurring there."

Zylphia laughed. "You love every minute of it."

"I do," Florence said with a broad smile. "Come for dinner. Richard and the children would love to see you."

Zylphia nodded her agreement as she paid for their drinks. They rose and ran outside to catch the passing trolley. They laughed like schoolgirls as they jumped on the rear platform and bit their lips as the ticket taker reprimanded them for their foolishness.

***

Upon their arrival at Florence and Richard's house, bedlam erupted the minute the front door opened. Little feet ran down the front hall, the boys screaming and waving small sticks in the air. Florence picked up one of her sons, holding him even when he wriggled to be set free. "What have I told you about running with dangerous objects?" she asked.

"It's not dangerous, Mama. It's a stick. And we're playin' cops 'n' robbers."

She kissed his head and let him down but kept a firm hold of one of his hands. "I fail to see what a stick has to do with it."

"It's my sword," Gideon said, brandishing it with pride and nearly hitting her in the face as he flung it upward.

Zylphia giggled behind Florence. "I hope I'm allowed to play."

"Zee!" he screamed, launching himself at her. "Oh, you're the best! Come!" Gideon ordered, dragging Zylphia down the hallway to what had been the dining room but was now a bedroom filled with chattering boys.

A roar of approval greeted Zylphia's arrival, and Florence shook her head as she walked into the kitchen, where Richard stood at the stove, humming lines from "Peg O' My Heart."

She paused as he burst into song, his deep voice forming a beautiful harmony as he whistled and sang a few lines from the chorus:

Peg o' my heart, I love you.

He whistled part of the chorus before singing, *"I love you."* He continued to whistle the rest of the chorus before he returned to humming, and Florence giggled. "You never can remember more than those lyrics. Hello, darling," she murmured as she wrapped her arms around Richard from behind and placed her cheek on the muscles between his shoulder blades. "Thank you for attempting to corral the boys' chaos."

He chuckled, setting down the spoon and turning to pull her into a hug. "Hello, my love. I've missed you and had to resort to singing love songs."

Florence laughed and gave him a quick kiss.

Richard heard his sons' voices and whispered, "Later," to Florence. He turned again to the soup pot, giving it another stir. "Ian is insistent he's too old to play with his brothers but then becomes caught up in running the whole show. He's a bit bossy, but he still looks out for his brothers, and no one's bled yet today."

"A successful day then," Florence said, smiling as she heard peals of laughter coming from the bedroom and Zylphia's softer voice in contrast to her boys' voices.

"How did you convince her to take time away from her day to come over?" Richard asked, pivoting to smooth a hand over Florence's curly black hair.

"Don't be rancorous, Richard. She's busy with the cause. With her painting. Attempting to not mourn her young man. We need to be patient with her," Florence said.

He kissed his wife on the forehead before returning to the stove again. "I know. But I've found I've missed her these past months, as have the boys." He turned down the heat and moved to the icebox, taking out a pitcher of iced tea. He waved for Florence to sit and set down the pitcher as Zylphia entered the kitchen.

Her blue eyes shone with mischief and delight after playing with her young cousins. Her hair was in disarray, coming free of its pins, and her stockings had a run. However, Florence hadn't seen Zylphia this carefree in months.

"Oh, it's wonderful to spend time with the boys. I should come by more often," she said. She rushed to Richard and grabbed him in a hug. "I've missed you, Richard."

"And I you, Zee. Come. Sit. Tell us what you've been up to." He motioned to the table, sharing a smile with Zylphia as she smirked at his stained apron.

"Oh, I have no interesting news. I paint. I write letters to England in the hopes one will come back to me with news of Teddy. And I work for the right to vote." She took a sip of the tea he poured her. "I can't believe you're a man of leisure."

He laughed. "I'm not. I thankfully have men at each shop who can run them without my presence. I stop into each location most days but take time off to be with my family too. Today was one of those days." He shared a smile with Florence, who sat next to Zylphia. "And we're never open on Sundays."

Zylphia took a handful of early peas to be shelled and began to work while she chatted. "Do you have any news from Montana?"

Florence placed a large bowl next to her that they could share for discarding the shells and a small bowl in front of her for the peas. "Richard just received a letter last night," Florence said, swiping her hands on a kitchen towel as she rose to retrieve the letter from the living room. She returned, handing it to her husband.

He flipped it open and smiled at the familiar handwriting. "It's from Gabe. I still can't believe he's so far away, even after all these years." He looked down at the letter. "He says that they're all doing well. The children are growing faster than he can believe, and they are excited for the fair later this summer." He scanned over the next few lines. "Clarissa still mourns Mr. Pickens, although it helps her to work part time again at the library. She and Miss Loken seem to have come to a truce." He smiled as she looked at Zylphia and Florence. "It appears that Miss Loken has an admirer in one of Colin's blacksmiths, and she's worried about the library if she were to marry."

Zylphia smiled. "I'm happy for Miss Loken. She deserves to find happiness after she had a rough start in Missoula." Zylphia frowned. "I can still hear Mr. Pickens sometimes. It's like he's there, giving me his irreverent advice when I don't know what to do. It's hard to realize he's gone, but I know he would be happy that Clarissa is again at the library. I never became well acquainted with Miss Loken, but I'm glad their animosity is behind them."

Richard nodded. "Gabe remains busy with work. He and Jer work on lots of fine molding and finish work on some of the finer houses in Missoula along with their furniture commissions."

"I'd think they'd take on someone else," Florence said. Richard nodded his agreement.

"How are Jeremy and Savannah?" Zylphia asked. "I loved staying with them last summer, and Melinda was a joy."

Richard set aside the letter. "I believe they are well. Enjoying Melly, but I think Jeremy worries what Savannah will do once their daughter is grown." He shared a glance with Florence. "I know Flo and I don't agree on this, but I think they should adopt another child. They would be wonderful parents, and I think it would help ease Savannah's hurts."

"She'll never fully recover from the loss of her daughter, Richard," Florence said, her voice harsh.

Richard looked down at his lap, momentarily chastised by his wife. His good humor had evaporated with her comment, and he sat there, somber and serious. "I know you never fully recover, Flo. I would never suggest that. Or that Sav should forget. I merely thought it might help ease her sorrow."

Zylphia watched the two of them, and her hands, busy shelling peas, stilled. She reached one hand to Richard and one to Florence. "I'm sorry if I've made you remember a time you'd rather forget."

"As Florence says, we'll never forget the daughter we barely knew," Richard said, rising and breaking contact with Zylphia. He reached for the stew pot and gave it a quick stir before whacking the spoon on the pot's edge. "I, for one, refuse to live in the past, dreaming of what could have been. I far prefer to live in the present."

He turned to face the two women, Zylphia with a look of entreaty and Florence glancing at the table, her hands continuing to prepare the peas for dinner. Zylphia shook her head at him in dismay and rose, mumbling something about seeing how her young cousins were.

Richard moved to Florence and sat across from her. His large callused hands, battered from years working at the smithy, reached forward and stilled her erratic movements. "Florence, I wasn't criticizing you. I never would. Nor would I ever forget our daughter. I never could." He waited long moments for her to raise her eyes to meet his worried gaze.

"I don't know why I'm so prickly," she whispered. "I love our boys. I love our life. I'm sorry."

He stroked a hand down her cheek, his caress soothing a part of her ache. "There's never a need to apologize," he whispered.

"Yes, there is. Especially when I've nurtured a resentment in my heart toward you. And it was wrong of me. I know it," she said, lowering her gaze.

His brows furrowed as he studied her. "You've hidden your anger well. Are you unhappy with me? With our life?"

She flinched at the pain she heard in his voice. "I'm not, not really. There are moments when the grief overwhelms me." She rose and sat in a chair next to him, snuggling into his side. "But then one of the boys does something, and I laugh, and joy comes back into my life. Or you return home with a crazy story from the smithy, and it's like old times. But there's this ache in me that never goes away."

"It doesn't for me either," he admitted.

"It never seems as though you were as sad as me. And that hurts."

"It's also unfair," he whispered. "Would it have helped you to see me sob in my uncle's arms the weeks after we lost her? Would it have helped you to see Zylphia and Delia attempt to boost my spirits so I could return home to you, strong and able, as the husband you needed?"

He looked around the controlled chaos of the kitchen. "I love our life. I love our boys. Do you want to try for another child?"

"If we are gifted with another child, I will rejoice. But I don't want to tempt fate." Florence entwined her fingers with his.

"Be brave, Flo. Dare to grasp what your heart desires," Richard entreated.

"I must learn to be content with what I already have," she murmured. She smiled at Zylphia as she reentered the room, their quiet moment lost.

Richard rose and pulled down plates and bowls for dinner, handing them to Zylphia. She set the table, the previous topic of conversation ignored as they discussed the struggle for universal enfranchisement and the women they had met that day.

CHAPTER FIVE

Parthena stood in her bedroom, staring out the window dressed in her wedding finery. She fingered the lace curtain and ignored her three younger sisters bustling around the room. "Could you leave me alone for a few minutes before we have to depart?" She heard her sisters leave, the *click* of the door a signal that she was alone.

She closed her eyes as she battled nerves, envisioning the upcoming day. She took a deep breath as she banished thoughts of the wedding night, refusing to contemplate Morgan's touch after knowing such tenderness from Lucas. When her bedroom door opened, she swiveled to reprimand the person invading her last few moments of privacy as a single woman. However, the words lodged in her throat as she beheld Sophronia, vibrating with fury. The door shut behind her, nearly soundlessly.

"Well, my girl, you've embroiled yourself in a mess. What are you going to do to extricate yourself?" Sophie glowered at Parthena's silence.

Sophie wore an ice-blue dress that highlighted her regal bearing and enhanced her aged beauty. She marched to a lady's chair near Parthena and sat with an appreciative sigh.

"You failed to notify me or your uncles of your distress or of any need for aid. What could we do to help you if you refused to ask for it?" Sophie's aquamarine eyes shone with disappointment.

Parthena stood tall in her wedding finery, her veil undulating with her movements. "I made my choice to help my sisters and my family."

"Will it bring you happiness? Do you believe you should sacrifice yourself for those who should know better than to expect such actions by their daughters?"

Parthena glared at Sophie. "You know as well as I do that this is the common course of action for many of our class."

Sophie *thunked* her cane on the floor softly so as not to draw attention to her illicit visit on the morning of Parthena's wedding yet with enough strength to display her displeasure to Parthena. She gripped the handle as though she wished she could wave it about with her agitation. "That may be so, my girl, but I always thought you had a sturdier resolve to live the life you desired."

"I refuse to be the one to cause Genevieve to marry Mr. Carlisle, Sophie. Or Eudora. Or Isabel. My father would find a wretched man for all of them if he could. I will help them, in my way."

Sophie sighed, the anger and bluster leaving her. "I see you are determined." At Parthena's nod, Sophie heaved herself to her feet. "Then you must know your life will not be as you envisioned. Not married to a man such as Mr. Wheeler. He has a strength of will that even you will have trouble bending. I wish ..."

Sophie's eyes glistened a moment as she beheld Parthena standing tall in defiant determination of the course she had chosen. "I wish you all happiness and joy, my girl. I fear it may be some time before you acknowledge it exists in your new reality."

***

Zylphia slid into the empty pew next to Rowena in the church. She shared a long glance with Rowena, her hat tipped forward, giving them the illusion of privacy. Bright sunlight streamed in through the high stained-glass windows.

Rowena wore a pale green dress with matching hat and white gloves. She fanned herself, as the summer heat had failed to abate. She spoke at a volume barely loud enough for Zylphia to hear. "I can't believe you didn't tell me about P.T. and ..." She broke off her whisper and made her eyes big.

Zylphia's smile failed to reach her worried eyes as she attempted to maintain the charade of chatting with a friend before eagerly awaiting another friend's wedding. "I keep hoping he'll march down the aisle and demand the wedding to stop." Zylphia's light-blue dress highlighted her dark hair and her brilliant blue eyes.

"I'm thankful she'll have her sisters beside her as she marries," Rowena murmured.

Zylphia coughed in an attempt to hide a snort. "God forbid we had to participate in this farce," she whispered in Rowena's ear. "I'm having a hard enough time reminding myself I have to hold my peace and refrain from yelling out my dissent."

Rowena fought a chagrined smile as she nodded to newcomers in their pew, effectively silencing their conversation. She and Zylphia spoke of the weather and Zylphia's recent suffrage canvassing as they awaited the heralding blast from the church organ.

As the minutes ticked by with no evidence of Parthena's arrival, Zylphia fought an amused smile. "Do you think … ?" she whispered to Rowena.

Rowena shook her head. "No, she'll be here." They sighed in unison as the organ's blast put an abrupt halt to the murmured conversations within the church. They rose and turned toward the entrance of the church for their first sight of Parthena.

Parthena walked down the aisle with her head held high, her dress made of layers of white satin that enhanced her curves. Her face was largely hidden by an elaborate lace veil, and a long satin train dragged behind her. She rested her hand on top of her father's arm, but it appeared she barely touched him. When she arrived to the front of the church and an awaiting Morgan, she backed away before her father could kiss her on her cheek.

Zylphia sighed as she saw her friend stand with rigid formality before the pastor throughout the wedding ceremony. Although her voice trembled, her vows were clearly heard by all present. "It's done," Zylphia whispered mournfully.

Rowena gripped Zylphia's hand a moment and shook her head in solemn solidarity. They rose as the newly married couple walked past them, Morgan smiling to his friends and business associates as though triumphant, Parthena with a vapid smile and staring straight ahead. She failed to acknowledge the supportive smile Zylphia gave her as she marched down the aisle.

***

Lucas wandered the expansive first floor of a grand house in Cambridge. He knew the hostess had hoped he'd play something—as she'd set up a piano in a place of honor in the large drawing room—but he'd avoided venturing in that direction ever since he'd caught sight of it upon his arrival. He roamed, searching for a petite woman with straw-blond hair. When he caught sight of Parthena, he tracked her through the small parlor and followed her to the edge of the ballroom.

"Mrs. Wheeler, it's a delight to see you," Lucas said when he stood next to her, his jacket sleeve brushing against her arm.

"Mr. Russell," Parthena said, looking forward at the crowd. She edged away from him so that they were no longer touching.

"Please forgive me for having to forego the pleasure of attending your wedding." The hum of voices from the ballroom and the lilting music of the musicians formed a pleasant backdrop. "I was devastated to miss your joyous celebration."

"As were we," Parthena said. "We had a very pleasant day, celebrating with family and friends."

"I hope you will be able to attend my performance this fall at Steinert Hall," Lucas said as he smiled at a distant acquaintance. He frowned as Parthena stiffened upon hearing her husband's voice.

"She'll have no need to hear you perform," Morgan said. "She has no further need of the piano."

Lucas raised his eyebrows at Morgan's comment. "Well, if you have the opportunity, I'm sure Miss McLeod would enjoy attending with you."

Parthena nodded and walked away, moving from sight as she joined the throng in the ballroom. Lucas watched her leave with a frown, before turning to study Morgan. He vibrated with tension, unlike the relaxed newlywed Lucas imagined the groom would be. Lucas frowned as he remembered Savannah after her marriage to Jonas.

"I'd appreciate it if you would cease any overtures to my wife. She has many other duties to occupy her time," Morgan said. He and Lucas were virtually the same height, and they shared intense stares from matching brown eyes. Morgan stiffened further when Lucas refused to back down from Morgan's silent challenge, even though he had broader shoulders and a reputation as a fierce fighter from his sparring matches at his boxing club.

"Do you understand what you are asking Mrs. Wheeler to forego?" Lucas asked, in a low, challenging voice.

"She tinkers at the piano. There are many other hobbies that will equally satisfy her artistic inclinations."

"I believe I was told you've known her since infancy. If that's true, then I'd think you'd know of her need to play the piano." At Morgan's determined silence, Lucas continued. "It's not simply a passing fancy for her. Have you ever heard her play? She has a genuine talent."

"Next you'll tell me how she could perform," Morgan said with a snort of disdain.

"If she practiced more and had a good tutor, rather than having to depend on her innate talent, yes, she could. I wouldn't be surprised if she surpassed my abilities, if only given the chance." Lucas frowned. "Let her try."

"This is exactly why I'd prefer you to keep your distance from my wife. She doesn't need to have her head filled with your nonsense about dreams that will never be fulfilled. She's competent, at best, and there's no need to give her any unwarranted delusions." He took a sip of his champagne. "I need something stronger," he muttered and moved toward the library, where gentlemen played cards, drank whiskey, and escaped the demands of dancing.

Lucas watched him go with a frown, recalling Parthena's lack of exuberance. "Only two weeks," he muttered. Two weeks since her marriage to Morgan. As the hostess approached him to perform, he pasted on a pleased smile. He allowed her to lead him into the large drawing room with chairs filled with interested partygoers. The small orchestra in the ballroom ceased playing a moment before she began to speak.

He stood next to her as she showered effusive praise on his playing and then pushed him onto the piano stool. He sat, staring at the keys for such a long duration that a few women giggled nervously, and he heard one man mutter about the validity of the reports of his lunacy. Lucas smiled and played a piece that always reminded him of Savannah. Sweet, yet filled with torment and sadness. At the last note, he sat back and raised his head, seemingly surprised to see a crowd gathered to watch him. He smiled again and rose, bowing to the crowd.

Amid cries of "Encore," his gaze met Parthena's as she lingered in the doorway. He held up his hand to the crowd for silence. "As much as I'm delighted that you enjoyed that small performance, I'm certain you'd enjoy something different tonight. For Mrs. Beaupre's guests deserve the best in entertainment. I offer you a duet, with the unequaled Mrs. Wheeler." He held out his hand to her, waving her forward, his gaze daring her to decline as the crowd clapped in approval.

He saw her pale and then flush as she was pushed forward by those standing near her. Her hazel eyes were huge as she attempted to conceal her discomfort at being in the center of attention. "Let's play the Brahms," he murmured to her. He nodded to his hostess who came forward with sheet music.

"Did you have this planned?" Parthena whispered.

"No, she did. She heard me play a duet years ago and bought the sheet music." He nodded to the young man arranging two small stools in front of the piano. "She hoped I'd play the piece alone."

"And rather than do that, you thought to humiliate me in front of Boston society?" Parthena hissed.

"You play this piece better than I do," Lucas whispered as he smiled to the crowd. "We are just about ready." He motioned for Parthena to sit and then sat beside her. "There's no one here but you and me, and our love of music."

Parthena took a deep breath, muttered the count to the music, and shared a long glance with Lucas. They began playing, in perfect synchrony, and didn't stop for nearly twenty minutes. As the last note faded away, Lucas shared a long look with Parthena and beamed. "You did it," he whispered. "You performed."

The roar of the appreciative audience snapped them from their momentary reverie, and they stood to take their bows. He noted Morgan, standing toward the back of the room, frozen as a pillar as he glared at the two of them. Lucas nodded in Morgan's direction and stepped to the side to allow Parthena to bask in her momentary glory. He waved away requests for more music and melted into the crowd as he watched Parthena become surrounded by her peers who had had no inkling of her hidden talents. He smiled as he accepted his coat and slipped out the front door to catch the trolley for home.

CHAPTER SIX

Parthena smiled vaguely to the butler who opened the door to Morgan's home. *Her home*, she reminded herself. She slipped up the stairs and into the bedroom she shared with Morgan. She'd hoped to have her own room, but he'd insisted they share a room and use the adjoining room as a sitting room.

After quickly changing into a nightgown and wrap set out for her by her maid, she sat in front of her vanity, taking off her jewelry and brushing her hair. She'd sent her maid away, preferring to perform these mindless tasks herself. She closed her eyes at the click of the door, signaling Morgan's arrival.

"It was a nice gathering," Morgan said with a searching glance at his wife.

"Yes." She tensed as he placed his hands on her shoulders.

"I hope you enjoyed yourself." He met her wary gaze in the mirror. "I was surprised to see you disobey me, Parthena."

She raised her chin in defiance. "I had every right to play. I brought no shame on your family."

He watched her intently, his hands softly resting on her shoulders. "You performed beautifully. However, I expect this to be a one-time-only performance. My wife is not a performer. You do not need to peddle your talents to survive, unlike some." He watched her frown at his criticism of Lucas.

"I am talented."

"As you showed tonight. However, I want your promise there will be no repeat performances." He met her mutinous gaze in the mirror, waiting until she nodded with reluctance.

"Good, now we can focus on the more pleasurable aspects of the evening." He leaned forward to kiss the back of her neck, exposed by a vee in her nightgown and wrap. He kissed her again before meeting her gaze in the mirror's reflection. "I would hope by now my touch wouldn't fluster you so much."

Parthena licked her lips and swallowed. She shivered as his long, lean fingers eased her wrap off her shoulders, leaving it pooled around her hips on the vanity's bench. Her shoulders and arms were bared to his touch as her nightgown was short-sleeved and diaphanous, perfect for the summer's warm evening. Or the ardor of a newly married husband.

"I love this gown," Morgan murmured, his hands tracing the lace at the edge of the gown, along the vee on her chest.

"I know," Parthena whispered.

Morgan's eyes flashed with desire and pleasure. "It pleases me that you wore this for me," he whispered, kissing the side of her neck.

She tilted her head to the side, granting him access as he'd taught her to do. She shivered at his touch and kisses.

"There's no need to feel embarrassed that you enjoy my touch."

She shivered again at his words.

He reached his arms around, spinning her to the side and then lifting her into his arms. He carried her to their bed, placing her on the turned-down sheets. He shucked off his jacket, waistcoat, and cravat. He frowned as he watched Parthena, holding herself stiffly as she awaited his next caress.

When he'd freed himself from his clothes, he slipped onto the bed with her and pulled the sheet over the two of them. "There, my darling. We're in our own little world now." He kissed her, long and passionately, provoking a mewl of frustration from her when he broke the kiss. He smiled as he moved lower, raising her nightgown and tossing it to the floor.

At her gasp as his skin touched hers, he bit back a groan. "I love that my touch brings you pleasure," he whispered, surprised by a tear down her cheek that he brushed away as he caressed her face. "Hennie?" He leaned up to kiss her cheek, finding it wet with her tears.

She shook her head, her body suddenly rigid under his. "It's nothing, please," she whispered.

He held himself above her, his ardor extinguished at her evident dismay. "What's wrong, Hennie?" Although his arms and legs bracketed her, she was able to move beneath him and she curled into herself, onto her side.

He settled behind her, tracing patterns along her hip, frowning as his touch provoked shudders and goose bumps. "Would you prefer I slept elsewhere tonight?"

"It doesn't matter."

"I believe it does. I refuse to be the cause of your torment," he said as he rose, walking to his dressing room for a robe. He returned to their bed, pulling the covers fully over her. "We must talk in the morning." He waited for some sort of acknowledgment from her, but, when none came, he moved to the adjoining room's door and slipped through it.

Parthena sobbed as she heard him in the other room, her tears soaking her pillow before she succumbed to sleep.

***

Parthena awoke the following morning to the other side of the bed dipping under a heavy weight. She cracked open one eye and beheld Morgan, studying her. He wore his robe from the previous evening, and he appeared as exhausted as she felt. He reached out a hand to her, tracing her eyebrow.

"I know you're awake, Hennie," he murmured.

"I don't want to be."

"Because you're still tired?" He paused, his touch falling away from her. "Or because you'd prefer not to speak with me?"

Parthena pulled the sheets under her chin but opened her eyes to face him. "Forgive me for last night. I know it wasn't what you had planned."

His frown turned into a glower as her gaze became guarded as she measured his reaction. "Have I ever given you any reason to fear me?" He relaxed as she shook her head no. "Why were you crying, Hennie?" He reached forward and traced a finger over her cheek.

"I don't understand why you care." Her eyes widened, as though she couldn't believe she'd blurted out the truth to him.

"Of course I care. You're my wife."

She leaned away from his touch and sat up, the sheet clutched to her chest by one of her arms. "Those are just empty words, spoken to obtain your momentary desires."

Morgan flushed as he watched her. "What's overcome you?"

"You said last night, when you left, that we should speak this morning. I spent the entire night thinking."

He nodded his encouragement for her to continue.

"In the two weeks we've been married, you've never once concerned yourself for my opinions. You've proclaimed what I should like. What I would do. What my hobbies will be. You've never once asked me what I would like." She exhaled a long breath at his shocked expression.

"I saved you from that man," Morgan hissed. "I saved your family."

"And for that I've paid with my body and my obedience," Parthena snapped. "Must I also pay for it by foregoing what brings me joy?"

Morgan scowled, his hand now fisted next to her hip.

"I heard you last night, talking to Mr. Russell." She met his surprised gaze. "Yes, I listened as you advised him to keep his distance from me and to not fill my head with foolish notions about my abilities. Which were, at best, competent."

"Parthena—"

She waved away his attempt at appeasement. "Why act as though you care about me? As though you want me to find contentment living in your home when you deny me what will help me to find such happiness?" Her face flushed with her pent-up frustration. "Will you also deny me the right to champion a woman's right to vote? Will you insist I sit and do nothing while my friends struggle for a right all people should have?"

"Parthena, you knew who I was when you married me."

"Yes, an overbearing, rigid man who must maintain control of his environment at all costs. I'm now just one more thing you must struggle to control."

He paled as he listened to her. "This is how you see me? As a man, eager to subvert you to my will?"

"When have you ever shown me otherwise?" Parthena raised a brow to him.

Morgan leaned farther away from her. "I see." He raised a hand, running it through his disheveled hair, and then scratched at his day's growth of beard. He frowned as he studied her, naked but for a sheet in their bed. "And you never—" He shook his head before finishing his question, his posture stiffening as he became resolute. "I beg your pardon for wishing to save you from the aspects of yourself that will only lead to pain and disillusionment."

"The parts of me that make me who I am," she retorted. She saw disappointment mirrored in his eyes. "I warned you that we should never marry. We've never agreed on anything since we were children."

Morgan nodded again. "I will leave you to enjoy your day," he murmured. "I will endeavor to avoid marring it further with my presence." He rose, the door to his dressing room shutting with more force than necessary.

Parthena leaned against the pillow, her thoughts whirling.

***

Zylphia sat with Sophronia in her back sitting room. Sophie detested the recent redecoration to her front sitting room and chose to use her private sitting room as much as possible, particularly when she had close friends call.

Zylphia frowned as she read the front page of one of the daily newspapers. "Why must they be so shortsighted?" She shook the paper in frustration.

"They're the Catholic church, darling. It's what they do best. You can't expect the leaders of the church to envision another role for women when they've preached for centuries that a woman is to produce babies to fill the pews at their churches." Sophie snatched the paper from Zylphia's hands and read a few lines. "Although I'd think by now, with the number of women working outside the home, the church leaders should realize that the role for women is changing."

"Has already changed," Zylphia muttered. "When I go to church with my parents, the number of women who agree with me grows. But the men are the ones who vote, and they agree with the priests. I don't know how to sway their thinking."

"We must show we are above reproach. That women voting is respectable and will only strengthen the family." She raised her eyebrows as she met Zylphia's frown.

"And how are we to do that?"

"Why, show them society out West hasn't dissolved into chaos with women having the vote."

"They're already prejudiced against anything occurring in the West. I doubt we'll be successful." Zylphia sighed as she sat.

"What did the Montana legislature do after women earned the right to vote last year?" Sophie asked with a raise of one eyebrow. She picked up a letter from Clarissa and scanned it. "Your cousin informs me they enacted crucial legislation for women, including a mother's pension law, an equal guardianship law, and an act giving married women control of their own property."

"Many would argue that Montana was merely behind the times and that their legislators were finally catching up to the laws already passed in other states." Zylphia reached for Clarissa's letter and began to read it.

"The particulars aren't as important as the fact that laws affecting women, championed by women, are being enacted. Especially so soon after garnering the vote. That is the crucial information that must be extolled to the women you speak with." Sophie glared at Zylphia. "Don't act in such a defeatist manner. You, almost more than anyone, must champion this cause and show that you have no doubt we shall succeed."

Zylphia sighed and sat back in her chair. "I know, Sophie. It's only with you—and Florence—that I express my doubts and fears. With everyone else I'm nauseatingly optimistic."

Sophie nodded. "Good. And you must expand that optimism to your young man. It does no good imagining the worst. Save your energy and emotions for when you need them, dearest."

Zylphia nodded her agreement before she focused on Clarissa's letter. "Oh my!" She raised luminous eyes to Sophie. "Why didn't you tell me about her news right away?"

Sophie grinned. "I was going to but thought uplifting news should be saved for after we finished discussing the business of the day. Isn't it wonderful?"

Zylphia focused on the letter again. "I can't believe she'll be a mother again. Gabe must be ecstatic."

Sophie cackled. "I imagine he's terrified. Just as he has been for the last four births. However, he'll be fine once she's delivered a healthy babe." Sophie sobered. "I worry for Savannah. She's desired a child for so many years, and I fear this will be difficult for her."

Zylphia tapped the letter on her knee. "Oh, poor Sav. I know she'll be happy for Rissa, but I imagine she'll be wistful too."

Sophie *harrumphed* and snatched her letter back from Zylphia. "Although you distracted me from our business at hand, there is more to discuss. I plan to escape this infernal heat. At the same time, I hope to pursue those who might be able to sway influential men to the vote. I need you to travel with me to Newport next week. New York is also having a referendum for the vote, and it should prove quite entertaining."

Zylphia stared at the small bouquet of yellow roses on Sophie's desk. "Returning to Newport would prove too painful."

"I know you met your Theodore there two years ago, but you must know he'd want you to continue to live a full life. Confront that ghost, Zee."

"He's not dead," she snapped.

"I know that. But the ghost of your regrets walks beside you every day. You must find a way to let it go."

Zylphia nodded as she met Sophie's concerned gaze. As the door to the parlor burst open, she turned her head to look over her shoulder. "P.T.!"

"About time you joined us," Sophie said, her brusque words masking her concern.

"Are you still plotting ways to improve our chances of success in November?" Parthena asked, her cheeks flushed.

"Yes, of course. I've just invited Zylphia to travel to Newport with me next week." She studied Parthena's reaction. "Why don't you join us?"

"I—We're already planning to travel there in a few weeks. Mr. Wheeler is unable to travel any sooner due to business concerns."

"Why don't you come with us, and he can join you later?" Zylphia said with a broad smile. "That way you won't miss any of the meetings, and we can have some time together, like before."

"I'm uncertain Mr. Wheeler would be in agreement with such a plan," Parthena said.

Sophie slapped her fan against the edge of the table, causing Zylphia and Parthena to jolt with surprise. "Stop acting the part of a meek, biddable wife. We know that's not who you are. Show the man your spirit, and he'll respect you for it."

Parthena shook her head. "I doubt that to be true." She leaned forward and helped herself to a biscuit. She smiled at Zylphia, teasing her. "You should have your cook spend a few days with Sophie's. Maybe she'd learn important lessons."

"I wouldn't want Sophie's cook to quit, claiming cruel treatment," Zylphia said with a giggle, then turned to Sophie. "Have you invited Rowena to Newport with us?"

Sophie nodded. "Of course. Her father was hesitant to allow her into my care, but, when he heard you would be there, as would your parents for part of the time, he relented."

"Why bother asking me if you already knew I had to come?" Zee asked.

"You always have a choice, darling Zee," Sophie said with an indulgent smile. "If you prefer to stay in sweltering Boston, by all means, remain behind. I know your mother was looking forward to meeting patronesses who might aid her orphanage."

"If Mother put one-tenth of her energy into fighting for the vote as she did in securing funds for the orphanage, we'd all have the vote by now," Zylphia complained.

"We all have our callings, Zee, and that is your mother's. It's unbecoming to disparage it," Sophie scolded.

Zylphia ducked her head in acknowledgment.

Sophie looked from Zylphia to Parthena and heaved herself to a standing position. She waved at Zylphia and Parthena to remain seated, and leaned heavily on her cane. "I must speak with my cook for a moment. If you'll excuse me." She thunked from the room.

"Not very subtle of her," Parthena remarked.

"No, but I'm thankful she's granting us this time together. Morgan doesn't like me to call at your house."

Parthena raised her eyebrows at this news. "I beg your pardon?"

"He advised Rowena and me, well, and Sophie too, that it would be better if we abstained from calling, as you were learning your new duties, and you didn't have time for our incessant chatter about nonsensical topics." Zylphia watched Parthena as she flushed, then paled, then flushed again.

"I had hoped your absence from my life was merely to grant me time to adjust to my new circumstances. Not a reflection of your disdain for my acquiescence to my father's wishes," Parthena whispered. "I know I hurt Lucas, and I feared you were angry with me."

"P.T., you have to know how worried we all are for you. If we'd been able to, we'd have been present on the morning after your wedding to give you support."

Parthena laughed, although it was more sorrowful than mirthful. "I wish you'd been there."

"Was it horrible?" Zylphia asked, reaching forward to grip her hand.

"Horribly embarrassing." She flushed from her neckline to hairline, accenting her straw-blond hair and hazel-colored eyes. "I didn't want to be with him. Not after ..." She broke off and bit her lip.

"Not after you'd been with Lucas?" Zylphia asked in a soft voice.

P.T. nodded. "The entire time, it was as though he suspected I wasn't a virgin, and he was angry."

"Did he hurt you?" Zylphia clasped Parthena's hand.

"No, that's the worst of it. It was as though he was even gentler, more solicitous of my enjoyment. Every time since, it's as though he's taunting me with his touch to show how I enjoy it. Daring me to like it more than Lucas's." She raised hands to her face as she blushed beet red.

"How does it compare?" Zylphia asked, unable to battle her curiosity.

Parthena looked down, her hands now clasped together in her lap. "Lucas touched me with a reverence. As though he believed I were special and wanted me to believe it too. However, I feel like Morgan's goading me to reveal my feelings. And I feel disloyal to Lucas every time I feel any pleasure from Morgan's touch." She again covered her reddened cheeks with her hands. "I can't believe I'm talking about this with you, my unmarried friend. It's not proper."

"Why would you be embarrassed, P.T.? It's something almost everyone will do at some point in their lives." Zylphia flushed before whispering, "I'm not as innocent as I look."

P.T.'s eyes bulged. "You and Teddy?" At Zee's nod, P.T. shook her head in confusion. "Then why'd he leave? Why'd he go to war?"

"I said hurtful, hateful things and pushed him away. To the point he wouldn't listen to my apology. He refused to read any of the letters I wrote him until he'd enlisted and was on his way to France."

P.T. squeezed Zylphia's hand, still clasped in hers. "What was it like? When you were with Teddy?"

"Wonderful," Zylphia breathed. "It was uncomfortable and awkward and strange, but Teddy made it all better."

Parthena blinked rapidly, battling tears. "That's what I don't have with Morgan. I worry that I could be any woman to him."

"Did you have that special bond with Lucas?" Zylphia whispered.

Parthena lost her battle with tears as she swiped at her cheeks. "Yes. I felt like I mattered to him."

Zylphia sat in silence a moment. "What confuses me is that I don't understand if you want to be with Morgan or not." At Parthena's determined silence, Zylphia asked softly, "Is it because he doesn't affect you, or that you won't allow him to affect you?"

P.T. stiffened. "That's not fair."

"Isn't it?" Zylphia asked. "I see how he watches you. It's as though he's constantly trying to figure out a way to reach you. Every time I see you together, he grows a bit gruffer, a bit more desperate to provoke a reaction from you. You're always so cool and emotionless around him."

"That's not because he cares for me."

"I wouldn't be so certain," Zylphia said, running a soothing hand down her friend's arm.

"If he truly cared for me, he'd not forbid me from performing, speaking with Lucas, or participating in any suffragist activities."

Zylphia smiled at the irony of what Parthena said. "You can't expect your husband to be overjoyed in his wife speaking with her lover. No man, if he cares at all for his wife, is that understanding."

"Nothing untoward has happened between Lucas and me since my marriage. I'm trying to abide by my vows. The more I give in to Morgan's demands, the more he expects me to change." She rubbed a few tears off her cheeks again.

"Your husband understands you have a close bond to Lucas forged by your love of music. Something he'll never be able to share with you. That would terrify most men."

"Do you know what it's like to have the one thing you are most proud of constantly ridiculed?"

Zylphia paled. "He truly doesn't understand you, does he?" She watched her friend, the vibrancy leaching from her little by little. "What if you continued to play the piano with the goal of performing?"

"He threatened to inform my father of my inability to honor both my father's and my husband's wishes to give up the piano. If I perform again, my father will happily marry Genevieve off to an onerous suitor." She and Zylphia shared a grimace as they contemplated Mr. Carlisle and other such men of their acquaintance who'd enjoy having someone as young and innocent as Genevieve at their mercy. "And I had hoped to play one song with Lucas at his performance at Steinert Hall in the fall."

"When did Morgan deny you this?"

"At breakfast this morning. We've barely spoken for the past week. After a disastrous evening out at the Beaupres' home last week. You might have heard about it. I played a duet with Lucas." Tears coursed down her cheeks.

"Oh my," Zylphia breathed. "You taunted your husband with your lover, in front of a roomful of the worst gossips ever created?" At Parthena's guilty nod, Zylphia shook her head in shock. "How could you? Why would you?"

"Do you know what it's like to have this talent, this desire to shine, in front of your peers? I'm so tired of living in the shadows and acting as though the most important thing I can do is parrot whatever my father or husband believes." Her mouth turned down mutinously.

"Parthena, I appreciate that you have a tremendous ability and that you are tired of hiding it. But it was folly, absolute folly, to act as you did. How could you expect your husband to rejoice in you performing when that makes him feel a fool?" Zylphia studied her. "How would you feel if he walked through a ballroom with his lover on his arm?"

"He doesn't have one," Parthena protested.

"It would hurt, wouldn't it? And, more important, you would care," Zylphia said, watching her friend closely. "You don't live an isolated life where your actions have no effect on those around you. I thought, after you acted to save your sister Genevieve, that you understood that."

Parthena closed her eyes and tilted her head back, as though reliving a memory. "You don't know what it's like to play with Lucas. It's intoxicating to match my skill with his. His is superior, but I can see my improvement every time I play with him."

"Do you desire Lucas because of his piano prowess or because of himself?" Zylphia clenched her jaw as she fought against saying anything more.

Parthena blinked in shock. "That's patently unfair." At Zylphia's implacable stare, she blushed. "I don't know. I love how he makes me feel when I play the piano. How he gives me confidence."

"If he never kissed or touched you again, would you mourn their loss?" Zylphia bit her lip, unable to hide her concern from her gaze.

"Yes. I can't imagine never being in his arms again. Morgan thinks his demand that I not perform is the greatest sacrifice he is asking of me. He doesn't realize that means I never see Lucas again. Giving up Lucas will always be my greatest sacrifice," Parthena whispered.

"But you will give him up?" Zylphia asked, her brow furrowed in confusion.

"I have to. I'm not a woman who thrives on deceit. I like to believe I have some honor, thus an affair is out of the question. Plus I can't divorce as I have no real cause." Parthena lowered her head in shame. "I'm not strong enough, Zee, to live with the notoriety or to live outside of society. I know playing in public with Lucas was reckless, and I know Morgan blames Lucas for that decision." She closed her eyes. "It's unfair of Morgan to blame him when I derived such joy from it and Lucas fulfilled one of my long-held dreams."

"Will his blaming Lucas help Genevieve at all?" Zylphia asked.

"I think so. Morgan thinks I was overpowered and had no real say in the matter." She shared a rueful smile with Zylphia.

"They don't know you well," Zylphia said with a wry smile.

Parthena smiled her agreement. "As it is now, Lucas is the villain, I'm the poor woman who was taken advantage of, and Viv is still safe because I'm being exonerated due to the events being out of my control. My father is angry, but Morgan was able to talk him out of announcing Viv's betrothal." She sighed and clenched her hands together. "I must now attempt to act as though I am docile and in agreement with my husband's dictates. I hate that I need Morgan to contain my father's idiotic plans."

"Oh, P.T." Zylphia clasped her hand. "I still don't understand."

"This is the world I was born to, and I want to live in it." She brushed away a tear. "I will always love Lucas. But it's a love that was never meant to be."

Zylphia shook her head in disappointment. "Wealth and standing mean more to you than love? I know what it is to be poor, Parthena. But not to have love? That is true poverty."

Parthena swiped at her cheeks. "My father advised me on the morning of my wedding that, if I acted in a shameless manner or caused any scandals, he'd happily consent to a marriage between Genevieve and Mr. Carlisle. He's more than willing to earn money off his remaining unwed daughters. Only Morgan is able to talk him down out of one of his vengeful moods."

Zylphia clasped her hands together to prevent herself from throwing one of Sophie's knickknacks. "You can't continue to allow your father to control you."

"I can't leave Viv to such a fate, Zee. She's young and has her whole life ahead of her. She should never be exposed to a man like him." She lowered her head.

"So you make three of you miserable to protect her?"

Parthena sighed. "My hope is that, one day, Morgan and I won't be miserable, and that Lucas finds a love worthy of him."

"Oh, my poor Parthena," Zylphia whispered, brushing away a tear. "And poor Lucas."

"I didn't use him," she protested. At Zylphia's incredulous snort, she protested again. "I didn't. He knew ... I hope he knew what we were to each other."

Zylphia leaned against her seat back, exhaustion and disappointment evident. "Now that we've ascertained you'll not struggle for a future with Lucas, what do you feel for Morgan? The man you've married."

"I don't want to appreciate his touch. I don't want to feel anything when he's near."

Zylphia smiled with sympathy. "And yet you do."

"I've always known, for years, when he entered a room. When he was looking at me." She shuddered. "It's a thousand times worse living with him. Sharing a life with him." She paused. "I pushed him away last week. Froze him away would be more accurate. And he slept on the floor that night, and every night since, in the adjoining room, rather than provoke gossip for the servants."

"That's chivalrous of him," Zylphia said with a raised eyebrow.

"It spares him gossip as well as me. What I realized, as the week has passed and he's become even more remote and cold, is that he doesn't want to know who I am. He wants to change me into who he imagines I should be. And that's not who I want to be."

"Would he ever hurt you?"

"Every day that he refuses to acknowledge who I am and what I like hurts me." She met her friend's worried gaze. "No, he'd never harm me physically. Even when I yelled at him this morning about his threat to tell my father if I performed again, he refrained from raising his voice. He's a very controlled man."

Zylphia was silent a moment as she thought about what her friend said. She then smiled wickedly. "What would happen if he lost control? If you took it from him?"

"I don't know what you mean."

She held up her hand as P.T. opened her mouth to interrupt her. "It's been a week since things have worsened between you, correct?"

Parthena nodded.

"How has that changed him?"

"He's more short-tempered. He acts as though he'll touch me, then snatches his hand away. He watches me but now with a glower."

Zylphia smiled as she shook her head. "I'm no expert in men. If I were, Teddy would be here with me. Anyway it seems to me that your husband is frustrated he can't have the marital relationship he wants."

"Why should he? He's taking away everything I want!" Parthena crossed her arms over her chest, like a petulant child.

"Parthena, you have to decide—now—what you want in your marriage. Do you want a cold, distant marriage where you come to loathe each other? You're on the path to just that sort of marriage. Do you want a marriage where you sneak away to be with your lover? Or do you want to forge a good relationship with your husband?"

"I can't imagine never seeing Lucas again. Never playing with him. Never hearing him tease me." Parthena closed her eyes. "I barely know Lucas. We spent a few short weeks together before that blasted announcement. Yet it was as though everything changed in my life."

"You had your chance to marry him," Zylphia said. "You declined him. You must own your decisions as they are yours and no one else's. You chose to protect your sister Genevieve from a perceived threat. You can't be certain it would ever have come to fruition, but you did what you thought was necessary. You choose to refrain from causing any scandal now. Is it fair to continue to keep Lucas in such turmoil? Or to mar your marriage forever?"

Parthena slouched in her chair as though in defeat. "I hate that Morgan wins. That he believes he can control me as he controls his world."

"No matter your infatuation with Lucas, you must admit you are equally intrigued by your own husband, even if it is against your will."

Zylphia tapped Parthena on her hand. "I know you believe he is too controlling, but perhaps it is the only way he can convince himself you'll continue to pay attention to him." Zylphia's smile became wicked as Parthena blushed. "You like his touch, even though you hate admitting it. Rather than wait for him to approach you, to touch you, why don't you shock him and take the initiative?" Her smile blossomed into one of true deviltry. "Shock him, and then seduce him into submission."

Parthena scoffed. "That only works in novels."

"You're both miserable now. I don't see how it could make matters any worse."

Parthena flushed. "It would give him the idea I want more from him."

"I think that perhaps you do." Zylphia raised her eyebrows as she reached for her teacup. "But you'll have to be the one to make that decision."

CHAPTER SEVEN

"Lucas, there is no need to antagonize your mother," Martin Russell chastised. He sat in his office in his fine linen store in the South End. Stacks of inventory lined one side of his desk, and the house shook every few minutes from the passage of one of the overhead trains. His brown eyes flashed with irritation at his son as he shut the door behind him. "When she calls on you, I would expect you to treat her with respect."

"I've no wish to see her, Father," Lucas said. He swiped a hand over his perfectly pleated gray pants, unbuttoning his matching jacket to sit with more comfort. "Which she knows and yet she continues to visit me."

"Lucas, she made a mistake years ago, and you must forgive her."

"What mistake is that, Father? Marrying you or having Savannah and me?" Lucas flushed at the wounded look that flashed across his father's face at his words. "Forgive me."

"This isn't like you, Lucas. We've supported you in your desire to perform and compose music. We've understood your need to travel the world and no longer work here with me in the store. You'll never understand how proud we are of you, son."

Lucas shook his head with disbelief. "You are proud of me. You understand. Mother isn't and never will be." His fierce glare and scowl silenced his father's protest. "She wishes I remained a store clerk, under her control."

Martin took a deep breath, his gaze distant. "Your mother had very little control over her life when she was younger. It's why she attempts to cling to it now."

"Even at the expense of losing her daughter? When was the last time Savannah wrote you? When did you last see her?"

Martin's eyes shone with repressed grief. "I saw her with you. When she left for Montana with her Jeremy. In 1903." He looked over Lucas's shoulder, as though envisioning that scene, his attempt not to clasp his daughter to him and never let her go as he bid her good-bye at the train station. "You don't understand what it's like for a father to know he'll never see his daughter again."

"She'd visit if not for Mother," Lucas said. Perplexed, he furrowed his brows and watched his father. "Why do you stay? She watched you, wounded and bleeding on the floor, and did nothing. She failed to visit you in the hospital. She mourned the man who would have gladly killed us all in his intent to regain Savannah. Why do you stay?"

"Your mother and I have forged a truce."

Lucas frowned as he studied his father. Rather than the vibrant man he'd worked with side-by side, his father appeared diminished. His shoulders stooped somewhat; the lines around his eyes appeared to be from frowns rather than the ever-present smile from Lucas's childhood, and his face held a deep resignation. "You've accepted that your son and daughter have the right to their heart's desire, but that you don't."

Martin sighed. "When you are a father, when you know what that deep, boundless love is, then you'll understand."

"Why would you think my love for you would be any less?" His voice broke with his deep emotion as he watched his father, for the first time seeing him as mortal. Even when Martin had been injured, Lucas never doubted his father's ability to recover. He fisted his hand on his armchair. "I hate that you sacrificed your happiness for mine."

"Life does not always follow the path we think it will. I never expected to meet, much less marry, a woman as fine as your mother." He opened his arms to encompass his office, the shop, and his home. "All we've had, all you've had the opportunity to experience, is due to my decision to marry your mother. Rather than tinker away at a back-breaking trade, you had an education and the time to learn to play the piano."

"Your father owned this shop. You would have been fine had you married someone other than Mother."

Martin's eyes flashed again at his son's impertinence. "I married your mother to save our shop. We were on the verge of losing it. Your mother saved my father's dream."

"What about your dreams? If you hadn't been tied to this shop, what would you have done?"

Martin closed his eyes a moment and settled against his creaky, comfortable wooden chair. "Travel. I would have continued working for my father, but I would have relished traveling to France or India or anywhere we purchased linens."

"Why don't you travel now?"

"When the world's at war?" Martin shook his head. "No, my opportunity is gone." His eyes shone with pride as he beheld Lucas. "It's part of the reason I encouraged you to accept the foreign tour. I knew you would be wildly popular. I also wanted you to live without restrictions." He shared a chagrined smile with Lucas. "Once you finally told me that you'd no longer work here."

After a moment's companionable silence, Martin said, "I want you to treat your mother better. She is your mother."

"Do you know what she's said about me? About how she's attempting to sabotage my career?" His eyes shone with hurt. He barreled on when his father shook his head no. "She's bandied it about that I'm slowly going insane. That it's a trait she's attempted to shield her husband from as I'm forced to face the harsh realities of my father's family's fate."

Martin tensed, his face reddening as Lucas spoke. "She said what about the Russells?"

"Why don't you ask her?"

Martin rose, his anger gifting him the agility of a man half his age. He strode to the door and bellowed for his wife. He waited, his head cocked to one side as he listened, nodding with satisfaction when he heard her heels on the stairs. He returned to his place behind his desk and took a few deep breaths, as though attempting to calm his erratic breathing.

Matilda entered the office, the staccato clicking of her heels an indication of her irritation. "Martin, how many times must I tell you that bellowing for me is not an appropriate manner to ask for my presence in your office?"

"Perhaps my latent lunacy is finally shining through," Martin hissed. He watched his wife, his face beet red and eyes glacially cold as he noted her paling at his words.

"Martin, you've been listening to nonsensical gossip."

"Of course he has, Mother. He's been listening to his son, who's purported to be going as insane as his father," Lucas said.

She started at seeing Lucas standing in a corner, one heel crossed over the other. She closed the door behind her, tilting up her chin as she regained her equilibrium and took her seat in front of Martin. "I have nothing to explain."

"Of course not. You never do. You simply wreak havoc in the lives of those you are supposed to love and protect, and then watch with glee as they suffer the consequences of what you've done."

"Lucas," Matilda said, her eyes shining with surprise and a hint of pain at his words.

"I tried, Matilda. I have tried to excuse your behavior after you invited Jonas into our house. After you refused to support Lucas in his dream. When I learned you wrote scathing letters to Savannah in Montana." He shared a look with a shocked Lucas at that news. "However, this ends now. Either you find a way to cease your meddlesome ways, or I will divorce you."

"Divorce?" Her voice rose to an octave just below a shriek. "Divorce? How dare you threaten me after all I've done for you? After all I've suffered?"

"I believe the suffering has been mutual," Martin said in a low voice. He motioned with his head for Lucas to leave his office, and Lucas nodded, silently moving behind his mother and shutting the door behind him.

***

Martin leaned forward, his hands clasped together in front of him on his desk. "You have a penchant for mischief. I'd hoped you'd worn yourself out, but it appears, with Lucas returned to us, you decided to attempt to bend him to your will." He clamped his jaw together in his fury. "At my family's expense."

"They aren't worthy of such concern," Matilda retorted.

His voice became softer but more potent for its controlled anger. "And you believe your family is? They who care nothing for the personal satisfaction of individual members as long as the family name and so-called honor is upheld?" Martin's eyes blazed with his ire. "After all these years, do you really feel no affinity for me or my family?"

"That question is not worthy of a response." She tilted her head a bit higher, her flinch barely appreciable when she noticed the agony in Martin's expression.

"My love for you, my devotion, my constant defense of you have meant nothing, have they? Because I'm not the one you wanted." He growled out, "Not some two-bit actor who had such little regard for you that he'd abandon you pregnant to pursue another conquest."

Matilda's calm facade cracked, and she snarled at Martin. "You have no right to even speak of him. He had more culture, more ingrained decency than I've ever known with you."

"What did he do when he learned you were pregnant? Did he approach your parents and say that he'd marry you? That he'd be delighted to care for you in Scollay Square?"

"How dare you!"

"How dare I? After I've dedicated my life to you and our family? After I've only shown you love and devotion, and this is how I'm repaid? By lies, deceit, and disdain? Yes, how dare I attempt to show you that the dreams you cling to have only ever been illusions. The reality you've lived with me is far superior to anything you could ever have lived with that bastard." He took a deep breath, his heartbreak and desolation clear.

"I want you to understand, Matilda, from this moment on, I will no longer excuse your poor behavior. I will no longer write to Savannah on your behalf. I will write on my behalf only. I will no longer encourage Lucas to treat you with respect. You've lost the right to his regard. If you want it, you must earn it back."

"Martin," she whispered, tears threatening.

"I'm afraid your tears are at least a decade too late. I would like you to move your things from our bedroom into Savannah's while you consider all you have done, all that you have failed to do. I hope you will come to the realization that you wish to be my helpmate, rather than my vocal opponent. If you'll excuse me, I have work to do." He reached for a ledger and bent over it, silently tallying columns. After a moment he raised his head and looked from her to the door. He watched her go, collapsing into his chair at the soft *click* of the door behind her. He glared at the paperwork in front of him, unable to focus on it as he relived the scene with his wife.

CHAPTER EIGHT

Parthena rose from the rear veranda at the rental house in Newport, quietly entering an open door. The silk curtain caressed her skin as she slipped inside. She paused for a moment to adjust to the darker interior before moving soundlessly through the room to the hallway. She peered down the hallway and walked on her tiptoes to a small room down the hall. The door eased open without a sound, and she entered, closing the door behind her.

Parthena glanced around, noting no one in the small parlor. She slid onto the piano stool, wincing as it squeaked when she pushed away from the piano. She raised her hands over the piano keys, tracing them with her fingers but failing to press down on them. She closed her eyes, swaying to the silent music she heard in her head.

"I don't see why you won't play," Aidan murmured, entering the room.

Parthena shrieked at his silent entrance, her hands dropping to the piano keys and producing a loud clanging noise. "It displeases my husband." She caressed the keys as she spoke, her head bowed.

"He's not here, Mrs. Wheeler. It would bring joy to this house to have beautiful music fill it." He waited for a few moments, but, when she remained resolutely still, he sighed. "Forgive me for intruding." He departed, leaving the door ajar.

Parthena listened for the sound of his shoes moving away from the music room, but silence ensued. She bit her lip as she traced the piano keys. As though against her will, her fingers pressed down, and she began to play. The sounds of Shubert-Liszt's *"Frühlingsglaube"* filled the room. She swayed as she played, her eyes closing and a smile spreading across her face as the romantic lyricism of the music enveloped her.

***

Morgan stood outside the music room, Parthena's romantic, passionate playing filling the hallway. Before he could take a step into the room, a strong arm gripped him and pulled him toward another room off the elaborate hallway. Morgan shrugged his arm but wasn't freed until the door closed quietly behind them.

"Let her be," Aidan McLeod demanded. "I encouraged her to play."

"You had no right," Morgan said. He glowered at Aidan who remained in front of the door, blocking his departure.

"Maybe not in the eyes of the law, as she is your wife. However, I refuse to remain silent as I witness your slow destruction of her spirit."

"Why do you believe you can speak to me in such a manner?" Morgan leaned forward, his jaw clenched and hands fisted at his sides. He quivered with suppressed emotion.

"Because I know when a man is being a fool, out of pride and spite." Aidan watched as a flush rose on Morgan's face, mottling his skin. He dodged to the side as Morgan's right fist flew, landing a glancing blow off his shoulder rather than on his chin. Aidan danced to the side and launched himself at Morgan, dodging blows and grunting as Morgan punched him in his ribs. After a few moments of grappling, Aidan pinned Morgan against the door, his hands holding Morgan's arms down, with his shoulder pressed into Morgan's sternum preventing much movement. Aidan's lower body canted away from Morgan, and the kicks and jabs from Morgan's legs did little to move Aidan, other than to tighten his hold on Morgan.

"I might be older than you, but I learned how to fight in the real world, not a fancy boxing club." He half smiled as he gave Morgan a shake. "And I worked on sailing ships, where I learned that I either fought and lived or lost and died."

Morgan continued to vibrate in anger and to push against Aidan's unwavering grip.

"Is this what your vaunted control has come to?" Aidan asked. "Is this what you would have unleashed on your wife?"

"Release me."

"Only when you promise me that you'll sit in the chair over there and calm before leaving." Aidan's blue eyes shone with a fierce intensity as he met Morgan's gaze.

"I have no wish to listen to your chatter, disguised as misbegotten advice."

"I think you have plenty to contemplate, without me adding to the clutter of your mind," Aidan said, easing away from him.

Morgan released a deep breath and relaxed when he was free to move as he pleased. He eased away from the door and approached one of the chocolate-brown leather chairs sitting in front of the desk and settled into it.

Aidan moved to a small sideboard, splashing in a few sips of whiskey into two glasses. "Here," he said. He settled into his own chair, the leather creaking with his movement. Aidan stared at the desk in the room, plastered with papers secured by paperweights. He smiled as one page seemed determined to break free as the afternoon breeze gusted into the room, billowing the curtains. He leaned his head against the chair's tall back, stretched his legs in front of him, and closed his eyes. "Don't think I'm not paying attention to you," Aidan murmured, when he heard Morgan shift in the chair next to him.

"I don't understand you," Morgan said.

"Of course you don't. You come from a world where little of consequence is discussed and all that should be openly stated is inferred." Aidan tilted his head to the side and met Morgan's confused stare.

"I speak what must be said."

"In business, most likely," Aidan murmured. "How has your acquisition of the timber prospects in Canada progressed?" He shifted, maneuvering to face Morgan, and watched him intently.

"Well, I think. Although I should never admit it, the war is proving a boon to commodities, and there is a great demand for them." Morgan shrugged his shoulders, either in apology or resignation to that reality.

Aidan nodded and continued to ask probing questions as Morgan spoke of his growing successes with his business ventures. Aidan made conciliatory noises as Morgan spoke of the few unsuccessful ventures he'd attempted in the past years and responded with quiet words of encouragement. The longer they spoke of business, the more Morgan relaxed.

"If I'd been smart, I would have bought into copper years ago. The demand is massive with the growing market for electricity," Morgan said.

Aidan snorted as he shook his head with chagrin. "If any man should feel embarrassed, it's me. I've been to Montana numerous times and refused to buy into commodities as I thought they were too volatile a market. I made a grave error by not heeding what was occurring in Butte." His gaze became distant. "However, by the time I traveled to Montana, all the claims had already been made there."

"But you could have bought cheaper stock in the early 1900s and made quite a profit today."

"Quite true," Aidan said. He watched Morgan with reluctant admiration at his business acumen. "You have a shrewd mind for business."

"Thank you. It's what I excel at."

Aidan nodded, idly swirling the last few drops of whiskey in his crystal tumbler. "Why is it you are allowed to enjoy what you excel at, but your wife isn't?" He pinned Morgan with a fierce stare. "Seems rather unjust to me."

Morgan stiffened. "I hardly believe the two are related."

"I believe they are. You allow yourself the right to pursue your interests, yet you deny your wife the same privilege." He glared at Morgan to prevent him from interrupting him. "I'm sure you justify it with the belief that she only tinkers away at what she does and that ultimately what she does has no real bearing on the world. In contrast, what you do is important. It is a man's job and earns good money."

Morgan glared at him, unintentionally nodding his agreement at Aidan's statement.

"If you go through life believing that the only things worthy of your notice or interest are those that will bring you a profit, you will end your life a pauper. You will have forfeited the opportunity to know beauty, joy, and wonder. No amount of money can buy those things." He paused as he watched the ease seep away that Morgan had attained during their discussion of business. "Your wife brings joy to herself and to others when she plays the piano. It is not a passing fancy. It is her life's passion."

"You will never understand, Mr. McLeod, how wrong you are," Morgan replied. "She plays merely to annoy her father and me."

Aidan shook his head in stupefaction. "You are poorer than I'd imagined."

"I have more wealth than you could ever dream of," Morgan growled as he rose, glaring down at Aidan.

Aidan's gaze was filled with pity as he shook his head in resignation. "You're unable to hear what I am saying. Your wealth means nothing when it fails to appreciate the beauty gifted to you freely every day." Aidan rose, walking to the door. He tilted his head to the side and nodded when he failed to hear piano music. "I bid you good afternoon, Mr. Wheeler. I'll see you at dinner."

***

Parthena sat on the window seat, the heavy curtain billowing gently with the breeze, but mainly obscuring her from the room as she curled on her side staring at the ocean. Her fingers tapped out patterns on the windowsill as though touching piano keys, and she shook her head as she hit a wrong note. She froze as the door opened.

"Parthena?" her husband called out in his deep voice, followed by his scent—a mixture of sandalwood, cedar, and sweat. He approached the seating area of the room and sighed. The tinny sound of metal cufflinks landing on a ceramic plate sounded, then two thunks followed as he removed his shoes. Any further indication of him undressing stilled.

She shrieked as he sat next to her on the window seat, his hip warming the side of her thigh. "There you are," he said with a wry smile.

She looked at him, her eyes wide as she tensed her muscles in anticipation of fleeing. "I wanted a few moments to myself."

"After you played the piano," he said, a challenge in his expression daring her to lie to him.

"I can't be what you desire, Morgan," she said, cringing at the defeat she heard in her voice.

He gripped her thigh, his implacable hold preventing her from moving away from him but not causing true pain. "You intentionally go against all my wishes. You know I despise the piano."

"For no good reason!" She struggled to free herself from him, and he leaned closer, backing her into a corner of the window seat.

"Do you really believe I want my wife, a Wheeler, consorting with the likes of artists and musicians? We are patrons of the arts but not the spectacle itself." His eyes flashed with displeasure. "I'd hoped your fascination with that musician had passed by now."

"He's my friend. He understands my need to play. To perform," she whispered.

"Yes, to perform. If I thought you played simply because you felt compelled to play, that would be one thing. However, I learned today from an associate that you are planning to perform at a concert this fall. Tell me that he was wrong, Parthena." When she flushed and looked away, he gripped her arms and gave her a shake. "Tell me he was wrong!"

"I can't," she gasped. "I can't! I want to perform. I want to show my talent. I ... Oh, how would you ever understand? You who have the soul of an accountant could never understand the desire to fill the world with beauty."

He flinched as though she had struck him, and his hold on her eased. "Have you continued to see him? To practice with him?" Morgan breathed heavily as though he'd just run up a flight of stairs as he awaited her answer.

"Of course I have," she said. She dashed away a tear from her cheek.

"And have you slept with him again? Is that why you are content for me to remain in the sitting room?"

Parthena shook her head. "I've been true to my vows, Morgan. I've only played the piano with him."

He released her arms and gripped his hands together. "I want you to cease practicing with him. I never want you to speak to him again."

"Or what, Morgan?" Parthena asked.

"I want to know that my child is mine, dammit," he snarled. "I have that right."

"Oh," Parthena gasped. "I'd never ... I wouldn't ..."

"You'd never think to foist his bastard off on me? Are you saying you're that honorable?" He caught her hand as she raised it to slap him. "I once would never have thought to ask you that question, Hennie, but now I can't help but torture myself every night with it."

"Promise me that you won't hurt him."

He sighed as she saw the desperation in her gaze.

"I never said I'd hurt him. I want your promise, as my wife, as an honorable woman, that you will cease your association with him. That you will forgo your infatuation with him." He met her devastated gaze. "I refuse to share you, Parthena."

"I will play the piano at home. I will attend suffragist meetings. I will see my friends," she declared.

"Fine," he conceded. "However, you will never bring shame on the Wheeler name. You will always act with decorum."

Parthena blinked away tears. "I have to see him one more time. To say things to him so that he knows our association is at an end."

"It ended the moment you married me, Hennie. I thought you understood that. I refuse to lose the good standing of my family name due to your obsession with those better left in the merchant class." When she nodded her agreement, he smiled. She gasped as he lifted her up and carried her to their bed. "Now, kiss me, wife," he rasped as he leaned over her.

"Morgan," she protested.

"Kiss me and show me that you've missed me," he demanded.

She turned aside her face as tears poured from her eyes.

He swore and rolled away, pillowing his head on his elbow. He stared at the cream-colored ceiling and gritted his teeth. "I spoke to you of honor, Hennie. I must also maintain mine. I will never force you." He rose and stalked from the room.

***

Zylphia ascended the steps to the Chinese Tea House situated on the coast behind the Marble House. Sunlight glinted off the sparkling blue waters of the Atlantic Ocean while waves crashed against rocks on nearby cliffs. Birds chirped from the peaks of the tea house roof which shone a bright green in the midafternoon light. On each wall of the tea house, glass doors were flung open in an attempt to catch the afternoon breeze. The tea house had been built the previous year by Alva Vanderbilt Belmont for smaller events on the Marble House grounds. Zylphia smiled as she envisioned the lively party that occurred the previous year to celebrate its opening.

Zylphia turned toward Parthena and smiled. "If it's this hot here, imagine how stifling it is in Boston," she murmured. "I can only imagine how miserable Rowena is, being forced to remain there."

Parthena swallowed a snicker. "Even among suffragists, we talk about the weather."

Zylphia laughed, and they moved farther into the room. The sense of grandeur was enhanced by the large vaulted roof with wooden beams along the ceiling. Ball-shaped chandeliers hung from the beams, while dark paneling lined the walls. A large oval table with fine china was set in the middle of the room. On a sideboard, a buffet of tea-time delicacies and bowls of fruit lay awaiting the adjournment of the meeting.

"It's too bad we never really eat at these things," Parthena whispered as they found seats next to Sophie and Delia.

Zylphia nodded her agreement before extracting a pencil and small pad of paper from her purse. Soon the meeting began after introductions were made.

The chairwoman, a Mrs. Aires, spoke. "I am thankful to Mrs. Belmont for allowing us to meet here today even though she was called away on family duties. I can think of no better place to meet than this." She cleared her throat and looked at her list in front of her. "I have an agenda, but the real purpose of our meeting is quite simple. We have, assembled in this room, women who are struggling to see our measures succeed in two states, New York and Massachusetts. I would like us to work together to ensure that each state has success. To pool our resources and our expertise."

She glanced at the women around the table. "Miss McLeod. I understand you were an integral part of Miss Paul's march in Washington, DC. I know you are planning a similar march in Boston in October. What insight can you give us?"

Zylphia paused for a moment before speaking. "I would recommend that there be sufficient police presence to prevent the sort of violence that occurred in Washington. I've also recommended to our march committee that we follow Miss Paul's example and have the parade resemble a pageant as they are quite popular. Floats, bands, and songs keep the crowd engaged."

A woman halfway down the table from Zylphia spoke up. "There is no doubt in my mind the Antis will try something that day. When we have our march in New York, I know they will attempt to disrupt our message."

"We can do nothing about those whose intent is to tarnish the grandeur of the moment," Sophie said in her scratchy, authoritative voice. "Although irritating, we must ignore their antics and fulfill our purpose of the day." She paused to glance around the table at every woman present. "Which is to show the members of our respective states that women desire the vote and can be trusted with it. If we react to each attack from someone opposing us, we will diminish the validity of our appeal."

"I agree," Delia said. "We must hold our heads high, walk with a purpose, and not respond to whatever the Antis do."

Zylphia tapped her pencil against her paper. "I agree, of course, with Mrs. Chickering and Mrs. McLeod. However, I also believe we should have women or men in the crowd who are selling our pamphlets and attempting to sway the onlookers' way of thinking."

The chairwoman nodded. "Although peddling our pamphlets and selling paraphernalia is important as it raises money for the cause, it can't be the purpose behind our march. The reason must always be to promote our vision. We do not want another disastrous parade like the one in Washington, DC. Although it swayed public opinion for a time, I do not believe it led to any lasting change in voter's convictions."

"The most effective manner to sway the voters would be to have an influential politician speak favorably about suffragism," Parthena said. "In Boston, too few are willing to espouse the notion."

"It is much the same in New York," Mrs. Aires said. "Besides the march, that is the task ahead of us. We must speak with our elected officials and persuade them to publicly support universal enfranchisement. Among us, I'm certain we know many of the men in our state legislatures.

I suggest we have them dine with us and broach the topic of universal suffrage with them."

Sophie *harrumphed.* "I doubt the men who are against suffrage would care to dine with women known to be for the enfranchisement of all." She glowered at the table. "The task is much more difficult than inviting recalcitrant men to our tables and showing them the way. They are used to their place in society. They relish their role in the world as they perceive it. We are wishing to set it topsy-turvy with our notion we have the same right to vote as they do. Let's not be naive in believing this is simply a matter of having our chefs outdo themselves for an evening."

A pinched-face woman frowned at Sophie, her mouth turned down in a perpetual frown. "I think you do a disservice to our chairwoman by insinuating that she believes this is an easy undertaking. She was merely suggesting we act with the class and decorum we are known for."

Sophie bit back a smirk. "Class and decorum will win us no battles. Hard work and plain speaking will. For some of these men, we'll have to bludgeon them with the truth of our words. Repeatedly. Talking around the rosebushes won't help."

Mrs. Aires held up a hand before further caustic words could be exchanged between Sophie and any others sitting at the table. "We aid no one if we argue among ourselves."

The conversation turned from discussing the march to discussing which legislators would be most amenable to a suffragist intervention. Zylphia laid a hand on Sophie's arm as the older woman became increasingly agitated. Finally the chairwoman decided enough discussion had been accomplished for one day, and the women rose to speak with others at different areas of the table. After a few moments Sophie rose with an intense look at Zylphia and Parthena. "If you'd like a ride home, I'm leaving."

Zylphia said a hasty good-bye to a few of the members and followed Sophie, Parthena, and her mother down the steps. She paused to take in the grandeur of the Marble House from the back lawn, its white marble limned by the late afternoon sun. She jolted from her reverie and trotted to catch up to her party when she heard Sophie muttering about "dawdlers." They wandered along a side path to the front of the house and the waiting driver of their car.

"Home," Sophie barked. Parthena sat in the front while Zylphia and her mother sat with Sophie in the back. "I thought this meeting would be of substance," Sophie growled.

Zylphia smiled and shook her head, looking at the grandeur of other large houses and mansions as they made their slow progression down Bellevue Avenue. "You can't expect everyone to agree with you, Sophie. Most are hopeful that their quiet defiance will lead to real change."

"Quiet defiance, my foot. We need decisive action. We do not need to seem as though we are pandering for consideration."

Delia laughed. "I can see why my daughter likes you so much, Mrs. Chickering. You are a force to be reckoned with, and you do not abide simpering fools."

"It's why I'm close to all the McLeod women. They have the good sense to be women of substance." Sophie shared a smile with Delia.

The car turned into the long driveway to the home Sophie had rented for the summer. She had managed to rent one on the ocean side of the avenue. The long driveway and tall hedge obscured the home from the eyes of curious onlookers. The white three-story villa with a blue slate mansard roof had a small garden in front. However, the large lawn leading to the cliffs and the side gardens—concealed from those not welcomed as guests—were the hidden treasures of the house.

Zylphia breathed a sigh of contentment as she beheld the house. "Thank you for inviting us to join you this summer, Sophie. I can't think of a more wondrous place to pass the summer months."

Upon entering the house, Parthena, Delia, and Sophie ascended the inner stairs with the purpose of resting before changing for dinner. Zylphia wandered through the house and out to the back lawn. She meandered toward the cliffs, her mind filled with the voices of the women from the meeting. As she turned onto the cliff walk, she ambled down the graveled path. She came to a sudden halt as she approached a boulder.

No longer in the present, her mind was filled with Teddy, attempting to aid her after she had twisted her ankle. The cryptic conversation they had had while he walked her home. His quiet chivalry and dedication to her from the very beginning. A seagull shrieking brought her back to the present, and she felt the rock. It was heated warm by the sun, not cool to the touch as when she had met Teddy on an overcast day where the sun had been shrouded.

She sat on the rock, which she now thought of as Teddy's rock, and clung to the hope that he lived. That he would return to her. She stiffened her shoulders at the prospect of returning to the house and preparing for dinner. Living in the past or her hoped-for future would not bring him home any sooner, nor would it ease her torment. She rose, patting the rock once before she strolled back to the house with no apparent concerns.

***

Morgan sat on the opposite side of the parlor, watching as his wife interacted with the women present. He stifled a groan as Aidan sat next to him.

"I'll take from that reception to my arrival that you would prefer to remain alone," Aidan said with a sardonic lifting of one eyebrow.

Morgan motioned for him to remain sitting. "I am thankful for Mrs. Chickering's hospitality. It is a wonderful respite from Boston's heat."

Aidan chuckled. "I never thought you'd be brought so low as to have to discuss the weather, Wheeler. What happened between you and your wife since we last spoke? She looks distraught tonight, although she's attempting to hide it."

Morgan's jaw tightened, and he shifted in his chair. "I hardly believe that you have any right to question me about my marriage. Or my wife."

"I may have no right, but I only have your best interests at heart. I'm a remarkably good listener, and my advice has been known to bring succor at times," Aidan said.

Morgan chuffed out a laugh. "It's good to see you're as humble as they say."

Aidan laughed fully, catching the eye of Delia and winking. "I find it's easier to know one's strengths and acknowledge them, rather than trying to hide behind some facade society deems appropriate." He sat with his hands crossed over his belly, as though in perfect harmony.

"She loves the damn piano," Morgan rasped out. "I don't think I'll ever get her to stop playing it."

"Of course you won't. But you already knew that. What's your real concern?" Aidan asked.

"She told me that I have the soul of an accountant," Morgan whispered.

"Did you always?" Aidan met Morgan's startled gaze. "Before life and necessity turned you into a successful businessman, were you unable to appreciate a talent such as your wife's?"

Morgan shook his head.

"Then I'd suggest that your real self is merely dormant, and you have to allow those closest to you to set you free again."

"That brings chaos and destruction, Mr. McLeod," Morgan argued. "I can't live through that again." He nodded at Zylphia as she rose to play the piano. He noted Aidan beamed at her.

"She's horrible at the piano, but I always encourage her," Aidan murmured. When she played a piece by Beethoven, off tune and off pace, Aidan rocked to the music and smiled as though he were hearing a master perform. As though Parthena were performing.

"You take joy in all your daughter does," Morgan whispered.

"Of course I do. And in all my wife does. They are strong-willed women intent on changing their lives and the lives of other women. I respect and admire them, even though they've chosen a hard road." He shared a smile with Morgan as Zylphia's piece ended, and he called out, "Bravo."

Morgan saw Zylphia roll her eyes and reach out a hand to Parthena. He frowned when he saw Parthena hesitate. "I'm slowly killing her spirit," he said in a low voice. At Aidan's nod, his frown turned into a glower. Parthena looked at him right then and shook her head at Zylphia.

"Play for us, Mrs. Wheeler. Play for us your favorite," Morgan called out.

He relaxed into his seat when Parthena sat at the bench and began to play. "I have no idea what it is, but it is beautiful," he whispered to Aidan.

"Tell her that," Aidan suggested. "You need to start again with your wife. Woo her. Court her. And you may be fortunate enough to win her affections. Blustering and bullying won't." He slapped Morgan on the shoulder and rose, moving to sit beside Delia.

Morgan remained alone, watching his wife perform.

CHAPTER NINE

The following afternoon, Zylphia sat in the shaded sunroom at the back of the rented summer house. The women who had called for the afternoon had just departed, and Zylphia had flopped onto a padded wicker settee with delight after their exhausting visits. The scent of honeysuckle wafted in through the open windows and doors, while the distant, melodious roar of the ocean provided a soothing counterpoint to the birds trilling in the hedges. Lemonade, rather than a pot of tea, sat on the table in front of her. She fanned herself as she reached for a stack of letters on a nearby table and absently flipped through them.

"Anything of interest?" Delia asked as she entered the room. She sat on a comfortable wicker chair near her daughter.

"A letter from Rowena, venting her frustration that she wasn't able to travel with us." She set it aside. "Another letter from Teddy's cousin Eugenie." Zylphia opened her letter and smiled as she raised her eyebrows at her mother's amused expression.

"Finally a few moments peace where nothing is expected of us." Delia sighed as she rested in her chair. "This is a lovely room at this time of day."

Zylphia nodded, sighing herself with pleasure as a cool breeze stirred the palm fronds and ruffled the pile of letters next to her on the settee.

"What does Eugenie tell you?"

"Nothing much," Zylphia said as she scanned her letter before sitting upright. "Teddy."

Delia reached forward, placing a hand on Zylphia's knee. She shook her head impatiently at Aidan as he entered the room, silencing him with her quiet communication. "What about Teddy?"

"He's been found. He's home in England." She sorted through the pile of mail, tossing letters to the floor as she searched. She paused at an envelope covered in unfamiliar handwriting and ripped it open. "Oh, God," she gasped, a hand to her mouth as tears poured from her eyes.

Aidan sat beside her, heedless of the letters he was crushing and pulled her into his arms. "Shh. ... Shh, my darling girl. Whatever has happened, we'll help you through it."

Zylphia shook her head, rubbing her face against her father's chest. "No, he's alive. He's alive!" She turned toward her mother with impassioned, joyous eyes, raising the letter over her head as though in triumph.

She swiped at her cheeks and turned her attention again to the letter. "I didn't recognize the handwriting. But it's Teddy. He ... he injured his right arm and has to write with his left. He says he didn't want to dictate a letter to me."

"Of course he didn't. One shouldn't dictate sentiments of love," Aidan murmured, kissing her head. He backed away as Zylphia pushed herself to a standing position.

"Please excuse me, I have to ..." She failed to finish her sentence as she rushed from the room.

***

Aidan pushed aside the letters and scooted to sit closer to Delia, reaching to clasp her hand with his. "I couldn't have asked for more," he murmured.

"Thank God," she whispered, squeezing his hand and leaning into his shoulder.

"I simply hope he returns to Boston soon. I can't imagine trying to keep Zee here now when she knows he's alive and in England." Aidan sighed, sharing an amused, yet worried glance with Delia.

***

Zylphia shut the door behind her and collapsed to the floor. She read the letter again, attempting to savor his words.

My Most Beloved Zylphia,

I can hardly believe I am writing you. I know you will doubt this letter is from me, as I am writing it with my left hand. My right hand and arm are still badly damaged, and I am uncertain when I will regain full use of them.

Thank you for corresponding with my cousin Eugenie. Thank you for never losing hope I was alive. Even when unconscious and insensate, I knew, in some indescribable way, that you were waiting for me. I don't know what I would have done had I awoken to learn you had forsaken me.

I long to hold you in my arm. To cradle you to me. To smell your sweet scent and forget. Forget all the time we were apart and never look back. I miss you, my Zylphia.

I must close, as I don't want to miss the post. I love you, Zee. More than you'll ever know.

Your,
Teddy

Zylphia kissed his name and then held the letter to her heart. She curled onto the floor and sobbed. At the knock on her door, she attempted to plead for the person on the other side to grant her time alone, but her voice failed her. As the door pushed open, Zylphia scooted away from it, allowing Parthena to squeeze inside.

"Zee!" Parthena knelt beside her, running a hand over her back. "Is it Teddy?"

"No. Yes." She reached forward and gripped her friend's hand. "He's alive. He's alive!" Zylphia said in a louder voice. She nodded her thanks as Parthena gave her a handkerchief. After scrubbing her face, Zylphia tried to push herself up but then decided to remain where she was, curled on the floor.

"Come. Let's get you up, to the bed at least," Parthena said, gripping Zylphia's shoulders and helping to heave her upright.

Zylphia came to a standing position, swaying subtly as she stumbled to her bed. Although the day was hot and humid, and the windows were open to allow any breeze to enter, Zylphia shivered and crawled under the covers.

Parthena sat on the bed next to Zylphia, and stroked a hand from her shoulder to fingers and then back up again. "What did it say?" She glanced toward the door as it creaked open, and Delia crept inside.

"He's injured. His writing is different because he hurt his right arm. He misses me. Dreams of seeing me."

"Of course he does, my dearest girl," Delia murmured, running a hand over Zylphia's brow. She blinked away tears at seeing Zylphia so distraught.

"You'll see him again soon, Zee," Parthena murmured.

"When?" Zylphia asked, her eyes filling with tears she was helpless to fight. "Crossing the Atlantic is treacherous. I can't go to him, and he can't come here. I might not see him again until this war is over."

"At least you know he's alive, recovering, and dreams of you," Parthena murmured.

"I just want to see him. Touch him." Zylphia took a stuttering breath as she fought a sob. She shared a watery smile with her mother. "At least I know, when I dream of him tonight, he is recovering in England."

"That's my brave daughter," Delia murmured, embracing Zylphia as she continued to cry and shudder.

CHAPTER TEN

My Darling Zylphia, *August 18, 1915*

As I sit here, listening to the lark outside the window at my grandfather's house, my thoughts are filled with you. I envision you going from house to house, convincing the men of Massachusetts of the merits of women voting. Have you had any rows with your constituents? Have you been reprimanded recently? I imagine you must bite your tongue frequently as you listen to the arguments against the vote.

I see you tapping your paintbrush against your easel as you concentrate on your next masterpiece. Do you still paint in vibrant color, Zee, or have you muted your talent as you attempt to conform to the world around you? I hope you realize you are a woman incapable of muting. You deserve to shine, and, if those around you don't appreciate your talent and abilities, they can sod off. (Forgive my swearing—I've spent too long in the company of soldiers.)

I wish I had exciting news to impart. However, my routine remains unchanged. I like to believe I'm improving, but it's torturous in its slow progression. Eugenie has been an enormous help as she refuses to take pity on me in the days I don't want to do my exercises. She refuses to allow me to accept my current situation as my permanent reality.

Never forget, my love, the thought of being with you again, of forging a life with you, is all the encouragement I need to continue my rehabilitation.

Do you ever dream of the one night we had together? I relive it constantly, but, rather than ending the evening sitting alone, contemplating the coal fire, in my dreams I awake with you in my arms. For those sweet hours we had together, you gifted me with your trust and your true feelings. My only regret is that I did not have the opportunity to show you all the pleasures of loving without the pain.

I dream of the day we are together again.

Your,

Teddy

***

My Beloved Teddy,

Of course I relive the night we had together. It was the most memorable night of my life. I've never known such joy. Each morning I wake, aching as though your fingertips are hovering over me, on the verge of caressing me. The reality of my lonely bed is harsh.

This abject loneliness and yearning for you is from my own folly. Oh, Teddy, how I wish I could go back and change how I lashed out at your honest expression of love.

If only I'd had the courage to trust in you and in us that night. (The ghost of you, of us, is everywhere here, darling. I must change the topic or I won't be able to continue writing.)

I'm currently in Newport, although we depart soon for Boston. We've had many meetings about how to further our prospective causes, as there is also a referendum in New York state the same day as in Massachusetts, on November 2. I've enjoyed meeting like-minded women, although we remain stymied as to how to convince influential men to support our cause.

Canvassing wasn't progressing as well as I had hoped when I was in Boston. I like to think we'll be more successful than in 1895, but I worry. Every Sunday the priest rants against women wanting to change the natural order of the world as God had intended it. If I hear that one more time, I fear I'll rail at the priest, which would do little for the cause. My father, sitting beside me in church, has to lay a hand on my arm to calm me and keep me seated. These few weeks in Newport have brought a respite from the outrageous proclamations from the Boston pulpit.

I am considering moving to Washington, DC, for a while, to help Miss Paul after the vote in Massachusetts. From what Sophie tells me, Miss Paul's planning on ramping up her tactics. Never fear, dearest. I will not participate in any violent acts. It is the one condition my father has given if he were to help me.

I would like to no longer depend on my father. Should I have an art show and sell some of my paintings? I think it would be a way for me to experience true independence. What do you think?

My darling, know that the day you return to me will be the best day of my life.

Your,

Zylphia

***

My Darling Zylphia,

The best part of any day is receiving a letter from you. Reading about what you are doing does not replace being there with you, but it does bring its own succor. In everything I do, you are never far from my thoughts.

I know I expressed regrets about our night together, but please do not blame yourself for our current separation. My stubbornness, and profoundly injured pride, prevented me from reading your letter in time.

I try not to have many regrets. For, if I do, then I'd have to doubt what I've lived through, and I must believe there was some purpose to what I experienced in the war. I cannot doubt that, or I fear for what would happen. It can't have been for nothing.

Since the moment I saw your art, I've believed you should show it. Proclaim to the world your brilliance. You will be a wonderful success, and, for those who do not celebrate you, they are unworthy of your regard. I only wish I could be there to behold your triumph.

As for your desire to live independently, I think it is a brilliant plan. You need to know you can survive on your own. I have come to understand this is an essential desire for you, and my hope is that, once you have fulfilled it, you will realize the joys of sharing life's burdens with another. As you know, I will continue to pray I'm your choice.

I hope you are merely reluctant to see the success of your canvassing, rather than that the men of Massachusetts remain entrenched in their traditional beliefs. However, I fear you are correct in your sense that success is far from guaranteed.

I will worry if you travel to Washington, DC, to work with Miss Paul. I trust in you and know that you will always act in a way to bring success to your movement. However, I don't trust in others. I don't trust in how they will react to your insistence in your right to vote and to your own voice. Too many, men and women, remain who fear a woman free to speak her mind.

In my eagerness to return to you, I caused an inflammation in my arm. Now, rather than exercising and building strength, I must settle for rest. Rather than the rest relaxing me, I'm filled with frustration at prolonging our separation.

I miss you. I dream of you. I yearn for you. I love you, my darling Zee.

Your,

Teddy

***

"Oh, how you slay me," Zylphia murmured as she read Teddy's latest letter. She was curled up on her favorite sofa in the family sitting room under a throw blanket on a cool September day.

Delia, who sat across from her daughter, reading a letter from Clarissa, raised her eyebrows. "Is Teddy well?" she asked.

"Yes, he's slowly improving. He's injured or reinjured his arm by overworking it in his eagerness to come back to me."

"That sounds promising, after what Eugenie wrote."

Zylphia held Teddy's letter to her, unconsciously clasping it to her breast. "I've been worried since she wrote."

"I'd call it frantic," Delia said.

"How would you expect me to be when Eugenie tells me that he's in a special rehabilitation center and refuses to admit it?"

"I'd expect no less, considering you love him. I'm not condemning you, Zee. However, you must be honest with yourself and with Teddy. He most likely will not be the same man who returns to you as the one who left."

When Zylphia's eyes filled with tears, Delia moved to her daughter, squeezing onto the edge of the sofa and putting an arm over her legs. "Why does that worry you?"

Zylphia shook her head in frustration as she swiped at her tears. "I'm being foolish, but I have this sense Teddy is making me into an idol. And I don't want that. I couldn't live up to it."

Her mother watched her with exasperated affection. "Anyone who loves you is suspect, aren't they? You believe your father and I have to love you, so we do. It's the same with your cousins. You're still confused as to why your friends like you."

Zylphia glared mutinously at her mother but remained silent. However, her mother was better at using silence as a tool than she was, so she eventually spoke. "You're being ridiculous."

"Am I? Do you fill your letters to Teddy detailing your faults so that you give him plenty of time to run if he wants? Do you truly believe he's coming back to you?"

"I don't think he wants to," Zylphia whispered, her gaze showing her devastation. "Last month it was a hurt knee. Now it's his arm. Next month will be another ailment, the submarines, his grandfather. Something. I'm terrified he feels obligated to return to me."

Delia squeezed Zylphia's legs and sighed, her gaze distant. "Have you ever considered that his reluctance has nothing to do with you? Or rather it has everything to do with you, just not in the way you imagine?" At her daughter's confused expression, she leaned forward and brushed curls off her forehead. "He's been through a war. Seen the unthinkable and done it too. Not only that, he was injured badly enough he couldn't be sent back to fight again.

"The man you love won't be the same, physically or emotionally. And my guess is that he's terrified you're going to reject him because the reality of him is a far cry from your memories."

Tears ran down Zylphia's cheeks. "That's even worse," she whispered. At her mother's inquisitive frown, she said, "It means he doesn't truly trust me. Trust in my love. Or he'd know nothing could alter my love for him."

"Teddy is afraid, Zee, with as great a reason as the one you had last year. You must find a way to alleviate it."

Zylphia's eyes glazed over as she considered all her mother had said. "I can't travel there. It would be sheer folly. Teddy and I have tempted fate enough." She shook her head. "I don't know what to do."

"There's nothing to do at the moment, except to continue to show your steadfastness." Delia cupped her daughter's cheek a moment before moving to rise.

Impulsively Zylphia leaned forward and threw herself in her mother's arms. "Thank you. I feel like everything is falling apart. The cause. Teddy's faith in me."

"Those are temporary feelings, my darling. All will turn out as it should."

CHAPTER ELEVEN

Lucas entered his rented rooms, stilling when he saw someone inside. "How did you get in?" He smiled with joy at the sight of her. "I hadn't realized we were practicing today."

"Your neighbor was generous enough to let me in," Parthena said. She stiffened when Lucas approached her, jerking her head to the side so he couldn't kiss her on the mouth. "Please, don't."

"I don't understand," Lucas whispered. He ran a hand down her arm, eliciting a shudder, but he couldn't discern if it was one of passion or distress. "Parthena? Why don't you want me to touch you?"

"It's not proper, Lucas. It's not like before." She moved away from him, placing the piano between them.

"Thena, I don't understand why you won't leave him. You don't love him." Lucas gripped her upper arms and then sighed as he realized he sounded as though he were begging.

"I married him, Lucas. It's what women of my class do. We marry. We provide children and a soothing home environment. We don't care too much about anything."

"And you've failed to match any part of that description." Lucas let her go, lest he begin to shake her. "You're my equal, my partner in life."

"I'm so sorry, Lucas," she whispered, shying away from his touch again.

He froze. "You don't see me the same way." At her persistent silence, he laughed mirthlessly. "Of course not. I was simply the musician you entertained yourself with for a time. No one of true consequence for a woman like you."

She began to shake, and she gripped the edge of the piano to remain standing. "How was I to know my family's circumstances would change?"

"You should demand more than to be married off to the highest bidder by your wretched father," Lucas growled.

"I wish you wouldn't speak of my father like that. He's done what he has to do to see his family maintain its respectability."

Lucas appeared flummoxed a moment and incapable of speech. "Are you serious? Are you speaking about the man who's complained of having to care for his daughters for years? Of the man who would sacrifice your happiness so he can continue to live the life of leisure he believes is his due?"

"He knows no other way," she whispered.

"Dammit, Parthena, what's happened to you?" He shook his head as he battled scorn for the woman he loved. "You've allowed your time among Wheeler and his cronies to make you believe you're worth less than your own happiness."

"You and I are not separated because of my father or Morgan," she rasped, battling tears. "It was my choice. One I'd make again."

He paled as he stepped away from her. He held a hand to his head, his gaze lost as he beheld her as though for the first time. "Why?"

"You wouldn't understand." She turned away.

"Make me," he demanded, spinning her to face him. "I expected better of you."

Parthena launched herself at him and beat her fists on his chest, pushing him back until he was against the wall. "You expected better of me? Of me?" Her voice rose to a shriek. "How can you stand there in all your disgusted glory and expect that I would turn my back on my family? When you would never have done the same. Not for Savannah. Not for Clarissa. Don't you dare hold me to a different standard than the one you hold for yourself."

Lucas blinked, furrowing his brows in confusion a moment.

Parthena shook her head in frustration. "How do you think it made me feel to have my father foist me on another man as though I were a problem he had to rid himself of? As though I were some prized animal, his to do with as he pleased? How do you think it made me feel imagining what could happen to my sisters?"

Lucas watched her as though poleaxed. "You never meant to marry me, did you, Parthena? When you visited me after the announcement and asked me to be patient, you never meant to accept me. I was never good enough."

At her damning silence, he paled further. "You never meant for me to be anything but a diversion. You knew an announcement was coming. That's why you were desperate for us to make love." He stared at her, his passionate anger fading to icy disdain as he held himself away from her. "You never really wanted me, did you? It was always the piano, the things I could teach you, but never about me."

He shook his head at his stupidity. "I always held myself back, convinced that women were after my fame, my fortune, anything but me." He leaned forward until they were nearly nose to nose. "How right I was."

When she attempted to protest, he reached for the door handle and pushed her away from him as he pulled it open. "Leave, Thena. Our association is over."

"What about the show? Our piece?"

"The show?" he roared. "How dare you ask me about the concert after confirming all my beliefs about women."

"Lucas, you don't mean this." She outstretched her hands, but he batted them down before they could touch him.

"I might have the misfortune of having you watch me perform, but, if you attempt to join me, ever again, on stage, I'll walk off it. Notoriety be damned."

He nodded to the door, a grim satisfaction lighting his eyes as he heard her stifled sob a moment before she rushed from his rooms.

***

"You're being a fool, Parthena. If there's anything I know about you, you're not a fool."

Parthena leaned back and laughed without humor. "I'm the biggest fool of all." She rose, walking toward the door. Sophie relaxed when Parthena turned from it and approached the windows, staring at the back gardens of Sophie's neighbors. "I found my defiance of my father's dictates exhilarating. And Lucas was an eager teacher."

Sophie sighed. "Did you, even once, consider the harm you would do Lucas?"

Parthena glowered at Sophie. "He's a man. He can do what he likes, with whom he likes, whenever he likes."

Sophie sputtered a moment, giving Parthena the impression this was one of the few times in Sophie's life she'd been speechless. "Do you believe he doesn't have feelings? That, because he's a man, he's heartless?"

Parthena blinked, as though she were attempting not to cry. "He said I was his equal. His partner in life."

"Oh, my dear. What have you done?" Sophronia watched her with a mixture of despair and anger.

"You believe I'm selfish because I acted without thought for anyone but myself when I was with him," Parthena said.

Sophie growled. "No, that makes you human. Remember, I know you. I've followed your upbringing even though your father detested me and wanted none of my influence to rub off on you. You aren't spoiled. You aren't inclined to hurt those around you. You aren't mean."

Parthena stared mutinously out a window.

"What you say is all a bunch of nonsensical drivel that you're feeding yourself in an attempt to ease some of your own agony. I know your father faced financial ruin. That he planned to marry you off to the highest bidder, no matter how lecherous the man was. However, you had a choice, Parthena. You always have a choice. Why did you treat that Russell boy so shabbily?" Sophie slammed her hand on her armrest. "Why delude yourself that you are worse than you are? Most strive for the opposite."

"I hurt him, Sophie. It's like I ripped his dreams to shreds, and I could do nothing to prevent it." She met Sophie's gaze with her shattered expression, battling tears. "I had to protect my sisters, especially Genevieve."

"If there's one thing Lucas understands, it's protecting family." Sophie's voice was gentler. "Why did you have to hurt him?"

"He can't have any hope of me," Parthena rasped. "I'm married."

Sophie snickered. "That's never stopped the majority of our class from behaving as they'd like. I don't know why that would be an impediment to you and Lucas."

"In exchange for the ability to play the piano at home and to continue to work on the causes that matter to me, I promised Morgan that I'd cease all contact with Lucas. Morgan is desirous of believing any pregnancy is due to him." Parthena flushed as she spoke. Parthena moved to sit next to Sophie, taking solace from Sophie's gentle clasp of her hand.

"Morgan has his pride too but don't let it stamp out your desires." She chucked Parthena under the chin, forcing her gaze upward. "You did what you believed you had to do to protect Genevieve from a horrid situation. That is honorable. Treating Lucas as you have done is dishonorable. You may have come to the painful realization that you won't be with him. That he can play no large part in your life. However, is it fair for him to believe all that you experienced was a lie?" She pinned Parthena with a severe stare. "Or worse, that you were merely using him?"

"I can't give him hope, Sophie. And I thought it best if he believed he was breaking things off with me."

"No, you can't give him hope. But you didn't need to be cruel. Even when we must let go of someone we love, it helps them to know they were loved." Sophie took a sip of tea. "What do you feel for your husband?"

Parthena stiffened.

"I can sense it's more than nothing."

"I wish it were nothing," Parthena admitted. She paused as though thinking about her husband. "He's present more than when we first married, and I have the sense he isn't as annoyed about my piano playing as before. He doesn't complain like he used to."

Sophie studied her closely. "You seem perplexed."

"It's as though he's trying to woo me. But I've already married him." Parthena flung her hands up in frustration.

"I'd imagine he'd desire more than your grudging presence in his life. And in his bed."

Parthena frowned at Sophie's subtle criticism. "Buying me flowers and increasing my dress budget is little consolation."

"For what? For what you've perceived to have sacrificed? Parthena, you must either accept what you've done or make a change. You've done irreparable harm to your relationship with Lucas. Do you desire to do the same with your husband?" Sophie frowned as tears streamed down Parthena's cheeks. "Decide what it is you do want. And then embrace it. Life is too short for such dillydallying."

***

"Sophie, will you be with me at the opening night of my art show?" Sophie roamed Zylphia's studio, *harrumphing* her agreement at the paintings Zylphia had selected for her show. "I'd only present one or two of these. They highlight your tremendous talent, but they're too depressing."

Zylphia frowned as she beheld the gray, green, and black paintings. "I'd think that, while we're in the midst of war, people would stay away from color."

Sophie pinned Zylphia with a fierce stare. "You forget. We're not involved in the war." She held up her hand to silence Zylphia's argument. "Yet. Yes, I know. It's inevitable that we'll become involved. However, even during times of war, people want to be reminded of beauty. Of why we're willing to sacrifice our youth. These paintings"—she tapped the small pile of muted paintings—"do nothing to alleviate that yearning."

Sophie sat on Zylphia's red tufted chair. "I've heard from Alice." She smiled as Zylphia rallied and abandoned studying her paintings to focus on Sophie's news. "She is grateful you are willing to travel to DC, but she's uncertain she needs you now. She'll write you when she has need of you."

Zylphia nodded.

"As for your art show, I've never seen another man prouder than your father."

Zylphia shared a rueful smile with Sophie. "I thought I'd have a show, be successful, and thus proclaim my independence."

"Your father has invited everyone he knows."

Zylphia raised her brows at the word invited.

"With the expectation they show up and purchase at least one piece from you."

Zylphia sighed, collapsing against the back of her seat. "He doesn't ... He refuses ... to understand that he undermines my ability to show that I can be independent."

Sophie heaved out a sigh, looking her age for a rare moment as she watched Zylphia with concern. "At some point you must come to understand, just as your cousins before you, that independence is an illusion. One way or another, we are dependent on each other."

"I hate that," Zylphia whispered.

"If you were truly independent, you'd have no concern, no love, neither for nor from your parents. Your cousins." As Zylphia paled, Sophie said, "From Teddy."

When Zylphia remained silent, Sophie said, "I'd think you'd regret what your desire for independence has already cost you."

"That's extremely hurtful, Sophie."

"I know it is, but someone has to force you to face the folly of your beliefs. Your father won't because he has too much guilt over the years he was away from you. Your mother won't, for reasons unfathomable to me.

You don't esteem your friends enough to listen to them. Thus, it's left up to me."

"I tell myself this is what I want. And I do. But I want other things as well. Things I never thought I desired."

Sophie watched Zylphia with kind eyes, nodding for her to continue.

"A home. Children. A husband. More than anything, a husband."

"Have you told your young man this?" Zylphia nodded, and Sophie watched her curiously. "Then why are you concerned?"

"Eugenie first wrote me about her worry, and then Teddy mentioned something I'm sure in his mind was innocent."

"But it's caused you to fret."

Zylphia fought tears as she stared at her blank canvas. "He's started a correspondence with a nurse who cared for him."

Sophie paled. "Oh, I see." Her gaze became distant.

Zylphia frowned, leaning forward to grip her friend's hand. "Sophie?"

"Of this, I completely understand." She blinked and shook her head subtly as though clearing her vision. "Did you know that my husband was a doctor? A successful surgeon?" She ignored any response Zylphia made, staring at the blank canvas as though seeing a scene come to life on it. "He went away to war. The Civil War. And had a nurse help him.

"It wasn't proper at that time for women to do that sort of work, but, amid the carnage of war, he wasn't about to refuse help when it was offered." She smiled, a hint of sorrow mixed with bitterness. "I could tell he was forming an attachment. How could he not? The immediacy of what he had experienced had to overshadow the memory of his home in Boston. Of me."

Zylphia growled her disagreement. "You're being far too understanding."

"No, I loved him enough to know that I would have welcomed him home with open arms and helped him overcome whatever he saw. Whomever he knew. Whomever he had to forget." She pierced Zylphia with a fierce stare. "I never had to live through such a challenge, as my husband died. For your sake, I hope you find a way back to your Teddy, no matter what. It will be one of your greatest challenges, but I know you are equal to it."

"I'm sick of challenges."

Sophie laughed at her grumble. "No, you're not. You'd be bored in a week if he didn't challenge you."

Zylphia watched Sophie with reluctant admiration. "I want to be you when I'm older. Parsing out sage advice to youngsters eager to hear it."

"You continue as you are, and you will be."

***

My Beloved Teddy,

I'm feeling melancholy and nervous, and needed to write you. It's as though, when I write you, I'm talking with you, and I don't feel as alone.

I've been lectured recently that my desire for independence is an illusion and that my love for you could be construed as a dependence. I am finally willing to admit that's true. And it is a dependence I embrace willingly. The only future I cannot envision is a future you are not a part of. I need you in my life.

I love you. I want you. I need you.

No matter how much this war has changed you, no matter what you are afraid to share with me, know I will accept it and you. All I want is you.

I am sorry. I know this letter must worry you as it is maudlin and pleading, but I wanted you to know how I truly feel. I have realized that I do not tell those I love how I feel nearly often enough.

I am terrified of the upcoming show for my paintings. Sophie will be there, as will my parents and all my father's cronies. However, I want my art to be appreciated due to its own merit. I know this makes me sound petulant and ungrateful, but my art is such a special part of me. To know that others might disparage it terrifies me.

If it were not for the constant canvassing or the preparation for my gallery show, I would travel to England. It seems that President Wilson has been successful in his negotiations with the Germans, and the number of ships sunk has decreased dramatically. My father would forbid me to consider it, as any risk is too great a risk for him, but I am desperate to see you again, dearest.

I pray that your recovery continues to go well, no matter that it is slower than you'd like.

I remain forever yours,

Zee

***

My Darling Zylphia,

I've never wished to surprise you with my presence more than after reading your last letter. I don't know what could have led to your insecurity about my affection and love. I want to reassure you that I've never loved you more than after I received your last letter. The fact you were willing to express the depth of your feelings to me ... There are no words to describe how that made me feel.

I know you love me. I believe and trust in it. However, to read your desperation to ensure I understood the depths of your affection soothes an ache inside me which I did not know I had. It helps me to know you feel the same as I do, for I could just as easily have written you that letter.

Every night I dream of holding you in my arm. Every morning I mourn to awaken as I realize you will remain an illusion. No one can take your place for me. You are a singular woman, Zylphia, and I want no other.

I agree with your father. Never risk your safety and health in an attempt to come to me. I could not bear it if something happened to you. I am considering upcoming travel, but I am uncertain where I will travel to as of yet. I am progressing with minimal benefit from my exercises, and I fear I must accept the limitations I will live with for the rest of my life.

I miss you, darling, and wait with the greatest expectation to hear about your triumphant art show. I know you will be a wonderful success.

Your,

Teddy

CHAPTER TWELVE

Zylphia sat in the formal parlor, watching as the knickknacks shook with the not-so-distant rumble of the elevated streetcar. A low fire emitted a gentle light to complement the decorative lamps throughout the room. The heavy red curtains were tied back to one side of the large windows, although a thin ivory-colored curtain covered the glass panes, muting any of the day's light that attempted to enter. Zylphia studied the sketches on the wall but quickly lost interest in their amateurish attempt at art. She sat up straight as she heard footsteps approaching the room.

Smiling as the short, sullen woman entered the room, Zylphia remained seated. "Hello, it's lovely to finally meet you." Zylphia's smile faded as the woman inspected Zylphia—as though she carried an infectious disease—and remained standing.

"Might I ask as to the purpose of your visit?" Matilda Russell asked in a glacial tone.

"I'm Zylphia McLeod, and I'm Lucas's cousin. I wanted to invite you personally to my art show that will occur in a week. I hoped to have as much family as possible attend my show." She jolted when the woman gave a discordant bark of laughter.

"You are no cousin to my son. And you are not my family. He would never have to stoop so low to find a relative." She looked at Zylphia from head to toe and back again, sniffing with disdain as she noted her mud-splotched shoes, the dirty hem to her navy skirt, and fingernails she was unable to completely free from paint.

Zylphia lifted her chin, her shoulders straight as she met Matilda's withering stare unflinchingly. "My cousin, Jeremy McLeod, is married to your daughter, Savannah. In my life, that makes me a cousin to your son. It makes us family."

"You McLeods aren't worth one-tenth of us. You should never have been allowed near my family. Why Sean allowed Gabriel to even speak with his daughter ..." She shook her head in disgust. "And then, when that worthless Jeremy enticed my Savannah away from her husband ..." She glowered at Zylphia.

"Yes, a wonderful man by all accounts. I've always thought it should be every woman's goal to be cherished so dearly that the man must beat you to show the depth of his feelings." Zylphia's cheeks flushed, and her eyes flashed with her anger.

"You're that horrid suffragist. Always sending around those pamphlets, even though they're unwanted," Matilda sputtered out.

Zylphia nodded with pride. "I take great pleasure in my attempt to educate the citizens of Massachusetts—the men and women—that they all have a voice that needs to be heard. That there are intrinsic rights that all people have."

"You have no right to come into my home, spouting such revolutionary nonsense." Matilda slammed her hand onto the back of a nearby chair. "I want nothing to do with the likes of you, and I pray my neighbors didn't see you enter."

"Appearances mean that much to you, don't they? That you'd consign your daughter to an early death rather than rejoice in the new life she's found with a wonderful man. That you'd reject your son who's found joy in his life's work." Zylphia shook her head in amazement.

"You, you who's never been challenged a day in your life, have no right to judge me and what I've done."

"I do. I do because it's women like you who've held women back for decades, if not centuries. You care more about what others will think rather than thinking for yourself and future generations. You are so small-minded that you can't envision a world where you are a man's equal."

Matilda snorted her scorn. "You will never be a man's equal. The sooner you learn that the better. The laws will always be against you. The social beliefs will always be against you."

"Yes, because we can't vote! Once we can vote, we can enact laws that will benefit us and the causes we espouse. We can vote in women as our representatives. We can change the way society views us because we will have more equal footing."

Matilda shook her head in disbelief. "You believe I've held women back? You're deluding an entire generation with your wishful thinking." She breathed heavily as she pointed a finger at Zylphia. "And when they are older and cynical and nothing has changed, they will look back at the likes of you and wish they'd never met you and that you'd never been born. For you will only bring disillusionment and pain. You will never bring hope. You will never attain your goals. Your lasting legacy will be that of failure."

Zylphia paled at the vehemence of her ire. "Mrs. Russell, I believe no more is to be said. I will leave the invitation with you, and I bid you good day."

***

Parthena sat in her parlor, staring at the used teacups, empty pot of tea, and half-eaten tray of tea cakes. She waved to the table as silent footsteps approached, indicating the maid would not be disturbing her if she cleared away the mess. At her husband's amused laugh, her gaze shot up to meet his. "Oh." She sighed. "Forgive me."

"I'm flattered you think me accomplished enough to remove this and find the kitchen," he teased.

She failed to laugh and watched him warily.

He sat in the seat across from her on the settee. "Who did you have for tea?"

"My sister, Genevieve, who I'd think you'd consider respectable enough to enter your house." Parthena sat with rigid formality, her hands firmly clasped on her lap.

"Our house," he said as he nodded for the maid who hovered in the doorway to enter and remove the tea items. He shook his head at her offer for a fresh pot of tea since he had just arrived. "Did you enjoy your time with her?"

"She's well." Parthena stared at the tabletop, now cleared of the tea items. She refused to elaborate, and long minutes of silence elapsed between them.

"Parthena, you are not a prisoner here. You are free to do what you like, as long as it does not bring scorn or infamy onto our family name."

She glared at him. "That's just it. I will bring scorn and infamy to you. By my actions. By my beliefs. The struggle for universal enfranchisement won't be easy nor will it be free of controversy. But I will participate. I will march in October."

Morgan's jaw firmed. "I wish you would see reason."

"I have, and that's why I must act and believe as I do. I can't imagine you'd want any less for me if you care for me as you proclaim you do."

He flushed at her barb and gripped the arm of his chair but exhaled deeply before responding. "I'm sure we will come to an agreement before such a time." He dug around in his waistcoat, extracting a ring with a large ruby. "I saw this and thought it would look beautiful on you."

He handed it to her, and she batted it away, causing it to land on the floor. "I don't want baubles. I don't want flowers. I don't want meaningless platitudes, Morgan. I want your understanding of who I am as a person. As a pianist. As a woman. Until that point, cease buying material things for me when I know it's a pathetic attempt to persuade me to change who I am."

She rose and stared at him with contempt. "I will never change." She stormed from the room, leaving Morgan to search for the ring and contemplate his relationship with his wife.

***

Zylphia departed the Russell house, her bag clutched to her side as she attempted to paste on a serene expression. She approached the stairs to the Washington Street elevated train and waited at the base of them, her thoughts roiling. Every time her mind replayed a bitter comment from Mrs. Russell, Zylphia formed a comeback. She kicked the base of one of the steps at her inability to barely form a coherent sentence to rebut the horrid woman's last attack.

She jumped as a hand tapped her on the shoulder. "Flo!" Zylphia clasped her friend's hand, and they walked down Washington Street to a corner a few blocks from the large Catholic church.

Zylphia pulled out pamphlets written the previous day, extolling the benefits of full enfranchisement and discounting the Antis' arguments about concerns related to loss of chivalry toward women. The pamphlets had a drawing of a blue-and-yellow-colored bird with the words Votes for Women emblazoned down the yellow belly and under the feathers of the bird. The sheet included information about donations and how to obtain a metal bird to display at home.

Florence grabbed Zylphia's sheet. "Where did you come up with this idea?" She traced the bird and smiled at it.

"At one of the latest meetings, we decided we wanted to have something decorative to send out to our supporters. I came up with the design and visited Richard at the forge. It was rather easy for him to prepare a mock-up." She shared a smile with Florence. "What do you think?"

"It's beautiful. I love it." Florence smiled, shaking her head ruefully. "No wonder Richard said you had a surprise for me today, and he seemed pleased with himself."

They shared a laugh as they approached people, handing out pamphlets to them. Most stuffed them in their bags or pockets; some flung them on the ground, while a few took them and then tossed them in the nearby garbage bin.

One man stopped and berated them. "You should be ashamed of yourselves. Standing on the street corner, like a woman peddling her wares. Your husbands must want nothing to do with you." He looked pointedly at Zylphia, who didn't have a wedding ring. "Although you don't have one and will never have one." He spat on the ground at their feet and walked on by.

Florence raised her eyebrows as she shared a long look with Zee. "Always pleasant when interacting with the public." She smiled at the next man, who was apologetic for the previous man's antics, although noncommittal about his intentions to vote for universal suffrage.

After an afternoon's worth of handing out pamphlets, Florence suggested they have a cup of tea before she headed home. They entered a small tea shop and sighed with contentment to no longer be on their feet. After ordering tea and a piece of cake each, Florence interrupted Zylphia as she began to speak about further canvassing and promotional endeavors. "No, Zee. You will tell me what is bothering you. Have you heard disturbing news from Teddy?" She reached out and patted Zylphia's hand softly a few times.

"No, thankfully. As far as I know, he is well. I visited Lucas's house. I wanted to meet his mother and hopefully his father, and to invite them to my art show."

"Oh, dear," Florence said as she prepared a cup of tea for each of them. "I imagine it was a singularly unpleasant encounter."

Zylphia laughed mirthlessly. "A part of me always thought that Savannah and Lucas exaggerated their mother. Now I know they actually attempted to diminish her vileness."

Florence took a bite of her cake, barely noting the sweet almond flavor as she beheld Zylphia's distress. "You need to understand that whatever she said is complete and utter rubbish." Florence frowned when Zylphia didn't readily agree with her. "Tell me what she said to you. I know you've been rehashing it in your mind since I met up with you."

Zylphia looked away, flushing. "She said the cause was doomed to fail. That I was raising women's expectations and hopes too high. And that, when they were cynical old women, they'd rue the day they ever met me and wish I'd never been born." She shrugged her shoulders. "More or less."

"That vile woman. Just because she gave up on her dreams and has clung to respectability as though it were her salvation, doesn't mean she should condemn the rest of us to her limited view of the world." Florence clasped Zylphia's hand, glowering when she saw Zylphia battling tears. "She knows what to say to induce the most pain."

"What happens if we fail, Flo? It will only prove horrid women like her correct," Zylphia whispered. She picked up her fork, playing with her piece of cake, rather than eating it.

Florence sighed. "I know you, Zee. I know the women truly committed to the cause, like Sophie. She'll never give up. You'll never give up. I'll never give up. I might not have a daughter, but I want my nieces to live in a better world. I want a better world." She smiled when Zylphia took a deep breath and battled away the tears. "We'll never stop fighting, Zee. You know that."

"I know. Please don't tell others of my doubts. I must remain positive and strong."

"But it does you good to be able to discuss your concerns with others. I understand. When your Teddy returns, you'll have him to turn to."

"I'll always need you and Sophie, Parthena, and Rowena. For you understand in a way a man never could." Zylphia shared a smile with Florence. "Now, tell me about the boys. How are they liking their new teachers?"

They spent the remainder of their time together laughing about Florence and Richard's sons and their antics. When Zylphia hugged Florence good-bye, her spirit was lighter, and Matilda's words were relegated to the far reaches of her memory.

***

A few evenings later Parthena sat at her keyboard, listlessly pressing keys. The discordant notes were almost melodic in their melancholy.

She sighed, her vision blurred by tears. She wore a simple at-home dress, and her hair was styled in a lazy braid down her back.

"If you insist on playing that thing, I'd hoped you could play something resembling music," Morgan intoned from the parlor doorway. The rich black walnut wood of the small parlor sparkled from a recent waxing and also added to the acoustic element of the room. A large crystal chandelier hung from the central part of the room's ceiling, while ornate molding decorated the corners and sides of the ceiling. The thick Aubusson rug covering the wooden floors silenced his footsteps into the room.

Parthena closed her eyes, thankful no tears escaped. "Why are you home?"

"Why must I explain my presence?" He walked into her parlor and sat down in the one chair not intended for a lady.

"You can come and go as you like, but you don't have the right to invade my private parlor." She slammed her fingers onto the keyboard, provoking a wince from him.

"This entire house is mine, including this parlor. Including you." He glanced around the room that had been largely unchanged since his marriage, with the exception of the large piano placed in the window alcove.

"I am not a possession you own."

"I spent enough obtaining you."

She failed to see his grimace at his flippant remark. Parthena spun on her piano bench to face him, her momentary sadness replaced by ire. "Yes, let's discuss just why you were willing to pay so dearly to obtain me when you knew the rumors that I was damaged goods."

Morgan steeled his expression into one of indifference and flicked a piece of lint from his immaculately tailored gray suit pant. "I had hoped you'd prove the rumors false. That you'd have enough respect for yourself that you'd resisted succumbing to that defiler's touch." His gaze warmed as he watched her. "However, you seem to have discovered that you don't despise everything about me."

"Against my will," she murmured.

His jaw clenched shut at her words. "I've never forced my attentions on you, or any woman, Parthena." When she met his gaze and nodded, he relaxed into his chair. "I'd hoped you'd have settled into your routine as my wife by now."

"Did you believe that by discouraging my friends from visiting that I'd adapt faster?" She shook her head with disbelief. "Why would you do such a thing?"

"If you had acceptable friends, I'd have no difficulty inviting them into my house. However, they are disreputable and only destined to bring infamy into our lives. That is not what I want."

"What happened to it being our house, as you said a few days ago? It seems you're done courting me in an attempt to change my errant ways. You've returned to who you really are. An overbearing tyrant who has to always be in control." Contempt laced her tone, and she glared at him as the barb struck. "It's all about what you want. In your house. How am I supposed to ever feel as though I belong here when you don't even acknowledge I have a place?" She shook her hand for him to remain quiet. "You say you want me to settle in, but you won't even allow me to do the things I've been trained for. I can't speak with your cook for fear that I'll choose a dish you disapprove of. I can't speak with the maids about the cleaning of the house, because you don't like to have any change occur. What exactly do you expect me to do?"

"I expect you to await me when I return, be a gracious hostess when I have guests, and be a willing bed partner when I so desire you," he snapped. "And I expect that, when I discover you are pregnant, I have no doubt as to its parentage."

Parthena sank farther onto the piano bench, her anger seeping away to despair. "You don't want a partner in life at all, do you? Someone who knows your faults and foibles and still exults in you," she whispered, brushing a hand down her plain skirt.

"They are highly overrated and only bring pain," he snapped, before flushing and looking away.

"Who hurt you, Morgan?" Parthena whispered. "I know we always fought as children, but you were still decent. And we were children, seeking any amount of attention we could garner from our absentminded parents. You had an interest in me, even then. Yet you weren't intent on controlling everything around you."

"Why would you betray me? Sleep with another man before our wedding?" he asked through clamped jaws.

"I didn't know we were to be married! I thought I'd marry him," she whispered, shocked at the flash of pain in Morgan's eyes.

"You speak of me not seeing you. When in reality, you never saw me. You never saw that, throughout all those years, I was right there waiting for you. I was waiting for you the entire time." He rose but came to an abrupt halt as she stood, moving to block the door.

"Morgan," she murmured, tears in her eyes, "I didn't mean to hurt you."

"And yet, living with you, day after day, only brings me more pain," he rasped, pushing past her and out the door.

CHAPTER THIRTEEN

Muted conversation and bursts of laughter flowed through the room where her paintings hung, displaying Zylphia's artistic talent, assisted by the gallery owner's knowledge of lighting which heightened each piece's beauty. Even the gray, green, and black pieces seemed to shine. Waiters circled with a never-ending supply of champagne and trays of small appetizers. The door and windows to the gallery were flung open on the warm September evening, enticing passersby to stop in to join the festivities. A discreet basket by the door was partially filled with the Votes for Women blue-and-yellow metal birds which Zylphia had helped to design. She knew her father had bought two hundred as party favors for the attendees of her showing, both of them relishing the thought of giving them to many of his associates who were staunch Antis.

Zylphia mingled with her prospective patrons—a mixture of friends, her father's business associates, and strangers interested in a newcomer's art. She remembered Sophie's adage to keep smiling, no matter what she heard. Her mother's advice of holding her head high and remembering that no one else had the ability to paint as she did gave her courage as conversations abruptly halted with each approach she made to a new group.

She saw Parthena and Rowena standing to one side and moved to them. She hugged them both and tried not to lean on them.

"I'm terribly upset with you," Parthena said, mischief glinting in her eyes.

Zylphia stiffened, and Rowena gripped her arm in support. "Why?" Zylphia asked.

"You're as talented an artist as I am, but you've allowed me to act as though I'm the only one entitled to the artistic temperament." She beamed at Zylphia. "Your paintings are brilliant, Zee."

Zylphia glanced surreptitiously at the crowd, sipping drinks and chatting. "If that's the case, why do they stop talking the moment I approach them?"

Rowena looked to Parthena. "Tell her. After all, I've never experienced anything similar to hosting an art show or a concert."

Parthena said, "They're uncertain what to say to you. They thought they knew who you were, and you've upended their impression of you. It's very confusing for them."

Zylphia snorted and then had to stifle a giggle as one of her father's business associates glared in their direction. "Of course it's inconceivable that women would be more than they appear." She donned her mask of interested artist as a female patron approached her.

The woman wore a slightly dated dress, faded at the trim and seams. Fine lines at the corner of her eyes and mouth hinted at her age. Golden hair shot with white suggested she was older than she appeared. "Miss McLeod, I've waited ages to make your acquaintance."

Zylphia stiffened against a shudder at her obsequious tone. "I was unaware I was known outside my small circle."

The woman smiled. "I find many are interested in the McLeod family and your numerous social vocations."

Zylphia shared a quick, startled glance with her friends. "We're no different than any other family."

"So you say. And, even though you are a talented artist, you also actively campaign for the vote. Isn't that correct?" At Zylphia's nod, the woman said, "How simply marvelous." She smiled at Zylphia's friends. "How did you learn your tactics that will bring success in a few short months?"

"I spent time with my cousins in Montana last year and learned from the women there about how to successfully campaign."

A flash of genuine interest shone in the woman's eyes. "I imagine the women of Montana have sense enough to know girls should not be involved in such endeavors."

Zylphia frowned before chuckling. "On the contrary. My cousins canvassed with their young daughters. I think my cousin Melinda will become an even greater campaigner than the rest of us, even though she's only to turn fifteen." Zylphia looked out at the crowd to see her mother approaching. "Let me introduce you to my mother as you have such interest in us." She looked back to where the woman had stood to realize she'd faded into the crowd. "How strange," she murmured.

"Do you realize you never even got her name?" Rowena commented.

Delia approached, on the surface smiling and exuding pride at her daughter's accomplishments. However, her eyes shone with annoyance and concern. When she was at Zylphia's side, she leaned forward and spoke in a hushed, urgent tone. "Zee, what were you doing speaking to that woman?"

Zylphia huffed out a laugh. "You're the one who told me to be sociable, no matter who approached or what they said. Now there are people here I shouldn't speak with?"

Delia frowned. "I expect you to avoid speaking with Clarissa's stepmother," she hissed.

Zylphia gaped at her mother, momentarily speechless. "That was the infamous Mrs. Smythe?"

"Yes, and, by how content she appeared when she left, you told her exactly what she wanted to learn."

Zylphia stared blankly over her mother's shoulder, absently noting that Sophie had waylaid Mrs. Smythe and prevented her departure with a few whacks of her cane. "I spoke about my time in Montana. About my family there."

Delia closed her eyes. "Oh, Zee."

"I didn't know!" she whispered, her wail a low protest but still loud enough to attract the attention of a few patrons. She smiled bravely at them.

Delia sighed and shook her head. "I don't know why I'm upset. It's not as though she couldn't have determined where our family is without speaking with you." She glared in Mrs. Smythe's direction. "I know that woman, and she's up to something." Delia straightened her shoulders and smiled at Zylphia. "This is nothing for you to worry about, dearest. You're a smashing success. All anyone can say to Aidan is that they want to commission a piece of work from you for their homes."

"You're not serious," Zylphia said, Mrs. Smythe forgotten at her mother's words.

"I am very serious."

Rowena leaned forward. "Why don't they simply buy a piece tonight?" Rowena waved a hand around at all the paintings present.

"Because almost all have been purchased," Delia said with a broad grin. "Can you imagine? Even those horrid dark pieces." She gripped Zee's arm as her legs seemed to buckle.

"I can't take it in," Zylphia whispered. "Do you think people bought them simply to curry Father's favor?"

Parthena barked out a mirthless laugh. "Such people may attend gatherings like this, yet they don't spend their money on paintings they don't like." She nudged Zee with her shoulder. "You're a success, Zee. Relish it."

Zylphia raised luminous eyes to her friends and mother and then clamped her mouth shut. "I want to whoop and yell my joy!" She tamped down her excitement as patrons approached her, and she transformed into the composed artist who had previously circled the room. As she shared one last smile with her mother, her sparkling eyes gave away her excitement, and she left the comfort of her friends to circulate.

***

"You have some nerve, showing your face here," Sophie barked. She glowered at an acquaintance to prevent her from approaching.

Mrs. Smythe simpered as she met Sophie's glare. "It's a relief to know that some things are constant. You haven't changed." Although her voice was candy-sweet, her eyes were as cold as steel. "However, you are older. I can always hope that means you'll soon no longer be here to badger me or to lead impressionable young woman astray."

"No matter by what name you call yourself now, you haven't changed either. I had hoped we had the good fortune of never seeing you again."

"I like to believe that I am free to come and go as I please." Mrs. Smythe's smile appeared to crack around the edges as she met Sophie's censure. She raised her chin in affront and began to walk away.

Sophie slapped her with her walking stick on the shin, earning a grunt of pain. Sophie smiled with satisfaction and thumped it on the ground in warning. "You would have no need to intervene here if you hadn't failed in your duty as a mother and if your life hadn't come to naught. Your apparition tonight proves you only mean to share your unhappiness with us," Sophie snapped, stamping her cane down with her displeasure. She watched for any signs of cunning.

"I am not a ghost," she hissed.

"It would be better if you were." Sophie leaned heavily on her cane. "Think very carefully about whatever you have planned, Mrs. Smythe. Clarissa is out of your sphere of influence. She has been for years. As is any member of the McLeod family, who have only grown closer over the years. You have no place in such a family."

"I have every right as my daughter is part of that family," she snapped, her cheeks taking on a ruddy color and detracting from any hints of beauty she might have had.

"You abdicated those rights over a decade ago. Leave the girl in peace with her adopted parents who love her," Sophie said, her aquamarine eyes flashing in anger.

"I would, but I worry that her father feels slighted because he has no place in her life. Just as I do." She smiled sweetly at Sophie.

Sophie frowned. "Her father's dead, you daft woman. Sean Sullivan died many years ago."

Mrs. Smythe looked at Sophie with a challenging, enigmatic smile. "I wish you a good evening, Mrs. Chickering. Always a pleasure to see you."

Sophronia glared at Mrs. Smythe's back as she exited the gallery. Sophie frowned as she thought through Mrs. Smythe's words but could not make sense of them. She watched the crowd, but her mind wandered to a cascade of memories involving Mrs. Smythe. Of battling wits with her as

Sophie attempted to convince the horrid stepmother to allow Clarissa to attend a suffragist gathering. Of Clarissa crying on her couch after Gabriel was forced away. Of Clarissa's quiet desperation after Mrs. Smythe left Clarissa alone in the parlor with Cameron only to be raped. Of Colin returning to Sophie's house with Melinda in his arms, rescued from an orphanage. "Meddlesome woman," she muttered.

"What was that, Sophie?" Parthena asked as she sidled up to Sophie. She held a glass of water as she surveyed the crowd. Her husband stood in the center of a large group of men, discussing business and reliving their antics at Harvard. She frowned as she watched him. He seemed to only lose his controlled facade when among his male peers.

"I wouldn't worry about the likes of Mrs. Smythe if I were you, Parthena. She's like an annoying gnat, always flying around and causing irritation but then gone again."

"I'd think she's more like a tornado. Appearing suddenly and leaving destruction in her wake." Parthena smiled wryly at her own wit.

"Ah, but that would be giving her too much importance in our lives," Sophie said. "And I refuse to allow that woman to have a continued presence in them."

"It would seem to me she's played an integral part in many of the McLeods' lives," Parthena argued.

Sophronia glowered as she thought about Mrs. Smythe. "I've decent friendships that have lasted less time than my acquaintance with that wretched woman."

Parthena watched Sophie with a sly twinkle in her eye. "I think you secretly like sparring with her. So few would attempt to match your wit. Or would dare to challenge you."

Sophie *harrumphed* before she cackled at Parthena's impertinence. "I've yet to determine why she came tonight, but I can guarantee it wasn't to admire a budding artist's talent." Sophie nodded to the expanding group in the center of the room. "I'd focus your energies on that man you've married," Sophie muttered. Her amusement faded as she noted Parthena sobering. "You've allowed him to keep you at an arm's length for too long, dear. You must break through that protective shield he wears. Unless this is the type of life you dream of living."

"I fail to see why I should be the one to make such an effort." She took a sip of her water and glared at her husband's group.

"One of you has to try, and I fear your husband believes he has been wronged. When a man's pride has been hurt, he's not about to broach a peace." Sophie smiled at a friend who approached them and wandered off with her cane *thunking* loudly.

***

Aidan McLeod froze as he beheld a woman hovering at the fringes of the showroom. He excused himself from his business associate and picked up a tumbler of whiskey as he approached her. Those turquoise blue eyes of hers seemed rapacious in their interest of the goings-on of Boston's social elite. Elegant, slightly outdated clothes hung off her thin frame, giving her an air of fragility. "Fragile my arse," Aidan muttered to himself as he smiled to another acquaintance and moved to stand in front of her. His outwardly friendly smile did little to conceal the animosity in his eyes.

"I wondered if you would deign to speak with me, now that you are among the upper echelons of Boston society," the woman said, her voice wheezy.

"I'd promised myself to do you bodily harm if I ever had the misfortune of seeing my nephews' wretched aunt again, but I can see time has already wrought its wrath on you." He glowered at her. "Mrs. Masterson."

"Ah, it seems you are incapable of forgiving small slights from the past," she taunted.

Aidan took a deep breath, forestalling his rising fury. "You call your mistreatment of my nephews while under your care a small slight? You lied to keep them separated from me all those years," he said, managing to control the emotion in his voice, yet his cheeks grew hot as they flushed with his anger.

She smiled as though she had won a small victory. "It was so well deserved, what you suffered. I lost my sister when she married your brother. It only seemed fitting you'd lose the same."

Aidan clamped his jaw shut for a moment, the muscles ticking. "By your own choice," he said. "You could have continued your acquaintance with her, but you chose not to."

She smiled triumphantly. "Just as you could have continued to look for your nephews, but didn't." She chortled. "To know they were right downstairs the entire time you had tea with me! Oh, the irony."

Aidan fisted his free hand and took a long swallow of whiskey. "Why would you come to my daughter's art show, Mrs. Masterson?"

She smiled at him. "I have an abiding interest in the McLeods. Your brother stole away my sister and ruined our chances of advancing our good family through an advantageous marriage. I'd hoped to see she was as great a failure as your brother."

"My brother was no failure. Neither is my daughter, nor are my nephews." He took a deep breath as he looked to the gathered crowd. "As you can see, many are capable of discerning her artistic talent."

She laughed with derision at his boast. "Just as I'm certain you paid them handsomely to prevent your daughter from suffering the scorn that was her due from the artistic community."

"What do you expect to gain from coming here?" He studied her. "You've had no effect on the boys' lives for fifteen years. We have all found love and prospered in your absence."

"I know of the inconsequential lives my nephews lead in Montana. It brings me tremendous pride to know that my own sons are men of superior standing and position than any of your relatives."

"You have no idea what kind of superior men my nephews are when compared to your offspring."

She smiled at Aidan as though he were a simpleton and unable to learn a simple fact. "My eldest knew better than to become permanently entangled with a shameless hussy. Your family seems to relish such liaisons."

"Fiona O'Leary Sullivan deserved better than your heartless son's attentions," Aidan replied.

She patted him on the arm as though offering comfort. "I fear we shall never agree. My Henry is destined for great things, and a woman such as that tart would never have aided him in fulfilling his destiny." She brightened as she focused on someone approaching them.

Aidan turned and groaned softly. He shook his head in an attempt to signal Zylphia to turn away, but she smiled broadly and linked her arm with her father.

After a moment's tense silence when her father refused to introduce her, Zylphia's smile dimmed but she introduced herself. "It's a pleasure to meet my father's acquaintances. I'm Zylphia, his daughter."

"I'm sure you like to believe you are, dearest," Mrs. Masterson said.

"Leave. Now," Aidan demanded in a low, clipped voice, his eyes cold and his body tensed with pent-up anger.

"Oh, I couldn't depart before furthering my acquaintance with your somewhat lovely companion here. Does your wife know you carry on with other women? I hope she is an understanding sort." She smiled benevolently as Zylphia paled.

"Who are you, and why are you saying such horrible things to my father?" Zylphia asked, stiffening at the unforeseen attack.

"My dear, I'm certain you're intelligent enough to have determined that this man couldn't possibly be your father. He's a McLeod, and they are feckless and unfaithful. I'd never trust a McLeod."

Zylphia frowned as she studied her father a moment before turning a calculating stare to the woman. "I agree. The McLeods are the worst sort. They have you believing in things such as duty, compassion, honor, and love." She smiled at the woman. "Life would be so much better if we could be like you. A heartless witch who relishes causing disharmony wherever she goes."

"Why, I've never—"

"Never had someone tell you that your opinions and beliefs are worthless? You are a woman not to be trusted. Not to be listened to. And certainly not to be esteemed. I would like you to leave my art show—which has been a great success because I am a great painter—and never return." Zylphia stood at her full height, a good half foot over the woman and glared her into abiding by Zylphia's will.

After Mrs. Masterson had departed, Zylphia leaned into her father's side, as though deflated. "Who was that awful woman?"

"Gabriel, Richard, and Jeremy's aunt. Aunt Masterson," Aidan murmured. He kissed Zee on her head. "You were magnificent." His eyes lit with pride. "Finally you proclaimed yourself more than proficient in your painting."

She laughed and blushed. "I don't know what came over me. I hated seeing her treat you like you were worthy of contempt." She squeezed her father's arm. "I must mingle some more." She smiled at him in solidarity as she moved into the crowd again.

***

Later that evening Aidan sat on a love seat beside his desk in his study so he could easily immerse himself in Zylphia's painting. He remembered the gull's cry, the briny scent of the sea, the heightened sense of expectation at pulling into Boston Harbor. Of returning home. He sighed as he lost himself to his memories, reluctantly returning to the present when his study door opened. He smiled his welcome to Delia and held out his arms to her. "Come, my love," he murmured.

"I don't want to interrupt," she said as she settled next to him, laying her head on his shoulder with a sigh of contentment.

He clasped her close, nuzzling her head. "I've missed you."

Delia chuckled. "I've been here the entire time." She kissed his neck. "I'm sorry if I was consumed with planning her show."

Aidan's hold on her tightened. "It was a roaring success." Pride resonated in his voice. "I had hoped my associates would buy a few of her pieces. I never imagined they'd purchase the entire collection."

"She'll be busy between her commissions and working toward the vote in November. I hope that will suffice as she frets about her separation from Teddy." Delia snuggled closer. "What bothers you? You're as tightly wound as when we first reunited."

"I saw you speaking with Mrs. Smythe tonight." His hold on her increased to the point he had to remind himself to loosen his grip so as not to harm her. "At nearly the same moment that Chickering woman was battling wits with her, I had an interesting discussion with Mrs. Masterson."

Delia started and twisted in his hold so she could meet his gaze. "You're not serious?" She flushed with indignation. "How dare she come to Zee's show!" She frowned when Aidan remained silent. "You know she's just like that Mrs. Smythe. Her goal is to provoke discord. I wouldn't give credence to anything she said."

"She met Zee," Aidan rasped. "I was so filled with rage, I was momentarily struck dumb." At Delia's gentle stroke of her fingers against his cheek, he met her worried gaze. "She intimated Zee wasn't mine. That she was really my strumpet and that you were an understanding wife."

Rather than the rage he expected, Delia burst out laughing. "Oh, she really doesn't know you at all, does she?" she asked with tenderness and love shining in her eyes.

Aidan grinned, lowering his forehead to rest against hers, the tension slowly ebbing from his shoulders. "No. She doesn't know Zee either. Zee was extraordinary, coming to my defense."

"It's humbling when the roles change, even for an instant," Delia murmured.

"Humbling and gratifying to realize how much she loves me," Aidan whispered. He leaned forward, kissing Delia softly on the lips. "I will never be able to thank you enough for the wonder and joy that you and Zee have brought to my life. You have enriched it immeasurably."

"Oh, Aidan," Delia whispered, her throat thick as she battled strong emotions. "I give thanks every morning that you returned to us. To me."

He smiled ruefully. "A few years late." He muffled their chuckles with another kiss, before rising and leading her from his office. "Come, my love," he whispered, walking with her to the privacy of their bedroom.

***

The capacity crowd gathered in the underground hall had become restless. Every available seat was occupied, those present understanding the privilege of having obtained a ticket to the exclusive for-one-night-only concert. The venue at Steinert Hall, although small, afforded the best acoustics in Boston and was ideal for an intimate concert. The elliptical-shaped concert hall was adorned with Corinthian columns along the walls. Small concave alcoves between the columns near the stage were like private boxes at the opera. A Greek-themed mural was on one wall, contrasting the others painted a soothing ochre color, reminiscent of the Mediterranean.

Parthena sat next to Zylphia in the second row of the balcony. She tried to fade into the shadows, causing Zylphia to snicker. "Lucas will know you're here whether he sees you or not," Zylphia murmured.

"As long as Morgan doesn't discover I came tonight," Parthena whispered.

Rowena stifled a snort in her handkerchief. "With all the Boston elite here tonight, I doubt that is a possibility. He'll know, and you'd better have a good reason for attending."

"The important thing is that you aren't performing," Zylphia breathed in a low voice. "If you had actually dared to perform ... I hate to think how your husband would react."

Parthena's eyes filled with tears. "I'm talented enough to be up there with Lucas."

Rowena gripped her friend's hand while Zylphia glared at a woman behind them who had leaned forward to better hear their conversation. "There was never any doubt of that, P.T. But you did what you had to do. And we'll never fault you for it."

"This is not the place to have this discussion," Zylphia whispered, making her eyes large. She snapped her fan open, inadvertently thwacking the woman in front of her who was stretching backward to listen in. The woman yelped and moved forward to avoid any further abuse from Zylphia's fan-waving. Zylphia winked at her friends. "I wish you'd taught me how to properly use a fan."

"I think you learned all you needed to from me," Rowena said as she bit back a laugh. "I thought your parents were in attendance tonight, Zee."

Parthena breathed deeply with relief at the change in topic, even though her hungry gaze watched the stage. She focused on Zylphia's comments when she was nudged, erecting a mask of polite boredom as she looked down to the small hall from her seat.

Zylphia pointed with her chin to the alcoves by the stage. "Sophie invited them to be her particular guests. Mother wonders what she's done to earn such an honor." They shared a giggle as they watched Sophie hold court with the McLeods. "I'm certain my father enjoys it more than my mother. She's used to playing Sophie's role." They stifled any further comments as the lights dimmed.

***

At the end of the concert, Martin knocked on the back door to the performer's private room, frowning when he was not asked to enter. He banged on the door, beaming at his son who answered his knock.

"Father," Lucas said, his momentary confusion lifting as he focused on him. He pulled him into a strong embrace and then tugged him into the cramped room. It stunk of sweat and had the humid, musty smell of an underground space.

"Your mother was unable to attend."

"You don't have to make excuses for her." Lucas nodded to the low settee and dropped onto a stool. "We'll never make amends."

Martin sighed but reluctantly nodded. "I'd like to argue with you and say you were wrong." He shook his head in consternation.

Lucas waited, not speaking, but his eyes were questioning.

"I've never known more joy than that I experienced tonight, hearing you perform. Listening to the roar of approval from the crowd. You're a master, Lucas."

Lucas's eyes grew shiny as though battling tears, and he cleared his throat. "Thank you, Father."

"Thank God you had the courage to leave the family business. You chose the more difficult path but the correct one."

Lucas bent his head at his father's benediction and reached forward to grip his hand. "Thank you."

Martin studied his son a moment and frowned. "You should be thrilled at your triumph. You should be celebrating out there with the throngs, waiting to meet you and shake your hand. I'd hate to think your association with that Mrs. Wheeler has caused you to become despondent."

Lucas raised wounded brown eyes to his father. "She never wanted me. She wanted my music. What I could give to her."

Martin sighed. "Your generation has such different notions now about relationships. In my era, it was always about what a man could offer the woman or the other way around. Affection, or love, had very little to do with it."

"You say that, but I know you loved Mother."

"I came to love her, after our marriage. But I resented her when we wed. She separated me from the woman I desired."

Lucas nodded. "I fear Mrs. Wheeler will come to love her husband. He's who she should love and the type of man she's been raised to love."

Martin tapped Lucas on a knee. "If all she appreciated about you was your music, she didn't deserve you. You're much more than that."

"Am I? Sometimes I think I'm only as important as my next concert or composition."

"Never let anyone take away your sense of worth," Martin said fiercely. "Now let's go and meet your fans."

Lucas sighed and stood. He slipped on his tuxedo jacket and smoothed back his hair. In a moment, he'd donned the mask of a musician's ennui, adding to his mystique. He slapped his father on the back and followed him to meet those who'd waited for him.

He stepped out a side door, taking a deep breath to see over half the audience had crowded around the small stage area. He relaxed when he saw Zylphia and Rowena but noted that Parthena was absent. He nodded to his cousin as he beamed at a group approaching him with effusive praise.

After shaking a multitude of hands, bowing to the men and air-kissing the women's knuckles, he inched his way to Zylphia. She shared an amused smile with him as he gripped her hand and looped it through his elbow. "Don't allow anyone to separate us," he whispered.

Rowena jauntily looped her arm through his other elbow and steered him toward the side of the room with the temporary bar erected for the evening. "I think you need a drink, Mr. Russell," she said. "All that bowing and scraping can make one parched."

"I thought you wouldn't have to go through this anymore," Zylphia murmured, beaming as she straightened even further for a photographer. She blinked a few times as the bright bulb momentarily blinded her.

"It's an artist's way of life, Zee. We must suffer events such as these or accept that our talents might remain in obscurity." Lucas nodded his thanks to the barkeep, freeing his arm from Rowena's hold to grasp his drink. He took a long swallow and smiled at those milling about. "I should think you'd know that now, after your successful showing."

"My talent doesn't require such antics," Zylphia argued. "And I can hide away in my studio. I don't have to perform to earn my accolades."

"Then you're the more fortunate of the two of us," Lucas said. "Besides, with the rumors swirling around me, I need positive publicity."

Zylphia fought a frown. "After tonight I doubt anyone could believe those rumors. You played nothing but your original compositions. You are no more mad than anyone else here in this room."

Lucas smiled, the tension leaving his shoulders at her fierce show of loyalty. "I hope you're correct, Zee." Martin joined them, and the only conversation Lucas overheard was the overwhelming fortune of their family to have two such artistic talents.

***

Delia mingled with the crowd after Lucas's performance, having had the luxury of sitting in one of the small boxes to the side of the stage with Aidan and Sophronia. Sophie motioned to Delia, and she moved in her host's direction.

"Sit, my dear," Sophie barked. She had settled on a comfortable tufted chair, unearthed from the bowels of the hall, and looked to be the most comfortable person in the room.

Delia sat on a hard wooden chair beside her.

"I'm certain you were curious about my invitation to join me this evening."

"I was, yes," Delia said as she squirmed in her chair in an attempt to find a comfortable position. "You seem to find more enjoyment in my daughter's company."

Sophie snorted. "Don't be petulant. Besides, I've found that few are clamoring for my attention lately."

Delia laughed and relaxed. An inebriated man sat at the piano and played a haphazard assortment of music while the remaining guests were content to wait their opportunity to speak with Lucas. "I feel fortunate I don't have to finagle a few minutes to speak with him."

"Yes, we are quite fortunate. He visits me quite often to ask my opinion on pieces he is working on. I fear he believes I have as valid a musical opinion as I do about everything else. A dear boy." After a moment's silence, she tapped Delia on her knee. "I had hoped you'd pay me a call after Zylphia's grand art show." Sophie *thunked* her cane in agitation. "We have a dilemma, and we must decide what to do."

Delia looked at Sophie in confusion. "Dilemma? Because Zee was successful?"

"Of course not. Because that horrid woman dared to resurrect herself." Sophie slammed down her cane again. "She'll mean nothing but trouble."

Delia let out a long sigh. "I fear you are correct. I've already written Clarissa to forewarn her."

Sophie studied Delia and nodded. "We know she will share the disturbing news with everyone in Montana."

Delia flushed and gripped her hands together until her fingers turned white. "I despise that woman. I don't want her back in our lives."

Sophie snorted. She held up her cane, waving away a friend who approached. "She's in our lives, no matter what we would like."

She shared a long look with Sophie. "Mrs. Masterson reappeared that night too. I have yet to determine why they reemerged at the same time."

Sophie glowered at the news. "Horrible woman. I can't countenance what she did to Clarissa and Gabriel. Then, I heard from Clarissa what her son did last year to Patrick's wife." Her gaze became distant as though envisioning her adversaries' untimely demises. "It's too much to believe their apparition on the same evening was a coincidence."

Delia sighed. "She attempted to ruin the evening for Zee. For that alone, I'll never forgive her."

"Zylphia is stronger than that woman. Now that she has fully accepted her McLeod heritage, she'll relish battling with that woman. With regard to that Masterson woman, I'd worry more about her offspring." Sophie shook her head. "No, our concern should be about the other one. That Mrs. Smythe." She gripped the neck of her cane. "Mischief is on its way West."

"I pray it is only mischief and not anything worse. I fear Aidan will be needed there soon." She shared a long look with Sophie.

Sophie *harrumphed* and Delia rose, joining Aidan as he spoke with Zylphia and Lucas. Delia slipped her arm through Aidan's, taking comfort from his presence.

CHAPTER FOURTEEN

A week after her art exhibit, Zylphia walked alongside the edge of a ballroom in one of the mansions in the Back Bay. Although Zylphia had not expected to dance that evening, the host's middle daughter had convinced her mother to hire a trio of musicians to play, and a small group danced on the parquet dance floor. Matrons, businessmen, and those disinclined to dance mingled throughout the first floor of the large mansion, freely moving from room to room.

"Miss McLeod," Owen Hubbard said, unable to hide a sneer as he looked her over from head to foot. "It appears you've learned little from your foray into society."

Zylphia came to an abrupt stop as he stepped in front of her. She ran a hand over her turquoise skirt, hiding a trembling fist in the folds of the fabric. "How pleasant to see you again," she demurred as she moved to walk past him.

He gripped her arm, leaning forward to whisper in her ear. "I'm surprised to find you so composed." At her bored stare, his smile grew, his ability to provoke pain sparking malicious joy in his gaze. He continued. "Considering the man you threw yourself away on has returned to Boston, with no apparent interest in seeing you again."

Zylphia blanched before forcing a smile. "I'm certain you are mistaken."

Owen's smile bloomed into a full-toothed malevolent glee, capable of ripping to shreds the hopes of the unwary. "I am rarely misinformed, Miss McLeod, especially where you are concerned. The only error I have ever made was to believe your sincerity regarding your growing disinterest in that miserable cause."

Zylphia flushed with indignation, grasping at anything to distract her from his earlier barb. "One day I will have the right to vote. All women will vote. And your perceived superiority over me and the women in your life will diminish. One day it will all disappear, and we will legally be your equal." She tilted her head to one side and fisted her hands in agitation.

"You have never been nor will you ever be my equal," he snarled, gripping her arm to the point of bruising.

A man laughed as he slapped Owen on his shoulder. He placed his hand on Owen's and freed it from his tight clasp on Zylphia's arm. "I fear you're correct," Morgan Wheeler said as he smiled and winked at Zylphia. "She's always been your superior, and it angers you to have to admit it." He winged his arm out to her and led her away from Owen.

She sighed as she moved farther from Owen Hubbard. "Thank you. Again. Although on this occasion I could have freed myself eventually, but the less time I spend in his presence, the happier I am."

"I know," he said. He led them from the ballroom into a sitting room crowded with other guests. Mauve-colored wallpaper shone in the bright electric light from overhead. The windows remained firmly latched, even though the room was nearly stifling from the multitudes present.

"I don't understand why you are gallant with me but are such a boor to Parthena." She bit her lip at her rash words.

He laughed again, his usual agitation absent at the mention of his wife. "I'm not married to you."

Zylphia shook her head at his evasive answer but did not press him for more information. As they circled the crowded room, Zylphia smiled to those she knew. "It seems ridiculous to continue with these events when men are dying on battlefields in Europe."

"I fear you are correct, but, until our boys are involved, we will continue to live as we always have." Morgan slowed his steps as they neared Parthena and Rowena. "What did he say that upset you?"

Zylphia turned toward Morgan, her confusion evident. "He told me Teddy is back." She paled when she saw the answering truth in his eyes. "He is? Why hasn't he come to me? Why didn't he tell me?"

Morgan held her arm, a consoling caress rather than Owen's taunting grip, and spoke with a soft entreaty. "For once be patient, Miss McLeod. Have faith in him. Don't let others, or any foolish doubts, tarnish what you know to be true."

Zylphia jolted when Parthena approached them, the cutting tone of her voice disrupting their quiet interlude. "Let my friend go, Mr. Wheeler. You hardly know what to do with one woman. You'd fail miserably with a harem."

Morgan stiffened and bowed in Zylphia's direction before glaring at his wife. "Come, Mrs. Wheeler. It is time we make our excuses to the hosts." A severe, quelling glance silenced any complaint from her.

Parthena thrust back her shoulders and pushed past him toward the foyer.

Rowena moved to stand next to Zylphia as they watched Parthena and Morgan depart. Zylphia shared a long look with Rowena as she rolled her eyes. "That one will never learn," Rowena muttered. "He thinks by keeping a tight rein on her that her fascination with Mr. Russell will fade."

"He doesn't understand love, nor does he care to," Zylphia said. "Although I don't know if that's fair. He seems to understand how I feel about Teddy."

"Do you believe Parthena still cares for your cousin? She's seemed content since she's set him aside." Rowena smiled impassively at a man who approached, and he walked past them to join another group.

Zylphia swallowed a snicker at Rowena's ability to dissuade unwanted company. "I no longer know. I thought she did, but now I'm uncertain." She sighed. "I thought I knew her. Before she married Mr. Wheeler, she was open and would share how she felt. Since her marriage, I can no longer discern what she thinks or feels." She faced Rowena. "When I was speaking with Mr. Hubbard, he told me Teddy's back."

Rowena gasped, reaching forward to squeeze Zee's hands as she tried to contain her joy in the crowded ballroom.

Zylphia relaxed upon realizing her friend had been unaware of Teddy's return. "Before she married, if Parthena had heard of Teddy's return, she would have told me immediately upon arriving here at this gathering, rather than allowing one such as Mr. Hubbard to impart such news." She paused as her roving glance met Owen Hubbard's glower. She smiled mischievously as she turned toward Rowena. "Mr. Wheeler might have no notion of how to treat P.T., but he was correct in his advice to me. I must ignore those who would only wish to cause me pain or to provoke doubt."

"I admire your steadfastness, Zee. If I were you, and I'd heard that the man I loved and I'd remained faithful to all this time had returned, I'd be at his door, demanding entrance."

Zylphia shook her head, as visions of doing just that flitted through her imagination. "I would love to, but we've already provided enough gossip for Boston society." She let out a deep breath. "For once in my life, I must be patient." Zylphia paused and studied her friend, realizing she had heard a hint of longing in her voice. "Who do you wait for?"

Rowena flushed and shook her head. "It is of no matter as nothing will ever come of it."

"You don't know that."

Rowena cut off Zylphia's burgeoning argument with a frown and quelling glance. "I do, Zee. I'm relegated to pining for someone who loves another."

Zylphia's brows furrowed. "If I were Sophie, I'd *harrumph* right now." Rowena laughed, and Zylphia smiled at her friend's return to good cheer. "However, I refuse to believe you'll never be loved for who you are."

Rowena shrugged. "I've long accepted I'm unexceptional. Unlike you and Parthena, I have no artistic talents. I am rather plain, and I parrot the ideas of brilliant women rather than write them myself."

Zylphia glowered at her friend. "I refuse to allow you to disparage yourself in such a manner. You are wittier than you give yourself credit for, and you intentionally hide your beauty from the unimaginative sheep gracing these ballrooms."

Rowena laughed. "Whether or not you want to face reality, Zee, I understand I'm wanted for my father's money and very little else."

"Then find a man who doesn't care about any of that. Find something that you truly enjoy. Whatever it may be. You have access to your father's fortune. You might as well use it for yourself, rather than letting it sit in a vault and multiply for your future spouse. If you even deign to marry."

"I've always been the most conventional of us all. I can't imagine not marrying."

Zylphia smiled. "Married or not, be the eccentric aunt to our children. I, for one, wouldn't bow to anyone's wishes but my own."

***

Zylphia sat in her studio, a sketch pad on her lap. She had used charcoal today, and her fingers were covered in the chalklike substance. She deftly sketched the public gardens in spring bloom, despite the fall season upon her. She frowned as she shaded in the pond, grimacing as she overblackened an area.

She sniffed and closed her eyes, the frenetic movement of her fingers stilling. The faint scent of peppermint, coffee, and sandalwood permeated the air.

"Zee," a man whispered, his voice low.

"Teddy," she breathed, leaning toward his voice, his scent, but not opening her eyes. Tears trickled down her cheeks as she sensed the air move near her.

She battled a sob as a finger traced a tear along her cheek. Her eyes fluttered open, meeting his tender, hesitant gaze. "Teddy!" she shrieked, tossing her sketch pad to the floor and throwing herself into his arms. She knocked him off balance, and he tumbled backward, laughing as she landed beside him on the rug. Both sat on the floor, refusing to let go of each other.

"Oh, my impetuous darling, how I've missed you," he whispered, peppering her head with kisses and holding her tightly with his left arm.

She kissed his shoulder, his neck, the side of his temple as she pushed herself upward to behold him. "How are you here?" she asked, unable to hide the wonder from her voice.

"I arrived yesterday." A soft kiss to her nape dispelled the hurt threatening to emerge. "I wanted to see you immediately, but Mother persuaded me to wait until today. She informed me that our reunion could wait another day as you had important plans."

Zylphia blinked away tears as she burrowed forward into his embrace. "Nothing could be more important than seeing you. Being with you." She felt him relax at her words and settled for a moment into his embrace. "Talk to me. Convince me I'm not dreaming."

"You smell like turpentine. Your hair is a mess, and you've just smeared my impeccably tailored suit with charcoal dust," he said as he kissed her head again. "I couldn't have dreamed such a wonderful reunion." He met her amused gaze as she rose up again. "And believe me, I've dreamed of our reunion more times than you can count."

Zylphia traced the furrows his smile created on his face, then the new wrinkles since she'd last seen him. "Let's not have a competition over who imagined more reunions."

"Or whose were more vivid," Teddy teased, rolling her under his arm and provoking a squeal. His gaze roved over her joyous expression a moment before he leaned forward and kissed her. It was at once tender and sweet, and yet a proclamation of his return to her life.

He jolted as the studio door opened, flushing with chagrin as he met Aidan McLeod's frown. "I beg your pardon, sir," Teddy rasped as he scooted away from Zylphia, who refrained from turning toward the door.

"I'll have to beg Zee's if I interrupted your reunion. Welcome back, Goff. You've been missed." His astute gaze moved over Teddy, and he nodded once before he backed from the room, the door *click*ing shut.

"Oh my, please tell me that wasn't my father," Zylphia moaned, covering her face with her hands while her shoulders shook.

"Zee, there's no reason to cry. Your father knows we belong together."

She lowered her hands, giggles bursting forth. "Can you imagine what he must have thought when he heard me shriek? And then when he saw us?" She blushed crimson red. "It's one thing for my father to know I love you. It's another for him to see the evidence of it."

Teddy's gaze intensified, his gray eyes lit with a fiery intensity. "Say it again. To me."

"I love you." She studied his face, sat up taller. Her gaze wandered over him, noting changes wrought during their separation. "What happened to you, Teddy?"

"I survived," he said, his left hand pulling the hair over his left ear.

She reached up, brushing away his hand. She sifted her hands through his silky sable hair. The only perceptible change in her expression was a slight furrowing of her brows as she catalogued the alterations that had occurred. Her fingers caressed a faint scar over his right eyebrow and a healed burnt patch behind his left ear that he attempted to cover with a shaggy haircut. Her hands continued to rove down his right arm, grasping his right hand where the tips of his three middle fingers were missing.

"Oh, my darling, how you have suffered," she whispered as she raised his hand and kissed first the palm before kissing each finger. She sat back and met his gaze, his more guarded by the moment. "I love you, Theodore Goff. Exactly as you are. Exactly as you have come back to me." She traced the scar over his eyebrow. "I will never wish for you to be any way other than you are."

His eyes glistened as though battling intense emotion. "I love you, Zylphia McLeod. The woman steadfast enough to wait for me and brave enough to never lose hope I'd return to her."

He clutched her to him, kissing her with over a year's worth of suppressed passion. His hands roved over her head, shoulders, back, and down to her hips. He pulled her hips more tightly into his, before pushing her away with a groan. He moved his arms around her upper back, embracing her, his hands ever moving as they relearned the landscape of her body.

"Zee, can you sneak out tonight? Visit me at my house?" he whispered into her ear. "I want privacy for our reunion."

She flushed as she saw passion's promise in his gaze. "Yes."

He rose and extended his left arm to help her up. She pushed it aside and reached for his right hand. She met his startled gaze and waited. He gripped her hand and tugged her to her feet.

"Did that hurt you?" she asked. At the subtle shake of his head, she stopped him from turning away from her by clasping his cheeks between her palms. "I don't want you to hide any part of you from me. I will attempt to do the same for you. I hate that you were injured in battle."

"I don't want to disgust you," he murmured.

"You've earned these scars in ways I will not ever be able to imagine. They are honorable, just as you are. They will never disgust me, just as you don't." She studied his gaze a moment and then smiled as she leaned on her tiptoes and kissed him.

He reached around her with both arms, pulling her tightly to him as he deepened the kiss. He spun them until she was backed against the door and kissed her until they were breathless. "Promise me that you'll find your way to me tonight." He kissed the side of her neck, and she arched into him.

"I promise," she said. She moved with him, her arms looped around his neck, as he settled them to the side of the door.

He backed away and ran a hand over his disheveled hair and charcoal-stained suit. He took a deep breath and fought a grin as he watched her attempt to compose herself. Tracing a finger along her cheek, he dropped his hand to grip hers and raised it to his lips for a soft kiss. "Until later, my love." Her eyes gleamed with love and the promise of what was to come as he backed out the door and closed it behind him.

***

"What is going on up there?" Delia asked as she moved to ascend the stairs.

Aidan placed a hand on her shoulder and shook his head. "Delia, come with me. Zylphia is fine," he said.

His wife frowned but followed him into his study. "Why do you seem so pleased with yourself?" She studied his contented expression.

"Because there is now the possibility for harmony in my house." He sat down and tugged Delia until she toppled onto his lap. "Teddy is home," he whispered into her ear.

Delia reared back, her mouth agape as she stared at Aidan.

He nodded. "It's a perfect reaction. There are no words created, not for our Zylphia, to express the wonder of his return." He smiled as Delia flung her arms around his shoulders and wept. "She'll be all right, love," he murmured.

"No matter what happened, I knew Zee was strong enough to survive it," Delia stuttered through her sobs. "But now she has the chance to thrive."

He nuzzled her head for a few moments until there was a gentle knock on his door. Delia remained perched on his lap. "Enter," Aidan said.

Theodore Goff entered the room, biting his lip as he beheld the scene of Delia McLeod sitting on her husband's lap. "I beg your pardon for interrupting."

"You weren't. Delia had just finished her celebratory sob at the news of your joyous return," Aidan said. He helped Delia to her feet before he rose. He extended a hand to Teddy, nodding with approval as Teddy held out his injured right hand. "Welcome back, Mr. Goff."

Delia moved around the desk to give Teddy a quick kiss on the cheek before opening the study door to depart. She shared a long glance with Aidan before she slipped out and closed his study door behind her.

"Would you like anything?" Aidan asked, waving toward a bar of decanters filled with amber liquid.

"No, thank you, sir." Teddy cleared his throat as he stood on the other side of Aidan's desk.

Aidan moved toward the decanters and poured himself a small tumbler of whiskey, waving for Teddy to sit. Teddy sat with casual elegance in a black leather chair that creaked with his movements. "I can't begin to tell you how relieved I was to see you today, Goff." Aidan took a small sip of his drink. "The rumor of your return had preceded your arrival to my house."

Teddy flinched. "I followed my mother's advice, most likely for the last time."

Aidan drummed a slow, silent tattoo on his chair's armrest. He settled in as he waited for Teddy to speak.

"I seek your permission to ask Zylphia to marry me," Teddy said.

Aidan nodded and took another sip of whiskey. After a moment he set down his drink and met Teddy's gaze. "Don't you believe this is a bit premature? You've been away for over a year, Goff. I'd think you'd want to ensure that you truly do suit before you bind yourself to a woman. Divorce might be more common these days, but I do not find it acceptable."

Teddy frowned. "Is it that you doubt my constancy? Or Zylphia's?" He flushed with agitation. "I fought in a damn war. Saw men blown to bits in trenches next to me. I lost the better part of the use of my right hand, and, through it all, I thought only of returning to Zee. Of what kind of man I wanted to be for her if I survived."

He nearly growled when Aidan continued to stare impassively at him. "A bomb landed not two feet from me, and, as I heard its whistling arrival, my only regret was that I hadn't loved Zee better."

"What happened to the bomb?" Aidan tilted his head to the side quizzically.

"A dud." Teddy stared blankly in front of him for a moment, lost in his memories of fear, destruction, hunger, and near-death. "I thought I'd lost my chance to love the most wondrous woman I'd had the fortune of knowing.

"I love your daughter, sir. I know you have reasons to doubt me. Reasons to believe we should wait. However, I've learned that fate can be fickle, and I want all the time I can have with Zylphia. I pray it is many years." He paused and took a deep breath. "I don't need your dowry. I can provide for her on my own."

Aidan smiled with triumph. "You'll do, Goff," he said as he held out his hand. "You always treated Zee well, and you challenge her in a way no one else ever has." He smiled fully as Teddy clasped his hand. "I welcome you into my family."

"Thank you, sir," Teddy said as he squeezed Aidan's hand.

"You and Zee acted like juvenile idiots before you left, and I hope the war taught you what is important."

"It did. It has."

Aidan settled into his chair. "You say you don't need the dowry I have set aside for Zee, and I believe you. You're an astute business man, and I look forward to working with you with more frequency once you are my son-in-law. However, I want Zee to have access to that money. For her causes. Her painting. Her daughters. For whatever she sees fit."

"Do you believe I wouldn't support her?" Teddy asked, gripping his hand as though battling indignation.

"Not at all. However, if something were to happen to you, I want to ensure that there is never any doubt as to who controls that money. I never want my daughter to worry about her future."

Aidan and Teddy shared a long glance, and an understanding was born, one forged from their mutual love for Zylphia.

"Nothing is more precious than family and those we love," Aidan murmured. "Nothing."

CHAPTER FIFTEEN

Zylphia poked her head into the laboratory on the third floor of the large mansion in Cambridge and found it empty. She silently backed out and tiptoed to the doorway farther down the hall. His study. She paused a moment as she battled memories. Rather than knocking, she tested the door and slipped inside when she found it open.

A soft fire smoldered in the fireplace, and the room was gently lit by lamps. She removed her heavy black cape and draped it over the back of a chair. She moved toward Teddy's leather wingback chair, tracing it as she remembered the last time she was here. The tears. The pleasure. The fear and then anger and pain as she had lied to him.

"You came," Teddy whispered from behind her.

She spun to face him and nodded. She remained mute, watching him lock the door behind him as he slowly approached her. He wore black trousers and a white shirt, partially open at the neck. She reached forward and touched his neck, finding his pulse point.

He frowned as he saw her battling tears. "What is it, my love?"

She moved into him, replacing her fingers with her lips. "I can't believe you're here. In my arms. I need proof that you're real." She kissed him again, before laying her head against his chest. "I fear I'll continue to need such proof for a while."

He traced a hand down her back and then to her loosely tied-up hair. His fingers found pins, and he deftly removed them. Her hair cascaded down her back, and he leaned in farther, burying his face in her long raven locks. "I don't mind as it means I am able to hold you in my arms," he murmured.

"Why did you want us to meet here?" Zylphia asked. She ran a hand over his back, earning a small shudder. She continued her caress, and he pulled her closer.

"There are ghosts in this room, Zee. Ghosts of our immature selves who must be vanquished. I want to create new memories here. Ones of joy. Where we have ..." He broke off as though he had said too much and chuckled. "You're a minx, encouraging me to say more than I'd planned."

She chuckled and attempted to move even closer to him. "I thought the reason for my coming here wasn't solely for conversation."

He laughed in her ear, and she realized that he'd been moving them slowly toward the carpet near the fireplace. "No, my dearest love. Although there's no one I'd rather speak with, there's so much more I'd rather do right now."

He eased her onto the carpet and paused as he felt her trembling. He backed away and met her gaze, frowning as he saw her attempt to hide her fear. "I won't hurt you again. I promise."

She nodded and bit her trembling lip. "I know. A part of me knows that. Another part worries I'll disappoint you."

Teddy laughed and then immediately sobered as a tear trickled down her cheek. "Oh, Zee, you'll never disappoint me."

She nodded, and her gaze became resolute. "Fine. Let's..." She waved a hand around as though indicating that whatever was to happen between them should begin.

He shook his head as he felt her becoming more tightly strung by the moment. "No, not like this," he whispered. He rose and reached for her hand, helping her up. "Come with me." Hands clasped, they walked through the study to the door. He unlocked it, peered down the darkened empty hall, and tugged her to a bedroom opposite his study.

He shut and locked the door behind them, then leaned forward and kissed her. Kissed her softly. Reverently. He traced featherlight caresses over her back, her sides, and her hips. He felt her tension ease as she leaned into him. Her hands roved over his back and soon became impatient with his clothing. He sighed with contentment as he felt her tug at his shirttails and pull them free of his trousers.

He worked loose the buttons on the back of her dress and broke their kiss as he grasped the edges of the opened dress, pulling it to her feet. They exchanged smiles as though sharing a secret while he urged her forward to step from her dress. He hooked his fingers into her chemise and pulled it up to her chin. He paused before easing it over her head.

He met her gaze, the fingers of his left hand reaching forward to trace the contour of her collarbone. "Do you want me to stop?"

Her smile bloomed while joy and anticipation filled her gaze. "No, my love, no," she said as she leaned forward to kiss him. He broke the kiss to lift the chemise over her head. His hands ran over the soft skin of her shoulders and upper chest before easing around to work on the ties of her corset. Soon that was discarded on the floor, and she was left in a thin undershift.

She pushed aside his hands to unbutton his shirt and drop it to the floor. She leaned forward and kissed his left shoulder exposed in the undershirt that covered his chest but bared his arms and moved to kiss his right shoulder.

He backed up a step and shook his head. "No, Zee." He backed up another step, and another, until he bumped into the bed. "I—this shirt needs to stay on."

Zylphia squinted in the darkened room and frowned. "I want nothing between us, Teddy. Not clothes, not secrets. Nothing."

Teddy caressed the side of her cheek, easing the warrior expression that had overcome her. "You'll never know how much you saying that means to me. You have to be patient with me, Zee."

"You're used to hiding away, and I won't let you." She met his gaze with one filled with fierce devotion, grasping the bottom of the undershirt between her fingers. "Trust me. Trust in us."

He swallowed and nodded. Rather than remove the shirt immediately, she dropped her hold on its hem and instead leaned on tiptoes and kissed him on his lips, before brushing quick kisses along his jaw, his neck, and upper chest. She caressed him along his back, arms, and chest as she kissed him. "I should have realized you needed courting as much as I did," she teased. He chuffed out a laugh, clenching his hands as she kissed him over his shirt down his belly.

"Take it off, Zee," he demanded.

She looked up at him in triumph, to behold him with his head thrown back in passion. She hooked her thumbs onto the edge of the shirt and caressed his bare chest with her hands as she raised his shirt.

"You truly are a minx," he said, pride and passion tingeing his voice.

"I've had plenty of nights to dream of our reunion." She threw his shirt to join her clothes on the floor and ran her hands over his torso, down his arms. She never hesitated as her hands rubbed over scars along the right side of his upper chest and shoulder.

"I would spare you these scars if I could," Teddy murmured.

She leaned up and kissed them before moving to his uninjured side. "They only make me love you more," she whispered as she wrapped her arms around him. "I hate to think of all you suffered."

"I'm suffering now," he teased as he pulled her even closer to him.

She laughed and pushed him backward, toppling him on the bed. She threw off the last stitch of clothing covering her and clambered onto the bed, straddling him. He pulled her down for a kiss, before rolling her so she was underneath him. He never broke the kiss, even as he wriggled to free himself of his pants and underclothes.

When he was as naked as she was, he broke the kiss to stare into her eyes a moment. "Do you want me? Do you want—?"

Before he could say anything further, Zylphia covered his mouth and quietly said, "Yes! I half undressed you. I want you. I want us. I want—"

She gasped as he kissed her deeply, ending all unnecessary conversation. They focused on their reunion as their gasps of joy and passion completed their homecoming.

***

Zylphia awoke, her head on Teddy's left shoulder. His hand sifted through her hair, gently tugging on it in a soothing caress. She snuggled closer and sighed.

"I'm hoping that is due to contentment," he whispered as he leaned down to kiss her forehead.

She raised her head, a small frown marring her expression. "Of course it is." She stared at him, her frown deepening as she failed to read his guarded expression. "It was everything I'd dreamed it would be and more."

"Will you lay with me here a while?" He brushed at her forehead, failing to ease the furrows between her brows.

She nodded and laid her head on his chest again. After a few moments, she traced lazy patterns on his chest. "I always dreamed of this. This quiet time together when no words were needed."

She felt him tense a moment before he rolled her onto her back, and he loomed over her. His expression was fierce, a determination and desperation in his gaze he was unable to hide. "I can't be quiet, Zee." At her nod for him to continue, he relaxed slightly. "I love you. I don't want to imagine a life without you in it."

Zylphia nodded again but remained quiet. He ran his hands through her hair until he clasped her head between his palms. "I wanted us to have our reunion in the study because I had a fantasy of rewriting the past. Of having a chance to create a different ending."

"I'm so—"

He dropped his battered fingers to her lips and shook his head. "Never be sorry, Zee. You showed me how I shouldn't be looking to the past. I should look to the future. Our future."

She nodded again, and he took a deep breath. "Give me a second." He rolled off the bed and ferreted through their clothes until he found his pants. He grabbed something before rejoining her again on the bed, this time lying beside her. She rolled onto her side, her gaze quizzical. She ran a hand over his hip, as though needing constant contact with him to remind her that they were truly reunited.

He took a deep breath, handed her a box, and waited. She leaned up on one elbow and popped it open.

Her eyes widened as she beheld the large sapphire surrounded by small diamonds. "What does this mean, Teddy?"

He reached into the box, clumsily grasping it with his thumb and damaged index finger. "Marry me, Zee. Accompany me through this life as my best friend, my love, my equal."

She raised luminous eyes, eyes that matched the sapphire, to his. "Yes, I'll marry you, Theodore Goff. You understand me, challenge me, and still love me."

He smiled. "How could I not love the most remarkable woman I've ever met?" His smile broadened as he slipped the ring onto her finger, before he raised her hand and kissed it. "I love you, Zee."

"I love you, Teddy," she whispered, attempting to blink away tears and failing. She flung herself at him, pushing him backward. "Hold me. Hold me forever."

***

He wrapped his strong arms around her and felt himself relax into her embrace. It was the first time he'd fully relaxed since their fight, over eighteen months ago.

***

Zylphia stood near the fire in Teddy's office one evening a week later, her dark cloak draped over the ottoman. She stared into the flames, swaying as though she heard music. She jumped and stifled a shriek when Teddy stroked a hand down her arm.

"Where are you, darling?" he asked as he pulled her backward into his embrace, looping his arms around her front and nestling her into him. "You're a million miles away." He shuddered as she settled into him, relaxing the longer he held her.

"I was thinking about the gathering tonight and envisioning that you'd been there to dance with me." She turned and snuggled into a full-bodied hug. "I miss you when I'm not with you."

"That's lovely. Thank you," he whispered into her hair. "I couldn't go. Not today. I have no desire to attend such events."

"I know, darling. But I fear you must go to one at some point as people are becoming curious, and the longer you refrain from attending, the meaner the rumors become." She leaned back to study his face, the tightening of his jaw belying his day's stress. "Did you have a terrible day?"

Teddy exhaled in an attempt to soothe the sudden tension gripping him. "It's all better now." He kissed her softly and eased her again into his embrace. "Is the gossip affecting you?"

Zylphia chuckled. "It doesn't matter to me. They already think I'm an oddity, and what they say about me doesn't hurt me."

He pushed her out of his arms to see her face. He ran fingers down her cheek and cradled her chin, his expression tender. "Yet what they say about me does hurt you." At her nod, he pulled her tightly into his embrace again. "Oh, my love, you don't have to fight my battles for me. The ones who speak poorly of me or speculate about me aren't worth our regard."

Zylphia sniffled as she burrowed farther into his embrace. "I know that rationally. Then someone comes up to me and says something snide, and all I want to do is hit them. Yell at them about not having any idea about what it was you lived through." She let out a stuttering breath. "Instead I have to smile and act pleased they took time out of their social obligations to speak with me."

Teddy moved toward the leather sofa to one side of the fireplace. He stretched out on it, and Zylphia laid down next to him, curling into him. "What else bothers you, darling? I can sense your worry."

"The march is in two days' time, and I have this fear no one will show up," she admitted. When his laughter filled the room, she stiffened and rose up on an elbow to glare at him. "I'm serious."

"I know you are," he said with another chuckle. "So many women and men will be there that you won't know what to do. It will be a roaring success due to the diligent work of you and the women on your committee."

Zylphia settled against him once more. She played with one of the sofa's loose buttons. "I love hearing you laugh. You comfort me when I can see you are in as great a need of comfort as I am." She stroked a hand down his chest. When he remained silent, she said, "The mansion tonight was festooned in red roses. All the men, well almost all, had red roses in their boutonnieres." Tears trickled down her cheeks. "If I can't convince any of those men, how can I convince others that universal suffrage is just?"

"What does the red rose mean?"

"It's a symbol of being an Anti. They took great pleasure in speaking of the beautiful floral arrangements and offering to give me the name of their florist." Zylphia sighed as tears continued to leak out.

Teddy moved so that Zylphia lay underneath him, his weight balanced on his knees and elbows as he swiped at her tears with jerky movements. "What color should I wear to show my support?"

"A yellow rose," Zylphia whispered. "Anything yellow really, as that is one of our colors." She leaned up and kissed him. "Oh, Teddy, thank you."

He kissed her fervently, his hands caressing her head and shoulders. "I'll always support you in what you do. Your art. Your suffragist work." He shared a long, passionate look with her. "I'll never stop loving you." He leaned forward, kissing her again as his hands attempted to loosen the buttons on the front of her dress. During the long minutes it took him to undo her buttons, he kissed her forehead, cheeks, the underside of her neck. As he slowly peeled away her dress, he kissed the newly exposed flesh.

She traced patterns over his back, ruching up his shirt to feel his skin. When he leaned away from her a moment, she worked at a feverish pace on the buttons of his waistcoat and shirt, pushing the shirt off and away so that he was bare-chested. His eyes glowed as he beheld the answering passion in her eyes, and he lowered his head, kissing her deeply.

"You have no idea how much your passion for me pleases me," he groaned out, his head tilting back as Zylphia kissed his neck down to his chest. He gasped as she worked on the remaining buttons of his pants and earned a gasp from her as he pulled her to him to straddle him. "Like this, love. Love me like this," he murmured, kissing her deeply.

She moaned, lost to their passion.

***

Zylphia smiled as she turned to kiss him before settling her back against his front. She was cocooned in a warm blanket with Teddy behind her providing even more warmth. "We've silenced one ghost."

Teddy's chest rumbled behind her as he laughed softly. "We have. I'd much rather remain here, all night, with you in my arms, than have you storm out of here like the last time."

"Forgive me ..." She bit back any further words as his fingers raised to her lips in a silent entreaty to say nothing more. "I love you," she whispered as she kissed his fingers.

"And I you, my darling," he whispered.

She traced a hand along the arm clasped around her belly and was silent for a few minutes. "We have to find other ways of seeing each other," she teased, breaking the contented silence. "I can't continue to sneak out of my house."

"It's only been a handful of times," Teddy murmured. "Besides, we'll marry soon."

She ran her hand down his arm, coming to his injured fingers. She traced her fingers over the healthy and the scarred skin, her fingers plucking and playing with his absently. "Thank you for insisting that we wait to marry until after the vote."

He sighed into her hair and burrowed through its thickness to reach her nape. He kissed her softly once, eliciting a shiver.

She felt his smile at her reaction, and more kisses followed.

"I had no desire to attempt to compete with the cause."

Zylphia scooted, bumping the back of her head against his nose and earning a grunt of discomfort as she turned to face him. "There is no competition, Teddy. Please tell me you understand that?"

"I do. But I will also admit to wanting you for myself for a while. I know that, after the vote occurs, whatever the outcome, I can steal you away from the cause for a little while."

"Only a little while," she murmured.

He ran a hand down her arm, eliciting goose bumps as his fingers followed imaginary trails up from her elbow and down from her shoulder. "Zee, there's so much I haven't told you about the war. The battles. The things I did."

She leaned up and kissed him on his forehead that had furrowed with worry as he spoke. "There's no need to tell me. It's all right," she soothed. She smiled at him, reaching up to run a hand through his locks of sable hair that fell over his forehead. "I love you no matter what happened or what you did."

"I know but ..."

"It's all right, darling," she whispered, leaning up on an elbow and kissing him deeply. After a while, she pushed him to his back and methodically kissed every one of his scars. "I love you, just as you are."

"That's a miracle, but I still need to tell you ..." He sighed as she kissed him and returned her kiss with a desperate fervency. Soon his protests were lost to their passion; any discussion of the war was silenced for another day.

***

Teddy ascended the stairs behind the silent butler and was shown into a rear parlor. He nodded to the butler who left him alone. He stared out the rear window at white sheets fluttering on the line in the warm October afternoon. His gaze became distant as he stared at the white sheets, envisioning row after row of sheets billowing in the sharp breeze outside his tent in France. The distant shrieks of children playing transmuted into the cries of agony from the nearby surgical tent.

"She left some time ago, with other committee members," Sophie said. "They are busy at work as the march is tomorrow."

He jolted at her voice. He shook his head, clearing it of his memories and attempting a smile.

Sophronia frowned as she beheld him perspiring and nearly gasping for breath. Yet she understood his travails. "I'm grateful you've decided to visit me." She moved toward her chair and nodded toward one near hers for him.

"I wouldn't have intruded, but I believed Miss McLeod was to be here today, and I desired to escort her home."

Sophie's eyes sparkled with mischief. "You were hoping to steal a little time with your betrothed, and I do not blame you. However, we had a short meeting today, and she left with Miss Clement. I believe you'd find Zylphia at home by now."

Teddy nodded, fidgeting in his chair. "Thank you for all you've done for Miss McLeod in my absence."

Sophronia *harrumphed* and batted her hand against the arm of her chair. "She is a dear friend, and I will always provide her counsel. Whether she desires it or not." At his protracted silence, she reached forward and gripped his hand. "I was never so glad as to hear of your safe return."

Teddy exhaled a stuttering breath and squeezed her hand a moment. "I don't know as I'd call a maimed man who jolts at certain sounds a safe return."

Sophie frowned as she beheld him. "Those of us who knew you from before can only rejoice that you are returned to us. That we are not forced to mourn you." At his confused shake of his head, Sophie asked, "Why are you perplexed by our joy?"

"There are those who believe it would be better had I not returned rather than to do so as I am."

"Then they are fools and not worth mentioning. Only an imbecile would fail to celebrate your continued presence among us." Sophie's brows furrowed as she watched his distress. "Are your parents celebrating your return?"

"My mother has barely registered the change in her household other than the slight uptick in the grocer's bill. I am again on the third floor, and she takes little notice of me." His gaze was distant.

"And your father?" Sophie asked. "I imagine he is delighted you have returned to help his faltering investment business."

Teddy snorted. "He's asked me to refrain from sending any advice as of yet as he doesn't want his clients to realize my influence."

Sophie smiled wickedly. "Then I'd cease providing him aid of any sort. Start your own consulting company and proclaim a concern for a conflict of interest." She shared a mischievous smile with Teddy before sobering. "Why should he benefit when he refuses to give you credit?"

Teddy's gray eyes were dulled as he met Sophie's fiery aquamarine gaze. "He paid me a consultant's fee. However, I think I'll put my energy into a business venture with Aidan McLeod. I'm uncertain as to what, but we'll determine something."

Sophie nearly growled with frustration. "It is their lack, not yours, dear boy. Those of us who care about you celebrate your return." She tapped him on his arm when he appeared dubious. "Do you doubt your Zylphia's reaction to you? Do you believe she was disappointed you returned?"

"No, not at all. I will forever give thanks for her. And my parents are not difficult to understand, Mrs. Chickering." He shook his head in resignation. "They will never rejoice in me or anything I do. They loathe Zylphia and her common beginnings. They think Aidan is an upstart with too much money. They wish I'd done glorious deeds on the battlefield or, barring that, come to a glorious end."

Sophie clasped his hands, now clenched on his lap. "Then they are fools, and I've always thought your mother a dithering idiot." She met his gaze. "Never allow their misconceptions and prejudices to become your own. Or for one minute to believe that others feel the same."

Reluctant gratitude shone in his silver eyes. "You are as formidable as Zylphia has proclaimed."

"Never doubt it, my boy. Never doubt it," Sophie said with a self-mocking laugh. She turned the topic to the next day's march and coaxed a few more smiles and laughs from him before he took his leave.

CHAPTER SIXTEEN

Teddy wove in and out of the crowd lining Beacon Street on the sunny Saturday afternoon of October 16. He looked up and saw people on balconies in expectation of the march, while others continued to arrive from the trolley stops. Police lined the sidewalks, and the route remained free for the marchers. He glanced up in consternation as many of the balconies were draped with red banners. He stumbled as a young boy rushed past him, carrying red roses pinned to cards, looking for interested parties to peddle his wares.

Teddy frowned when he came to a main intersection at Arlington Street and saw a parked car, facing Beacon Street. Festooned in red roses, placards proclaiming Vote NO were plastered on all sides of the vehicle. He noted that passersby plucked a rose from it to affix to their buttonholes as they moved to watch the parade. "Where are the yellow roses and pro-vote paraphernalia?" Teddy murmured to himself.

He smiled at an intrepid youth who navigated the crowd without running into anyone. He handed out sheets of paper with a broad smile and wouldn't allow a person to turn him away. Teddy sighed, resolved to reading a tirade against suffragism. Instead, he read lyrics to the songs the women would sing, with an invitation for the audience to join in. All the songs were based on popular songs of the day, and the harmony would be readily recognized. He laughed as he read the lyrics replacing the well-known "Yankee Doodle Dandy" with "Votes for Women, Sure to Win."

He jostled a few people as he moved through the crowd and was stopped by a strong arm gripping his shoulder. He frowned at the man holding him before smiling in recognition. "Morgan," Teddy said, holding out his hand.

"It's good to see you again, Teddy. It's been too long." They shook hands. "I don't have to ask why you're here."

"Of course not. I'm very proud of what Zylphia is doing. As I am sure you are with Mrs. Wheeler ..." He interrupted himself as he stared pointedly at Morgan's red rose, slipped into his boutonniere.

"I remain unconvinced that equal suffrage is the correct path for Massachusetts and the United States as a whole. I fear it has not led to the social changes the women thought it would in the West, and I cannot favor chaos." He nodded at Teddy's clothes and bit back a smile.

Teddy smiled, running a hand over his yellow waistcoat and fingered the yellow rose in his lapel pocket. "You'll never doubt who I'm supporting."

Morgan laughed ruefully, and they pushed themselves forward to carve out a space to better watch the parade.

"Did you receive one of these?" Teddy asked, holding up his sheet with the day's musical lyrics. At Morgan's shake of his head, Teddy shrugged.

"We'll share. And, if you have any sense, you'll ensure your wife sees you singing when she passes."

Morgan grumbled and refused to agree.

Teddy stood beside Morgan as the marchers filed past. The suffragist flag, striped in yellow, white, and purple, was proudly paraded past them, and Teddy cheered. "If you hope to gain any favor with your wife, this isn't how to go about it," Teddy said with a rueful shake of his head. He stood on his toes as he looked down the street for any sign of Zylphia.

He clapped loudly as he saw Rowena carrying the next banner. Made of yellow cloth with the words in purple it read, "Forward out of Darkness, Leave Behind the Night, Forward out of Error, Forward into Light." His enthusiastic cheering earned him curious glances from nearby onlookers, but they did little to dampen his enthusiasm.

The song "Come Vote, Ladies," was sung over and over as the women marched past. It was an easy marching song as it had few lyrics and was based off the song "Good Night, Ladies." Teddy sang along and encouraged those near him to join in.

"I'm sure you'll have no difficulty in seeing Miss McLeod. She has a wonderful ability to be in the center of all spectacles," Morgan said, yet had struck a detached, uninterested pose, even as his keen gaze rove over the marchers.

"You act disinterested, but I know you're searching for your wife. You're as concerned as I am." When Morgan stared at him with feigned boredom, Teddy said, "I hope it is more peaceful today than two years ago in Washington."

"If it isn't, it will only give the Antis more proof that women should not have the vote. One march with violence will provoke sympathy for the marchers. Two with violence?" He shrugged one shoulder. "That would only cause those with reason to suspect it is a ploy to garner support."

Teddy shook his head in exasperation. "I hope what you are saying is truly what you believe and not just something that you espouse to nettle Parthena. For this is no way to earn her trust." He sighed with disgust.

Morgan stiffened with indignation next to Teddy. "You've been gone a long time, Goff. You know nothing of it."

"I know enough." He turned to glare at Morgan. "Stop baiting your wife, and maybe you'll find more harmony at home."

"I was unaware that my marriage provided such interesting gossip for the likes of Miss McLeod." His brown eyes shone with fury as he glared at Teddy.

Teddy rolled his eyes as he looked at the marchers. Zylphia was in the midst of one of the groups. "Zylphia! Way to go!" he yelled, waving his arms about. Her head snapped up, and she broke into a broad smile. She waved back before her arm was whacked by the woman next to her, lowering it to her side. She flushed as she resumed looking straight ahead and marching in perfect solemnity. She snuck a peek at him from the side and gave him another small smile, before recapturing her serious demeanor.

"Did you see Parthena?" Teddy asked Morgan, exhilarated. He swayed to the lively music played by an approaching band, clapping and cheering them on. He looked at his sheet, singing along to the new lyrics to the harmony of "Yankee Doodle Dandy" and laughed as he stumbled through the unfamiliar words.

The women marching sang proudly and with vigor, the chorus ringing loudly. Although some near him muttered, "Blasphemy," at the use of a revolutionary song, others laughed and joined in.

Groups of delegates marched past from counties around Massachusetts, including the Men's League, plus varying professional groups and organizations. More bands and floats were interspersed, in an attempt to enliven the spectacle.

"She was in the same group as Miss McLeod." Morgan glared at their retreating backs.

"I'll never understand you, Morgan," Teddy said, refusing to allow anyone to ruin his joy in the parade's success. "You are married to the woman you've desired for years, and yet you are miserable. You wittingly sabotage your chances for a harmonious relationship with your wife." He waved his hand at the red rose in Morgan's lapel again.

"I wouldn't expect anyone to understand."

Teddy clapped as a float passed with Sophronia sitting proudly on a chair as she waved to those below. Her purple dress had a yellow sash across it, proclaiming Votes for Women. Women walked alongside her float, handing out yellow roses to members of the crowd. "In the end, Wheeler, it doesn't matter if I understand. There's only one person who needs to, and that's your wife."

***

Zylphia moved around the volunteers from the march at the postparade party at Mechanics Hall. The speeches had ended, and now it was time to thank everyone for their hard work, for marching, for their contributions to the cause, and for traveling a great distance to participate. She paused for a moment to arch her foot in her shoe, fighting a grimace as the muscles in her foot and calf spasmed before pasting on a smile when a sponsor approached her. She couldn't remember his name and hoped she wouldn't be forced to admit it.

"Miss McLeod, I can't believe how successful today was," the gentleman crowed. "You'd said thousands would be marching, and I thought you were overconfident in your abilities to excite women from around the state to join you."

Zylphia maintained a polite smile, although a feral glint had entered her eye. "All women want the opportunity to be heard. I am thankful so many joined us today and that the weather cooperated for our march."

"Yes, well, most impressed, Miss McLeod. Most impressed," he gushed before moving away to partake of punch and pastries.

Zylphia breathed a sigh of relief and arched her back. She stifled a shriek as she arched into someone, relaxing as she recognized Teddy's chuckle. He ran a hand down her back before moving to sit by her side.

"If you can sneak to my place tonight, I'll give you a back rub," he murmured as he raised his punch glass for a sip.

"Oh, don't tease me like that," Zylphia whispered. "It's all I'll be able to think about now when I have to focus on my role here." She met his gaze and the sensual promise within, and fought a smile. "I must continue to mingle," she said and stood.

He rose too and gripped her hand. "Let others do the busy work for now. You've been worked off your feet for days." He nodded as he saw Florence, Parthena, and Rowena moving through the crowd. "Sit," he ordered with a cajoling smile, pushing her into a chair and claiming the one next to her. He watched the women celebrate their success as they laughed, told stories, and relaxed after the march.

"I need to tell you something, Zee. About the march." He turned to meet her suddenly concerned gaze. "I've always been proud of you. Your passion for your art and your causes. But I've never been prouder of you than I was today as you marched past me." His chest puffed out as though he could barely contain his emotions.

She ran a hand down his yellow waistcoat. "Oh, Teddy," she whispered, blinking to fight away tears. "Thank you." She beamed as she focused on his clothes. "I can't believe you'd wear such a garish thing."

He laughed. "I had considered ordering a yellow suit with a purple waistcoat, but I thought that would be a little much." He raised her hand and kissed her palm. "I'm glad you appreciate my efforts."

"I wish more had done what you did. At times, it seemed as though I was staring out at a sea of red." She scowled as she envisioned the march in her mind again. "The Antis did a very good job of organizing."

She and Teddy jolted as Sophie joined them. "You don't have to seem so surprised by that, my dear. Although we never believed they were capable of such abilities, they proved us wrong. They are a more worthy foe than we gave them credit for." Sophie sat in the chair next to Zylphia and ran a hand over her sash proclaiming Votes for Women.

"I fear you'll never want to take that off," Zylphia teased, while Teddy grinned.

"You are correct. However, I already scare away too many of my acquaintances."

"I've never thought that bothered you," Teddy said with a chuckle. He relinquished Zylphia's hand as she rose to mingle. He scooted over to sit next to Sophie.

"You should be out there, young man, not sequestered here with an old woman." At his amused grin and continued presence, she sighed. "You appear in better spirits today."

His smile dimmed but failed to fade away completely. "Today was a good day," Teddy murmured. He met her frank gaze, flushing slightly at her assessment. "I'm having more and more good days."

Her eyes lit with an inner joy. "That's as it should be, my boy. No one should continue to suffer for things out of their control."

Teddy nodded. "I'm trying, Mrs. Chickering."

She patted him on the hand. "That's all any of us can do. I would warn you though. Don't find your joy only in Zylphia. She is a wonder, I will agree. But you need to find joy in your own pursuits. If you don't, I fear you may stifle her or become resentful of that which you admire today."

Teddy sighed. "I understand. After we return from our honeymoon, I'm entering into a partnership with my father-in-law. I will be busy every day with pursuits that I enjoy."

"Excellent. I know I am looking forward to partaking of your excellent consulting advice once again."

"How do you believe the march was received?" Teddy asked, smiling unconsciously as he watched Zylphia laugh with a fellow crusader.

"The number of women and men marching was impressive. I never thought we'd have thousands march as we did, and I'm most grateful for the careful planning of Zylphia's committee members. However, the Antis were out in force today." She shook her head in disgust. "The mayor and governor stood and watched us march past them with no evidence of being moved toward our way of thinking. Without endorsement from a high-level politician, I fail to see how we will succeed on November 2."

"Don't give up hope, Sophie," Teddy chastised gently. He grunted as her cane came down on his foot.

"One way or the other I will vote before I die. Even if I have to do what Susan did," she snapped, alluding to Susan B. Anthony voting in 1872, even though women were prohibited from voting in New York. "I'm hopeful I will be seen as a full member of my country and won't need to take such drastic measures."

"I do too," Teddy said, frowning. "And no talk of death on a day when we should be celebrating your triumphant march through Boston. As the struggle continues, I'll give all the support I can."

Sophie patted his hand in agreement, and they shared a conspiratorial smile before settling in to watch as the gathering slowly broke apart.

***

Parthena walked beside Morgan, shaking off his arm upon entering their house and striding up the stairs. She marched down the long hallway to their suite of private rooms and flung open the door. Her purple hat flew across the room as she approached the opposite side of the sitting room. "How could you?" Parthena screeched. She vibrated with pent-up fury as Morgan entered their sitting room and closed the door.

"I'm certain I've done nothing to earn your wrath, Parthena." He barely moved from the door before she launched herself at him, hitting him on his shoulders and chests with closed fists. He grasped her arms to prevent her from pummeling him further. She wrenched one arm free and ripped the red rose from his lapel. "How could you do this to me?"

"Why would it matter to you what I do?" He shook his head with disbelief. "For months, you've chosen to act as though we barely share a living space, and now you are concerned because I dared to express my opinion as to the upcoming referendum?"

She backed away from him, rubbing at her face. "It's important to me," she rasped through her tears. "It's important to the women I know to be able to have their own voice. To not depend on their fathers or husbands to vote for causes they believe in. For candidates who would represent us. Can't you understand that?"

Morgan ran a hand through his hair and walked past her, into the sitting room. "All I see is that universal suffragism will lead to increased societal chaos. I have no wish to be proven correct."

Parthena crumpled to the floor, her breath stuttering from the after-affects of her sobbing and rage. "Change always provokes some chaos, but it doesn't mean it's wrong or leads to a permanent state of disarray. How can you want so much for yourself and allow so little for me?"

Morgan stood with a rigid posture, his hands gripped at his sides, before he exhaled deeply. "Parthena, you are on the verge of becoming hysterical. I can't abide that. You must cease your activities with such women."

Parthena lowered her head as tears coursed down her cheeks. "I'll never stop my activities with them. I'll never stop playing the piano. I'll not allow you to change me into a person who is fearful of the future because of what happened in the past. I refuse to become you." The derision in her voice caused a flush to rise on his cheeks.

Morgan marched to her and lowered himself to kneel in front of her. He stooped so that he met her gaze, his broad shoulders hunched down as he matched her pose on the carpet. "Do you have any idea what it is like to lose everything? To have to live by deceit to survive?"

Parthena shook her head. He grasped her hand, stilling her instinctive movement away from him. She shook her head again, unwilling to speak.

"My father lost everything in the Panic of 1893. I was eleven. Do you know what that is like? To suddenly not have a home to return to? To have only the clothes on your back? To not be allowed to approach your friends because, if they knew the truth, they would not acknowledge you?" His jaw tensed at his recitation. "I was eleven, but I knew I had to help. I bartered. I begged. I stole. I did whatever I had to do to help my family survive." He closed his eyes. "The only thing I refused to do was murder."

Parthena stroked a thumb over his hand held in hers. "Oh, Morgan."

"I learned that my father had lost control of his company and his fortune. Lost control of my mother," he grated out. "And I swore I would always be in control."

"How?" At his perplexed stare, she asked, "How did he lose control?"

"Bad investments. Overextending himself." He clamped his jaw shut. "My mother wanted little to do with a poor man. She ran away with her rich lover to live in Europe."

"I thought your mother was dead," Parthena said, her eyes wide. "I thought they loved each other."

"She is now dead. She died a few years ago. In impoverished splendor in Luxembourg." He met his wife's gaze. "Although she died for me the moment she abandoned us and boarded that boat in 1893. Yet my father loved her. Desperately. He loved her until he died."

"How did you return to prominence?" she whispered. "My parents seem to have always known you and your father."

"Your family was the only one who knew the truth, and you never turned your backs on us. Your father lent me money for my first venture. He advised me what to do with the money. Thankfully I knew enough by then that he was a lousy businessman and didn't follow his advice, or we wouldn't be sitting in a grand house in the Back Bay. We'd still be in a tenement somewhere."

"But you were always dressed properly when you called," she whispered.

He smiled derisively. "Oh, how important clothes are. The first thing we did when we had any money was buy one set of acceptable clothes. I'm certain you never noticed that, for years, I wore the same clothes every time I saw you. That the seams had begun to show as I grew and that the cuffs were turned out."

Parthena shook her head at that detail. "Why does no one whisper about this? It's the sort of scandal everyone would love to bandy about, especially with me."

His gaze shrouded at her allusion to their discord. "When my father realized he'd lost everything, he had the sense to fabricate a story, promoted by your father, that we were selling up to further our fortune in New York City. Some didn't believe him, but, when we essentially disappeared from Boston, they lost interest in us."

Parthena looked toward the window, her gaze flitting as though reimagining old scenes. "Which is why my father was irate the one time I invited someone else over when your family was to call."

Morgan nodded. "No one was to know we were still in Boston. And no one ever did discover that, not where we were living." He sighed. "When I learned everything I could about trading and how to build a business, and subsequently rebuilt our fortune, we returned from New York in triumph."

"Which is why you never talk about your old boarding school days and friends," she murmured. "You didn't have those days the way other men, men like Owen Hubbard, had." Her brows furrowed. "But you talk about Harvard. You all talk about your Harvard days."

"I went to high school, but it was a public school. By the time I was old enough for university, I'd saved enough to go to Harvard, just like my father and grandfather. I attended, working every weekend and most nights, but I attended."

"Why?"

"Because then no one could doubt that the Wheelers were still successful. If I'd failed to go to Harvard, there would have been devastating rumors." Morgan's jaw tightened at the word.

"Of course. Appearances," Parthena muttered.

He gripped her jaw, forcing her to meet his gaze. "Don't make light of what I suffered when you've never had to sacrifice anything."

Parthena frowned but did not rise to his baiting. "I wished I'd known."

"I don't want your pity," he snapped, releasing his hold on her.

Her head jerked at his harsh tone, the intimate moment destroyed by the return of his cold demeanor. "You'll never understand me, Morgan. I wasn't offering you pity or scorn or ridicule. I was offering you understanding and compassion and ..." She broke off as she stood, her breath coming out in panting gusts. "You'll never understand because you won't even try." She stormed from the room and slammed the door behind her.

He lay backward onto the carpet, waiting for the harmonious music to sound from the piano. He smiled when he heard her begin to play. "Ah, but I do understand," he murmured. He settled onto the carpet, relaxing the more she played, listening to her impassioned performance.

***

Martin entered his store, smiling to the man behind the counter. "I hope all went well in my absence today, Joe." At the man's smile and nod, Martin breathed a sigh of relief and walked toward his office.

"Mrs. Martin was looking for you earlier, sir," Joe said before he turned to the customers entering the store, the bell on the door tinkling to announce their arrival.

Martin nodded in resignation and entered his office. He came to an abrupt halt as he beheld his wife sitting behind his desk. "What are you doing here?"

She raised her head from studying a ledger and frowned at him. "I should think it were obvious, Martin. I used to help more in the store, and I always had a better head for the figures."

After shutting the door, he took off his jacket and hung it on a peg behind the door. He eyed his wife warily. "You haven't shown an interest in the store in years. Why now?"

"You pay entirely too much money for help." She tapped at one of the lines in the ledger. "I had no idea we were so prosperous to need an attendant most days."

Martin groaned and sat in the rocking chair, what used to be her chair. "Mattie, I can't do the paperwork, the orders, and the inventory while also taking care of customers. You know it's impossible."

Matilda's mouth firmed in displeasure. "Yes, that's why we had a son. So he would help at, and one day inherit, the store."

Martin shook his head before scratching at his forehead. "We didn't have a son for that purpose. We had a son because ... because we were so fortunate to be gifted with a son. He has a wondrous talent, Mattie. I wish you'd hear him perform some day."

"I have no need of it. He is a disgrace, and there is no more to be said on the issue." Her mouth trembled with her agitation. She focused on Martin, and her eyes flashed as she noticed the yellow rose in his lapel. "I presumed you were running errands for the store. There is no other acceptable reason for you to be absent when the store is open."

Martin laughed and relaxed into the rocking chair. "You can try to reprimand me, but it won't work. I've given everything I have to this store and my family." He closed his eyes as he hummed a few lines from "Yankee Doodle Dandy." Then he spoke to his wife, without bothering to open his eyes to look at her. "I watched the march today. Zee's march."

At the intense silence permeating the room, Martin opened one eye. Matilda sat frozen, her face reddening with each passing moment. He smiled, closed his eye, and continued to rock as though in perfect contentment.

"How dare you attend such an event? It's disgraceful!"

He shivered at the high-pitched shriek, then sighed with resignation that she would never be agreeable. Her banishment to Savannah's room had not evoked any softening of her toward him, nor silenced her complaints. He smiled with steely resolve at his ability, at last, to take a firm stand with her, although the only refuges left to him now were his office, until today, and his bedroom. If she continued as always, he feared he'd have to make good on his threat and begin divorce proceedings.

"Everything that doesn't conform to your way of viewing the world is disgraceful. However, I disagree. We need discourse in our lives. We need those who challenge us to envision the world in a different manner. Universal suffrage does that. I am very much in favor of it, and I couldn't be more proud of the spectacle I witnessed today."

"When I think of what my parents would say..." she sputtered as she glared at him.

"Oh, they'd think it a disgrace, but they enjoyed supporting the Antis." He smiled, enjoying shocking her again. "I ran into them as I was moving through the crowd. They sat in a car on one of the streets that joins Beacon near the Hill as they are old and didn't want to stand. The parade marched directly in front of them."

"I imagine they were appalled to discover you were there."

"They were most disturbed by the fact I sang the suffragist songs and wore a yellow rose. Of course their car was festooned in red." He smiled. "This is a democracy, Mattie. We are allowed to have a difference of opinion." When she merely continued to glower at him, he sobered. "I don't understand why you don't want the vote for yourself. You are intelligent"—he pointed to the books spread out in front of her—"and you have your own opinions."

"That clearly are not in line with yours!"

"Exactly. So why wouldn't you want your own vote and voice when it comes to politics? It makes no sense to me." He waited as she remained resolutely silent. "It seems to me that you are terrified of any change, when the only constant is change. If you embraced it, you might enjoy life more."

"Don't lecture me about enjoying life," she hissed.

He held up his hand as he hefted himself to his feet. "And don't bother lecturing me about all you gave up to marry me. I've long since learned you have little regard for me, although I will always be thankful for the years you allowed me to live with the fallacy of my belief in your love. If you will excuse me, I will check on the store."

CHAPTER SEVENTEEN

The week after the march, Teddy agreed to attend a soiree with Zylphia. He paused as he faced the brownstone's steps, taking a deep breath. Zylphia looped her hand through his arm in silent encouragement. He firmed his jaw and ascended the stairs.

Upon entering the main parlor, the hum of conversation dimmed for a moment before swelling to a dull roar. His muscles tightened as he felt curious stares which he met with a straightforward intensity that caused the other partygoers to look away.

"Your glowering at them doesn't help," Zylphia murmured as she smiled at someone across the room. "Act as though you're having a good time."

"I hate these things. I always have," he muttered as he accepted a flute of champagne.

"Most of us do, but we play the part," Zylphia said. She smiled broadly as Sophronia made her way to them.

"Infernal gossips. So intent on getting their first sighting of you that they wouldn't get out of my way," Sophie muttered as she swung her cane around, nearly hitting a member of the hostess's staff with a full tray of champagne glasses. "I'd think they'd show some gumption and come talk with you."

"I'd rather they kept their distance," Teddy said, smiling for the first time that evening.

"Well, what you want and what happens are rarely in line. You must circulate," she said with a pointed stare at Teddy. "And you must not hover, Zylphia. Let the man go, lest they think he's an invalid and can only be present due to your assistance."

Zylphia reluctantly lowered her arm from Teddy's, running her hand down his arm and squeezing his hand once in support before she ceased all physical contact with him. "I see the theme of red roses continues," Zylphia murmured.

"There are those with such limited intelligence that it's not worth commenting," Sophia stated as she nodded and moved away.

Soon Zylphia was separated from Teddy as she was asked to dance. He watched as she moved into the ballroom to dance with a Mr. Danforth. Teddy chastised himself for not asking her to dance first and thus preventing being separated from her.

"How does it feel, Mr. Goff, to be home and reunited with Zee?" a man asked from behind him.

He turned to face a stranger with longer-than-acceptable brown hair in an impeccable tux with a yellow rose in his boutonniere. "I'm sorry. I don't know you."

"I beg your pardon. I'm Lucas Russell, a cousin of Miss McLeod's. Of a sort," he said with a smile. "I'm the pianist. My sister is Savannah McLeod, married to Jeremy."

"It's wonderful to meet you," Teddy said, extending his hand. He noted Lucas tracking a couple and his jaw twitching with agitation before Lucas smiled glibly. "What would you want with Mrs. Wheeler?"

"You have been out of society," Lucas said with a laugh. "No one is ever that blunt." He took a sip of his drink, effectively evading Teddy's question. "I received an invitation to your wedding yesterday. I'm delighted to attend."

Teddy studied him a moment. "Could you do more than attend? Could you write a piece of music for us that we could dance to at the reception? Mr. McLeod is insistent we have a large party after the wedding, and I would like to do something for Zylphia that is ours and not planned by someone else."

"I'd be honored," Lucas said. "Aidan wants to show how proud he is of his only daughter and her choice in a husband. You're fortunate to have such a man as a father-in-law."

Teddy nodded his agreement and nodded again as Lucas slapped him on the arm as a means of good-bye. Teddy looked into the parlor to see Parthena and Morgan approaching him, and he frowned as Lucas melted into the crowd.

"Mrs. Wheeler, wonderful to see you," he said. "Morgan." He saw Morgan's tight grip on Parthena's arm and her icy disdain for him. "It is wonderful to see you both again."

"It's about time you showed yourself in public rather than hiding away in that horrid lab of yours," Morgan said, gripping Teddy's hand with no indication he cared his hand was injured.

"I was at the parade last week," Teddy protested.

"We know that doesn't count for society," Morgan said.

"I imagine he's done more than hide in a lab," Parthena said as she reached a hand out to Teddy in greeting. "It's like old times, having you among us again. I can't tell you what it's done for Zylphia to have you back."

Teddy flushed with pleasure. "It's done wonders for me as well," he murmured, provoking a small flush in Parthena's cheeks and a throat-clearing by way of censure from Morgan. "Congratulations on your recent nuptials. I'm sorry to have missed the festivities."

"Seeing as you were wounded and missing, I think you can be excused," Morgan joked. He flashed a rare smile at Teddy. "I hope you are adapting to Boston upon your return."

"I am. It's quite a change, but I'm happy to be home," he said, his gaze flitting from one to the other. He looked at the red rose in Morgan's lapel, Parthena's yellow gown, and raised an eyebrow before shaking his head at his friend's obstinacy.

Morgan attempted to ignore him. "Come," Morgan said to Parthena. "I fear there'll be some horrid piano playing. We should make our excuses before we are forced to suffer remaining in attendance."

Parthena stiffened next to Morgan but bowed her head in obedience to his dictate and moved away with him.

Teddy remained to one side of the room, watching as those he'd called acquaintances, rarely friends, mingled and enjoyed themselves. He stiffened at the sound of a large crash of a plate of silverware falling to the ground. He stood still, breathing deeply as he searched the room for any sign of Zylphia. He continued to inhale slowly, attempting to envision anything that would hold the panic at bay.

"What's the matter, Goff? Or is it that you're as crazy as everyone whispers about, and we'll finally see the show?" Owen Hubbard asked with a sneer as he sidled up to Teddy.

Teddy focused on Owen, his expertly coiffed hair, his scarless face, his apparent perfection. The panic receded as righteous anger filled him.

"Wonderful to see you're as welcoming of the war wounded as you have always been of those less fortunate than you," Teddy gasped out.

"We don't need your sarcasm or attempt at wit here," Owen said as he flushed. He glanced around to ensure others weren't listening to their conversation. They stood in a small alcove, largely hidden from the main parlor area, cooler than the main room as the windows to the back of the alcove allowed crisp evening air to seep in.

"No, but you might need my decency. One day, you could be called to fight for your country." He clamped his jaw shut to prevent saying anything further.

"You're such a woman, Goff, complaining about what you suffered. Take it like a man and quit whining about it. No one cares." He raised his tumbler of whiskey and took a deep sip.

Teddy gripped Owen by the lapels and shoved him up against the side wall of the alcove, his movement hidden by a large bouquet of red roses. "Just as you believed no one would care that you attempted to abuse Miss McLeod last year when she denied your suit." His anger gave his injured arm increased strength, and he held Owen in place. He held one forearm to Owen's neck, effectively cutting off his airflow. "You are a letch who preys on those you believe weaker than you are. Fair warning, Hubbard. I'm not weak, and Zylphia McLeod isn't either. Keep your distance." He released Owen and stepped back a pace.

Owen gasped for breath but kept his arms lowered and refrained from attacking Teddy, his tumbler of whiskey spilled at his feet. "You're insane to believe you can return and be the most-sought-after financial advisor again. I've become something of a savant, and I refuse to have you usurp my clients."

Teddy chortled. "If you believe you'll be able to match your financial acumen with mine, you are the delusional one. You will not best me," he boasted.

"You will never be accepted into society. No one wants your advice or your fiancée's reckless beliefs for women."

Teddy's smile was triumphant. "There you are wrong, Hubbard. I have formed a strong alliance with Aidan McLeod, and I believe the two of us will form a partnership to be envied. As for Zylphia and her beliefs for women, one day her cause will meet with success. And I will have great joy standing beside her as she waits to cast her first vote."

Owen became so agitated at the news of Teddy's partnership with Aidan McLeod that Owen looked as though he were going to have a heart attack. Teddy smiled, feeling relaxed for the first time since entering the mansion, and departed the alcove in search of Zylphia. He found her on the other side of the parlor, speaking with Rowena Clement.

"Miss Clement," he said, bowing slightly in deference to her. She had changed little since he'd last seen her. A petite woman with somewhat plain features unless one focused on her remarkable brandy-colored eyes that failed to hide her intelligence.

"Mr. Goff. It's a delight to see you in Boston again," she said with a broad smile. "I'm thankful you have returned home healthy and whole."

He quirked his head to one side at her comment while Zylphia squeezed his injured hand. "Thank you, Miss Clement."

"Miss McLeod and I were discussing your wedding," Rowena said. "It will be the highlight of the autumn social calendar."

"I should hope not," Zylphia said. "We want a quiet affair with only our closest friends."

"I fear we'll be disappointed as Miss McLeod's mother is insistent we host a grand gathering for all our friends and acquaintances," Teddy said.

"You'll only marry once, Zee," Rowena said. "You might as well have a huge bash and enjoy yourself."

"I think I'd rather elope," Zylphia said.

"Hush!" Rowena gasped. "That's scandalous, and you know it. Everyone would wonder why, and you don't need that sort of talk, not if you want to continue to sell commissions for your paintings."

"And not if you wish to have influence among society for your suffragist activities," Teddy said. "I don't care what happens that day, except that you show up at the church and that we both say 'I do.'"

Zylphia fought a snicker as she saw the wicked intent in his gaze.

"I think it's wonderful you're waiting until after the vote," Rowena said. "It's very considerate."

Teddy laughed. "It's not considerate at all. I want time alone with Zee, and I refuse to compete more than I have to with her causes." He raised her hand and kissed her palm. He placed a hand to Zylphia's back and led them to a smaller drawing room to hear a pianist perform. Lucas had declined, having whispered to Zee that he wanted patrons to attend his performances, not hear them for free in the Boston ballrooms. She smiled at him as he stood to one side of the room, awaiting the first notes from the man sweating profusely, sitting on the stool.

"I'd hoped you'd knock over that display of red roses when you were speaking with Owen," Zylphia whispered to him.

Teddy choked back a laugh. "I was tempted, but I didn't want to create any more of a scene." He caressed her lower back, hidden from view from the other attendees. "He won't bother you again, Zee."

She leaned into his touch and turned so that only he would hear her. "He will, but we'll face him together." She schooled her face into one of polite interest as the man reached a crescendo finale with his piano piece. She clapped and sighed with relief as no one in the room called for an encore. She moved to leave the room and depart with Teddy, when she saw Lucas slip onto the piano stool. She gripped Teddy's arm, silently signaling him to remain with her to listen to Lucas.

Lucas turned to face the crowd and nodded once. He then set his fingers atop the piano keys, stretching them a few times but not pressing them. After a few moments, he began to play. At first Zylphia didn't recognize what he performed but was teased by the tune. Then she turned her face into Teddy's lapel, as though she were fighting a coughing spell.

"Why are you laughing?" Teddy whispered. He extracted his handkerchief for her to promote the fallacy that she was ailing in some way.

"He's playing a suffragist song. We call it 'Marching to Victory and Freedom,'" she breathed into his ear. "It sounds proper, like the great Civil War song it's styled after. But he knows that it's one of our most important suffragist songs. And he's taunting our hostess. Look at her."

Teddy glanced across the room and saw the hostess, a devout Anti, red with ire. However, the majority of the guests merely recognized the song as the triumphant "Marching through Georgia," which came to a resounding end. Lucas rose, bowed to the applause from the crowd, winked at Zylphia, and escaped the hostess who had murder in her eyes.

"Oh, he's fantastic," Zylphia said, as she fought another giggle, coughing into Teddy's handkerchief. "This is the sort of thing he did when Clarissa was first interested in Gabe. He loved taunting her stepmother. The stories are legendary in our family."

"That was fifteen years ago," Teddy said.

"I know. And some would argue he hasn't matured since then. I think it shows a steadfast commitment to our cause." She gripped Teddy's arm again, no longer as offended by the overflowing bouquets of red roses. "Come. Let's sneak out to celebrate his triumphant act of defiance." They shared a conspiratorial smile and slipped from the room and out of the stifling house.

***

Zylphia wandered Teddy's study, nervous energy roiling through her as she awaited his arrival. She glared at the small folder set on his desk, filled with details surrounding their wedding day, and paced away from it. With their ceremony a few days after the vote, little calmed her mounting anxiety. She huffed out a sigh and strode toward Teddy's desk, reaching for the folder. In her agitation, she knocked it and other papers to the floor. She knelt, separating the wedding information from Teddy's correspondence. As she picked up an envelope, she glanced at it and stilled.

"Oh my," she whispered. She glanced at the door and then hefted herself up to sit in the seat behind his desk, the wedding folder forgotten on the floor. Frowning at the envelope, she extracted the letter and began to read.

When she finished reading the letter, she sat, dumbstruck, with it lightly clasped between two fingers. Tears absently rolled down her cheeks as she stared at the fireplace. She jolted as the door burst open.

"Darling," Teddy said with a broad smile before stilling as his sharp gaze took in the chaos around his desk and Zylphia's devastated expression. "What's the matter?" He moved to her side and knelt by her. He held out a hand to touch her but frowned when she cringed away from his touch. "Zee?"

"How long did you expect to keep her a secret?" Zylphia demanded. At his blank stare, Zylphia waved the letter in front of him. "Do you profess to love her as much as you love me?"

Teddy blanched when he saw the letter in her hand before flushing red with indignation. "How dare you go through my private papers."

"They couldn't have been very private if you left them on top of your desk! I set the folder with our wedding plans on top of your desk." Zylphia paused as she fought a sob. "Our wedding, Teddy." She arched away from him as he attempted to swipe the tears off her face. "And when I knocked the folder to the ground, along with some of your papers, this is what I found." She waved the envelope in front of his face again.

"Zee ..." Teddy whispered. "It's not like it seems."

"How can you say that?" She ripped the letter from the envelope. *"I miss you more every day. I dream of your return. I can't wait to feel your ... touch again."* At this point Zylphia's voice broke, and she was unable to forestall sobbing. She bent over at her waist, holding herself as though she were preventing any further pain.

Teddy rose and moved away, toward the fireplace. He ran a hand through his hair and took a deep breath. "Will you let me explain?"

Zylphia raised her head, his calm demeanor in the midst of her sorrow enraging her. She rose, striding to him. "What is there to explain?" She pushed at his shoulders. "I waited for you. I stayed true to you! How could you?"

He gripped her shoulders, and she saw a reflection of her grief and despair in his eyes. "Please, Zee, let me explain."

She nodded, backing up a few steps to collapse onto a hassock. He pulled over a chair and sat on it, leaning forward so that he could grasp her hands and meet her gaze.

"Maud, Miss Stephens, was a nurse. Is a nurse." He closed his eyes for a moment. "They told you how I was missing in late 1914. I was, for a short time, before I was found, patched up and sent back to fight again. I never realized my letter to you, explaining that I was alive and well, hadn't reached you. I didn't write my family as I was sent back to fight much more quickly than expected. In my letter, I'd asked you to inform them I was alive.

"The second time, a month or so later, I was badly injured, Zee. You've seen the scars. You may imagine what that entailed, but you can never know what living through those injuries was truly like. The fear that I'd suffer an infection and lose more than parts of my fingers. The terror of undergoing the treatments. The horror of hearing those around me suffer. The bitter reality of waking up to new tentmates, aware that the previous ones had died."

He opened his eyes and met her gaze. "I lived in an agony of hope and despair, determined to live but terrified of returning to fight." He broke eye contact and glanced at the navy fabric of her dress.

"Tell me, Teddy," Zylphia urged.

"The first time I was injured, they were desperate for men to fight. I was deemed strong enough, even though I still required the occasional bandage. But I was healing well. I returned to the front quickly. That was the worst. The truck ride back to the front, knowing what awaited. Miles of trenches, the whistle harkening the arrival of another barrage of bombs, the never-ending death. When I was out there fighting, my sole focus became making it through each time increment. An hour. A night. The latest shelling. It didn't matter. Nothing did but survival. When I was injured again, my last thought was that I'd failed.

"When I first awoke, I thought Maud was an angel, and I fought like a demon. They told me later that it took three orderlies to hold me down before they could sedate me again."

After a long moment of silence, she asked, "Why?"

"I thought I'd died, and I didn't want to be separated from you. I kept screaming your name as though by sheer force of will I could bring you with me to wherever I was."

"Oh, Teddy," she whispered, tears coursing down her cheeks again.

"By the time my wounds had mostly healed, I was still more beast than man. I started at any little sound. A door slamming shut would make me cower in a corner for an hour." He swallowed. "I received no letters and thought ... thought it better that no one knew of my shame."

"Teddy, there is no shame. None. I would have rejoiced at any word from you."

He barreled on, ignoring her soft words. "I didn't want anyone to know I was alive. I was ashamed to be as I was, and I thought it better if no one knew that I'd lived."

Zylphia hit him on the shoulder again. "How dare you put me through months of misery! Your family and I, we had every right to know how you were."

Teddy grabbed her hand and held it to his chest. "I know now that you are right. However, back then, I was merely trying to survive. I couldn't have handled it if you or my cousin had shown up. I couldn't have borne the indignity of you seeing me like that."

"I love you, Teddy. I wouldn't have loved you any less," Zylphia whispered. At his subtle nod, she asked, "How does that nurse play into this tale?"

"Maud worked with the doctor who seemed to understand what I was suffering. She never looked at me as though I were damaged or pathetic." He flinched when he saw Zylphia's hurt expression. "Everyone else did. I heard their whispers. That I wasn't manly enough to handle what had occurred. That I needed to quit complaining and be strong." He shuddered. "I didn't understand ..." His voice trailed away.

"What?" Zylphia whispered in an attempt to coax him into speaking further.

"I didn't understand why others couldn't see the corpses of the men I'd gutted. Why they couldn't hear their screams of agony like I did. Why they didn't shy away from the incoming bombs." He shuddered again and shook his head and smiled forlornly. "There were no corpses or bombs. It was all in my head."

"What happened between you and that nurse?" she whispered.

"I can't lie to you, Zee." He reached forward and grasped her by her forearms to prevent her from fleeing. "I did come to care for her. Very much. She helped bring me back from the brink." He tilted up Zylphia's chin with his fingers, forcing her to meet his gaze. "I kissed her. Once."

"Once?"

"I thought I'd overcome the visions, the torment, whatever you want to call them. And then someone dropped a bag of tools onto the cement floor. I grabbed a metal pole, what I thought was my bayonet, and battled the men attacking me. Except no one was there, and I was hurting those trying to help me. I sent three to the operating room that day and concussed another."

He pinched the bridge of his nose. "When I finally snapped out of it, the shame was overwhelming. I ... There are no words to describe how weak and unmanly I felt. My mind betrayed me. I no longer knew what to trust. What was real. What was a figment of my imagination. There was no one and nothing that could ground me in reality.

"I needed to feel like a man, Zee. So I kissed her. I kissed her—and would have done more if we hadn't been found out. I nearly caused her to lose her position. And I'm ashamed."

"Why?"

"Because I didn't think of you when I was doing it." He met Zylphia's bleak stare. "I didn't really think of her either. I only thought of myself. Of what I needed. Of how I needed to feel."

"Would you rather her than me?" Zylphia's eyes shone with anger, pain, and fear. "If the two of us were side by side, in this room, right now, who would you want?"

Teddy smiled as he beheld her, his stress easing for the first time since he began speaking about the war. "You. Always you, Zee. No one compares to you." He clasped her hand. "When I finally emerged from the stupor that enveloped me after the attack, I was appalled at what I'd done. Who I was becoming."

"Why does she write you such letters?"

"She's lonely, surrounded by death and the carnage of war. She wants more. She wants the dream of more."

Zylphia sat in silence a few minutes. "Did you encourage her?"

"I left the hospital not long after that incident, it having been determined I should convalesce at my grandfather's estate. I dissuaded her from writing me, but I answered her letters when she eventually did write. In that sense I encouraged her."

At Zylphia's frustrated frown, Teddy clasped her hands between his. "She's the only person who understands all I experienced. I couldn't break the connection with the one person who ..." He shook his head.

Zylphia nodded in resignation. "Is there any hope for us?"

"Of course there is." His gray eyes were lit with a fierce intensity.

"I promised you, when you returned, not to hide any part of me. I meant it. It's nearly impossible to realize you didn't mean the same."

"Zee, of course I did. I promise I planned to tell you about the war. About her."

"When? After we were married? Did you think I'd be content sharing you?" She cupped his closely shaven cheeks between her palms. "You should know I'm greedy. I'll never be content sharing you."

His eyes mirrored the uncertainty and fear in hers. "What do you want to do?"

"I need to go home and think about what you've told me. I'll contact you when I want to see you."

"No, that's not good enough. We have to agree when to next meet. I refuse to wait with futile hope, uncertain when you'll contact me."

"In two days, Teddy. Meet me at my house. We'll have tea." Zylphia rose and moved toward the door. She paused and looked back at him just before she opened the door. Regret, longing, and pain flitted over her features before she slipped from the room.

***

Florence McLeod moved with a ballerina's fluid grace as she navigated her kitchen from the sink to the table to the oven and back. Zylphia watched Florence with unconcealed envy as she extracted a cake from the oven, poured boiling water into a teapot, and then sliced another cake for their afternoon snack. "Thank you both for making the journey here, rather than meeting at Sophie's house," Florence said when she finally joined them at the table.

"No need for thanks," Sophie said. "You have your young ones to consider, and it is much easier for us to travel than for you." She raised an eyebrow as she looked at Zylphia. "Thankfully I dissuaded Zee from taking the horrid trolley."

"I will admit that your automobile is much more comfortable than the trolley. However, there is much less cause for artistic inspiration than when riding public transport."

"I should hope so," Sophie said with a wry smile. When Zee remained silent and downcast, Sophie frowned. "I understand that it is essential in today's meeting to discuss the upcoming vote. We need a continued presence in the popular papers after our successful march. We must sway the undecided to our way of thinking."

Florence nodded her agreement but appeared to bite back her words at Sophie's swift jerk of her head to remain silent.

"After the success with the children's penny project, I'm certain I can convince the zoo to allow us the use of one of the elephants. I mean for you to ride the elephant down Beacon Street," Sophie said with a nod to Zylphia.

"An elephant, yes," Zylphia said. She started and focused on Sophie a second later. "I'm not riding an elephant!"

"Of course you aren't. However, little seemed to garner your attention, including the upcoming vote. Now, before we attempt to discuss plans for our part in ensuring victory, you are to tell us what is troubling you."

"They're just pre-wedding jitters." Zylphia took a sip of tea and reached for a piece of Florence's zucchini bread.

"Most brides starve themselves in their attempt to fit in the dress their modiste deems appropriate," Sophie said as she watched Zylphia devour the slice of bread.

"I'm not like most brides," Zylphia retorted.

"Exactly. Two days ago you carried around that dratted wedding folder as though it held the treaty to the Great War. Now you won't even mention your wedding." Sophie reached forward and gripped Zylphia's hand.

"You look like you did when Teddy was missing," Florence whispered. "Clinging to hope but afraid that you'd have that hope proven false."

Zylphia looked from Florence to Sophie, her eyes filling before she lowered her head to the table and sobbed. Florence scooted her chair around so she could pull Zee into her arms.

Zylphia leaned away from Florence, pulling a cream-colored handkerchief from her pocket to swipe at her face and nose. "He still writes that nurse."

Sophie nodded once. "I see."

"I don't," Florence said, shaking her head in frustration as Zylphia and Sophie shared a knowing look.

"When Teddy was injured in France, he became involved with a nurse. They continue to correspond. I was at his house yesterday, waiting for him in his library. I found a letter from her." She swiped at her cheeks as tears continued to fall. "I think she loves him."

"That's not your concern, dearest. Does he love her?" Sophie asked.

"I think so. He appreciates how she helped him." Zylphia took a deep, bracing breath. "He believes she is the only one who truly understands all he experienced and doesn't want to lose contact with her."

"Oh my." Sophie sighed. "What do you want to do?"

"I don't know. I thought I could accept anything as long as he was returned to me. Now I realize that was childish. I told him yesterday I can't share him."

Florence gripped her hand. "Of course not. You don't want to share him now. But you will have to accept that you shared him while he was away from you."

"I don't know if I can," Zylphia whispered.

Sophronia *harrumphed.* "You can and you must, if you love him." Her aquamarine eyes shone with a fierce determination and decades-old sorrow. "You must learn to live with the reality that you will never be the only woman he's loved. However, he's chosen you, Zee. He returned to you."

Zylphia pushed an errant wisp of hair behind her ear as she thought through Sophie's words. "He never would have told me about her, about his time in the war, if I hadn't found the letter. He didn't trust me."

"Is that true?" Florence asked. "Were there times he began to speak of what he suffered but you encouraged him to not dwell on the past?" At Zylphia's hurt expression, Florence squeezed her hand.

"Dwelling on the past never does any good," Zylphia said. "I've learned that."

"I agree. However, sometimes we must speak about our past and the horrors we've lived through in order to overcome them," Sophie murmured, gentle censure in her scratchy voice. "To know that those we love most accept us completely is an extraordinary gift."

"I promised not to hide from him when he returned, but he continued to hide from me!" Zylphia cried.

"Perhaps he did so because you didn't want to hear about what he'd suffered. Have you ever, even once, considered that he wrote that nurse because he felt as though at sea and needed someone, anyone, to talk to? That if you'd offered him your understanding, your compassion, rather than your determination to look to the future, he might never have turned to her?" Florence asked.

"Flo," Zylphia whispered.

"I'm sorry if I speak harshly, but you need to hear these things. No one is ever blameless when there is a disagreement. You must learn to take your share of the blame." Florence squeezed Zee's hand before rising for the kettle warming on the stove to refill the teapot.

Sophie watched Zylphia with fond amusement as a few tears trickled down Zylphia's cheeks. "I'd think those would be embarrassed tears. Flo has the right of it. You need to think of your young man in all this, not just you. He's suffered worse than you will ever imagine."

Zylphia took a sip of tea, holding the cup with both hands so it wouldn't shake and so she wouldn't spill the tea all over the table. "It's much harder than I thought it would be."

At her whispered admission, Sophie shook her head in exasperation. "You young ones think everything will be easy. Nothing is easy. Everything is hard. Even when life is going well, things are hard. You have to find your inner fortitude, Zee, and face this challenge. Be the strong woman Teddy needs you to be."

Zylphia paled and kept her gaze downcast. "I understand, Sophie. And I've always been thankful for your counsel." She paused as she swiped away a tear. "It's just that I'm so tired. I'm tired of being strong. Always putting on the brave face and being the one to prop everyone up."

Sophie's cane slammed onto the floor and caused such a jolt that Florence and Zylphia jumped in their chairs. "You're too young for such a pathetic display of self-pity. The fact is you are strong. You always have been, and you always will be. That is a blessing, Zylphia McLeod, and not something to bemoan. If you truly love this young man, and by all appearances you do, then you must regain your gumption and fight for him. And for you."

Florence took Zylphia's hand. "I can understand Zee's concern. Sometimes we want others to be strong for us. To fight the battles for us."

"Then you're a fool. No one can fight the battles for us the way we'd want them fought. And you'll never be satisfied if you don't fight, Zee."

***

Teddy paced his laboratory, staring at his previous experiments in an attempt to harness enthusiasm to restart them. He walked to his desk and flipped open his ideas notebook, pausing when he came to sketches he'd done of Zylphia. He traced her irreverent smile and marveled at the innocent enthusiasm for life in her expression. He flipped the pages, coming to details of his experiment, but then slammed his notebook shut in disgust.

He approached one of his workbenches and sat at a stool in front of it, picking up a mechanical part. He closed his eyes as his hands and arms remembered long-unused movements and manipulated the small wires and pieces of metal. Groaning with frustration, he slammed down the piece, breaking it, as his injured fingers were unable to accomplish what he wanted.

He moved to the window, bracing a shoulder against the frame, and glanced out at the treetops, the branches becoming more skeletal with each gust of wind. He held up his mangled hand and shook his head in disgust. Lowering his hand to his side at the knock on his door, he called out, "Come in."

"I wondered if I'd find you brooding in here," Aidan said as he entered and closed the door behind him. He appeared as debonair as always with an immaculate slate-gray suit and matching waistcoat over a white shirt. His bright blue eyes flashed with concern as they spied Teddy leaning against a window frame.

"Sir," Teddy said, moving to meet his future father-in-law. "Forgive this room for being such a mess. I have done little to clean it since my return."

"I imagine it's difficult to return to a place that seems unchanged, except for a few layers of dust, when you've been so altered." He nodded at Teddy's flush of agreement. "How do you manage to do the finer adjustments now?" He glanced at the smashed experiment on one table and tilted his head in concern.

Teddy flushed a brighter red. "I haven't determined how to successfully do that as of yet, sir. Not with my hand as it is. As it always will be."

"Perhaps you need to take time and discover other avenues you wish you investigate." He glanced at the tables, their experiments dormant. "I imagine other topics interest you more now." Aidan watched Teddy with a curious glint in his eyes, as though Teddy were the day's experiment.

"May I help you with something, sir?" Teddy asked, his flush transforming from one of embarrassment to annoyance.

Aidan pulled out a small card with an address scribbled on it. "I believe you would benefit from writing my nephew, Jeremy McLeod."

"Why should I wish to write a man I don't know?" He examined the card and frowned at the address. "A man who lives thousands of miles away in Montana?"

"It has come to my attention that you are quite adept at letter writing." He smiled at Teddy's chagrined expression. "He too lived through war. A different sort of war, but war all the same."

At Teddy's persistent silence, Aidan said, "I can imagine you believing it awkward to write such a letter. He knows who you are, as Zylphia stayed with him and his wife, Savannah, when Zee was in Montana last year. He consoled her when she received word you were missing."

"There is no reason for me to write a stranger."

"Isn't there?" Aidan asked. "I understand the desire not to burden those I love most with my deepest fears. With what I perceive to be my failures or personal shame. However, this isn't a business failing, Mr. Goff. This is much deeper than that, and you need to cauterize the wound. Jeremy understands, better, I believe, than that nurse."

Teddy exhaled a deep breath he hadn't realized he'd been holding. "You believe your nephew is more acceptable as a correspondent to your family than the nurse is."

"He should be to you also, Mr. Goff." Aidan watched him in confusion. "You profess to love Zylphia. To want her as your wife. You can't have divided loyalties, not with someone like Zylphia. You'll both become miserable, and I want joy for the two of you."

"No one's life can be filled with joy," Teddy rasped.

"No, but you can choose to want joy, rather than despair. You can make an active decision to see beauty and goodness and hope instead of decay and evil and desolation." Aidan gripped Teddy's arm and gave him a shake, his jaw gripped in anger. "Surely you see this. Surely you learned this after what you've suffered."

Teddy shook his head at Aidan. "I do. I've tried, every day since I've returned, to put the war behind me."

"Write Jeremy. I have every faith he will aid you, as he has had to overcome the same fears and doubts as you. Something that no one else, not even your nurse, has had to do." Aidan met Teddy's gaze for a long moment, coming to a silent accord before Aidan gripped Teddy's forearm in farewell and moved toward the doorway. "I wish you well, Goff."

Teddy collapsed onto the window sash at Aidan's departure and stared at Jeremy's name. He slipped the card into his pocket, uncertain as to what he planned to do with the information.

***

Morgan entered his mansion, giving his hat to his butler before turning so that his coat could be eased off his shoulders. He approached the stairs to ascend to his study but stilled his steps when he heard the plaintive music emerging from Parthena's private study. His approach muffled by a thick carpet, he peered through the partially open door. Rather than the proud, determined Parthena who passionately played the piano, his wife appeared devastated as she sat, ashen and defeated, her hands evoking a lament.

The door creaked open with his entrance to the room, and she glanced up at him. He glowered as he saw her grief, her expression even more grim than the day she had married him. Than any day of their married life.

He approached the piano bench and crouched down. He silenced her music, now appropriate for a funeral. "My Parthena," he whispered. "What happened?"

She exhaled a breath that sounded like a sob, shaking her head in denial. "I won't let it happen, Morgan. I don't care what I have to do, but I won't let it happen."

He tugged her to fully face him. "I don't know what has caused you such distress. Tell me."

"Of course you do! You planned the entire thing with my father. I was just too stupid to know better and went along with your plans." She curled down into herself. "Why I ever thought to be the dutiful daughter, I can't say. It's not as though he'll ever truly love me."

Morgan stroked a hand over her shoulder and back but retracted his hand as though from a flame when she reared up and glared at him. "Tell me."

"My sister Genevieve is to marry Mr. Carlisle. On the fourth of December. Amid much fanfare." Her cheeks became ruddy with her anger as she watched him pale.

Morgan rose, swearing as he spun to face the doorway. "No. That was never to happen." He ran a hand through his hair, disheveling it in his agitation. "She was to be spared." He pulled an ottoman close to Parthena and collapsed onto it. "What did your father do?"

At Parthena's blank stare, he leaned forward but refrained from touching her. "I gave him enough money to save him twice over, Hennie."

"You couldn't have. He told me that you reneged on giving him any money and that's why—" She broke off when she saw his irate expression.

"Do you really believe me so low that I'd do that? That I'd renege on a promise? A duty?" he asked. "For no matter what you are, Parthena, providing for you and keeping you safe is a duty to me."

He sat on the ottoman again, his elbows on his knees as he studied her. "I know we don't agree on much of anything. You want me to support you in all you do, although you don't like that I have the same rights to my opinions and beliefs." He smiled as her eyes flashed their ire at him. "However, I will always see to your care, Hennie. Even though you may not believe me, I will always want to see you happy."

She outstretched her hand, tentatively stroking his hand. It was the first sign of affection from her in their marriage, and he attempted to refrain from overreacting as his fingers twitched under her soft touch. "I think this is his way of telling me that he despairs of me. He hates that I marched in the suffrage parade."

"Then he's an even slower learner than I am." At her perplexed look, he traced a finger along her jaw. "He should have learned long ago that you are stubborn enough to follow your dreams and that nothing will prevent you from attaining your goals."

She frowned. "You sound almost pleased."

He leaned forward and kissed her forehead.

"What will we do?" Her heartbroken voice tore at him.

Morgan clasped her hand tenderly, giving it a soft tug.

She watched him warily but allowed herself to be coaxed into his arms, coming to settle on the ottoman between his legs.

"I don't know. Not yet. Have your sister for tea within the next few days. We have to find a place that's safe to send her. She must leave Boston and your father's sphere of influence." He sighed into her hair. "God help us when your other sisters come of age and we have to protect them too."

Parthena leaned into his strong embrace. "But you would protect them?" she asked with a hint of wonder in her voice.

"Always," he whispered, holding her close for long minutes of the first real peace between them in their marriage.

***

Zylphia sat at her vanity, staring at her reflection. She fidgeted with the brush set out in front of her and smiled at her mother when she poked her head in. "Good night, Mother."

Delia smiled at Zylphia, although she was unable to hide her concern as she noted Zylphia's agitation. "If you are worried about the wedding, I can do more to help with the planning. I know you are very busy with canvassing and preparing for the vote."

"I will look through the folder tomorrow and see what help I need. Thank you, Mother," Zylphia said. "I know I should feel nothing but exhilaration at the thought of my upcoming nuptials."

Delia smiled. "If you didn't feel some trepidation about how your life will change, I think I'd worry even more about you." She caressed one hand over Zylphia's loose raven hair. "Would you like me to braid it for you?"

"No, I want to brush it a bit more." Zylphia picked up the brush and swiped at the ends of her long hair in an absent manner.

"I forgot to give you a letter I found mingled in with my correspondence. Let me know in the morning if there is any interesting gossip from Montana." She held out an envelope and leaned down to kiss Zylphia on her forehead.

Zylphia set aside the brush and opened the letter. She scanned it quickly and realized that it was from both Savannah and Jeremy.

Dearest Zee,

I hope this finds you well. I'm sure you are still ecstatic with your Teddy's return, and I cannot wait to hear more about your reunion. When is the wedding? I only wish we could all travel to be there. However, with school for Melly and Clarissa's children, and with the threat of inclement weather, we have decided to remain here.

You can imagine it was quite a gathering we had to discuss whether or not we'd venture East! We met in our front living room and debated for a few hours. We ate and drank quite a bit more than we should have, but had a wonderful time. I think we all realized we couldn't travel, but we wanted the illusion of truly discussing it.

I fear Araminta was hoping we'd make the trip as she wanted Colin to come with us quite desperately. He had said he'd remain behind to help care for the children. I'm uncertain what has transpired between them, but whatever sweet feelings once existed there continue to sour. Jeremy has advised me to quit my meddling, but I can't help it. I want them both happy, and, at the moment, they're only becoming more miserable.

Miss Loken, on the other hand, is relieved we are not traveling. If I remember correctly, you didn't come to know her well. However, she and Clarissa have become fast friends since Rissa began working in the library again. Miss Loken, for reasons unknown to us, is resistant to marrying a very eligible blacksmith who works with Colin. She hides in the back rooms of the library when he comes looking for her, happy Rissa is there to run interference. I think she was dreading having Rissa leave for that reason. Again Jeremy advises me not to meddle, but I wonder what would happen should Rissa be absent for any length of time. What do you think?

Bravo on your successful art show! I never had any doubt of your success, and Jeremy is as pleased as he can be that we have one of your pieces hanging over our mantel. I received a letter from Amelia recently where she told me that Sebastian keeps your painting in the family rooms as he doesn't want his neighbors to be jealous of the beautiful artwork he has! Your painting of their mountains was majestic and a perfect thank-you for our time with them last summer.

Melly misses you and hopes you will visit again soon. I encouraged her to write a small missive in this letter, but she is a horrible correspondent. She takes after Colin. She's also determined to keep Mr. Pickens's memory alive by continually making up misspoken words. It's rather endearing, although I try not to encourage her.

I miss you, dear cousin, and look forward to seeing you again soon.

Savannah

***

Dear Zylphia,

Savannah informed me that your Teddy has returned to you, although he has been altered by wounds and battle. I know what that is like, as I remember well what I lived through on my return after serving in the Spanish-American War. I fought in the Philippines, and I did things I never knew I was capable of.

I know you are one who is determined to push forward and not become mired in the past. A word of caution, dear cousin. Allow your Teddy to speak of his fears. Accept them, and do not dismiss them out of hand as nonsense. They are real to him and must be acknowledged. When a man returns from war, his fears may seem irrational at times. You may have the desire to tell him to buck up and move forward. However, you would be doing him, and your relationship, a grave disservice.

Life is wonderful in Montana. We are preparing for winter, but it is always one of my favorite seasons as it gives me an excuse to cuddle near a fire with my Savannah while Melly reads us stories long into the night.

I miss you, cousin.
Jeremy

Zylphia traced Jeremy's words and recalled her conversation with Sophie and Florence. She sighed as she acknowledged to herself what she needed to do

CHAPTER EIGHTEEN

Zylphia stood hidden by the partially open doorway and watched Teddy roam the back sunroom. He strummed his mangled fingers along the edge of a chair back as he moved to stare at the dreary back alley. After a moment, he removed his glasses and ran a hand over his face, his shoulders hunched and head bowed. "Please, God, please," he rasped just loudly enough for her to hear.

She entered the room, silently closing the door behind her. "What do you pray for?"

He twirled to face her, his eyes unfocused without his glasses, the gray even steelier without the reflective glass. "Absolution."

She remained closer to the door than the window, far from his touch. "Why do you think you need it?"

"Because I hurt you and betrayed your trust." He replaced his glasses, and his gaze roved over her stoic posture. He frowned in frustration at not being able to discern her expression.

Zylphia took a step toward him. "Do you think you are deserving of forgiveness?"

Teddy froze, the momentary joy at her approach toward him forgotten. "No. I'll never deserve forgiveness for what I've done."

"Do you believe that all men who've fought should live in torment forever?"

"Of course not."

"So, it's simply a special form of hell you've fashioned for you and you alone." At her glower, Teddy remained silent. "I refuse to live my life with someone who doesn't believe he deserves to be happy. Who doesn't grasp at every happy moment we have with both hands."

"You don't understand what I did," Teddy whispered.

"I have a better understanding after listening to you the other day. I realize that I discouraged you from speaking with me the few times you tried to talk with me about the war, and I'm sorry for that. I want to understand your pain, your sorrow, and then help you to leave it in the past." She took another step toward him, inhaling a deep breath. "Did my desire to focus on the present and not listen to what you'd lived through lead you to reach out to that nurse?"

Teddy closed his eyes and nodded.

"I thought you'd stopped writing her," Zylphia whispered.

"I had. For a long while. When I received your letters, proclaiming that you'd love me as I was, no matter what had happened and what I'd lived through, I realized I needed to let her go. I wrote her, informing her that I was committed to you and our future."

Zylphia moved close enough that she could feel the heat of his body but refrained from touching him. "What happened?"

He raised tormented eyes to her. "I had one of my fits. I nearly attacked my mother. I'd never felt more alone, among the grandeur of Boston with no one who wanted to understand." He sighed. "I can't blame them. Who wants to understand the horrors of war and the lunatic who returns with the tale?"

"That was the day you tried to tell me. When you looked rung out. And I pushed aside your concerns," Zylphia said. She reached for his hand and clasped it with her own. After a moment she lifted it, cradled between her hands, to her chest. "You consoled me that day."

"You eased me with your love," Teddy said.

Zylphia attempted to blink away tears. "Don't excuse what I did. I refused to listen to you when you desperately needed me to hear what you'd lived through. Forgive me, Teddy." She raised his hand and kissed it. "I proclaimed that I didn't want us to hide anything from each other, but then I refused to allow you to share yourself with me."

He raised his other hand and caressed the side of her face. "Forgive me for being like this. I'm doing all I can to overcome these attacks."

Zylphia shook her head. "There's nothing to forgive, my darling. You must always tell me in the future when I am ignoring you, when there is something you need to say—even if it's something I might not want to hear." She tugged on his arm and pushed herself into his embrace. He freed his arm from her clasp and held her tightly to him. She muffled a sob against his chest as he choked out a deep breath into the side of her neck.

"I'm sorry for writing her, Zee. I felt so alone. No one here understands what the war is like. What that fear is like." He relaxed as he felt her tight hold on him as he held her. "Thank you for wanting to soothe me with your love, darling, but no embrace, no matter how fierce it is, will ever undo what was done."

Zylphia sighed into his chest, kissing him through his clothes. She held him closer, each moment her arms incrementally tighter around him. She pressed her fingers into tight muscles along his spine. At her persistent touch and presence, he shuddered, and she heard a small sob escape. "Cry, my love. Cry."

She felt him shake his head in denial. "It doesn't make you weak or less of a man to cry in an attempt to dispel what has been done to you," she murmured, running her hands over his shoulders as he finally collapsed into her arms and sobbed. She sank with him to the floor and held him to her breast as he cried, rocking him as she crooned in his ear. She stroked his hair off his forehead, kissing the scar along his scalp, murmuring her love for him over and over.

When his crying abated, he stiffened and tried to extricate himself from her grasp. She maintained her firm clasp of him and refused to release him.

"This isn't to be done, Zee," he said.

"What? Receiving comfort when you need it?" She met his chagrined gaze with her supportive smile. "I will never abide by your English sensibilities and agree that you should hide behind an aloof wall while you are suffering. Never, Teddy." She stroked a hand down his cheek and leaned forward to kiss him on the forehead.

He gave up his struggle to move from her embrace and laid on the floor, his head pillowed on her lap. "I dreamed of such moments. Of the contentment of hearing your voice. Of laying my head on your lap and having you caress me as you are now."

Zylphia's hands continued to stroke his shoulders and face when he leaned into her for more of her touch. "Did it help you to dream?"

"When I was in the trenches, everything was so horrible. The memories and dreams of us, for us, are what sustained me." He sighed at her gentle caresses. "I've missed this. Just being with you."

She bent over him as though she could shelter him with her body. "I would do anything to take away your pain. Your torment."

He raised a hand and brushed the hair off her forehead. "Don't you realize you already do?" He arched up and kissed her before laying back down, momentarily content in the cushion of her lap.

***

Teddy sat in his study at his desk, reading a stack of letters, mainly from family in England. A fire crackled in the grate, and a small lamp shone light from the corner of his desk. He attempted to ignore his office door but remained hopeful Zee would sneak through it at any moment. Their wedding was in three days' time, and he wanted a few moments with her before the spectacle.

He set down a letter from his cousin Eugenie, updating him about his grandfather, their mutual friends, and her suffragist cause. He smiled as he considered introducing her to Zylphia. He pulled out the next letter in the stack with unknown handwriting scribbled on the envelope. He ripped it open and settled into his chair.

Dear Mr. Goff,

I know you don't know me, and a letter from me is presumptuous. However, Zylphia is my adored cousin, and I feel compelled to write. My uncle wrote me last week, advising me that I should expect a letter from you. As I've yet to receive one from you, and because I know your wedding day approaches, I thought I'd write to you.

My uncle wrote about your recent return from the Great War. It brought back many memories for me as I recalled my experiences in the Spanish-American War and my time in the Philippines. I know that what we each lived through is quite different. However, I believe that war is war and what men are asked to do to each other hasn't changed.

It took me quite some time to overcome the memories and the self-loathing that I felt upon returning to the United States. My family's faith in me helped. Savannah's love helped. Time helped. No one thing acted as a curative balm. It was a combination of everything and nothing. I don't know if that makes any sense.

However, what I would advise is that you try not to compare who you were with who you are now. It's unfair to you and to those who care for you. Just as Zylphia changed while you were away, you did too. Embrace the change, and let go of the memory of who you were for you are no longer that man.

I wish you all possible happiness as you marry Zylphia and begin your life together.

Sincerely,

Jeremy McLeod

Teddy set down the letter, his gaze distant as he stared at the painting Zee had gifted him the spring before he went away to war. He lost himself in the bright pink cherry blossoms and the memory of walking down a similar street with her. He remembered their growing friendship that grew into a brash, impulsive love. He closed his eyes as he thought of himself in his laboratory, happily tinkering away on his experiments. He opened his eyes, understanding, if not yet accepting, that some things were no longer possible for him.

He looked to the door as it opened. He rose, moving toward Zylphia and enfolding her in his embrace. He held her as she cried against his shoulder, murmuring sweet nothings into her ear in an attempt to soothe her as yesterday the Massachusetts men had voted against giving women the same right. "I'm sorry, love. I'm so sorry."

She pushed away from him and rubbed at her face before turning from him and swinging her arms around in agitation. "I'm so angry. Sad. I feel listless, and then I'm filled with such a rage that it's as though I could march all the way to DC." She spun to face him as he chuckled at the thought. "I feel like screaming, yet no one cares what I have to say. I'm just a woman. What does that matter?" She bit her lip as tears coursed down her cheeks.

"It matters a great deal, my love, and you know it." He grasped her shoulders to prevent her from pacing away from him and tried to face her. "Never denigrate yourself to me." He waited until she met his gaze. "You will find a way to win the vote for the women of Massachusetts. For the women of this country. Of that I have no doubt."

"Oh, Teddy." She sobbed into his chest as she fell into his embrace. "I worked so hard. I don't know what more I could have done. I keep thinking, if I'd canvassed more, visited more houses. If I'd written more compelling articles. Maybe we would have had success."

Teddy sighed, leading her toward the fireplace. He settled onto the couch with her beside him. "I hate to disagree with you, but I doubt you could have done anything to persuade the men of Massachusetts to vote differently this time. The party leaders were against it as was the church. Not enough influential men were willing to take up your banner."

Zylphia played with his waistcoat, her sobs subsiding to stuttering breaths. "Not this time. But we'll be better prepared next time."

Teddy smiled as he kissed the top of her head. "That's my Zee. Always ready for the next challenge." He held her in contented silence as she relaxed into his embrace on the couch. "Speaking of our next challenge, how are the plans for the wedding?"

Zylphia sighed as she attempted to nestle farther into his embrace. "They're coming along. My mother is ecstatic, planning all the final details. I hide upstairs in my studio, painting."

"Good," Teddy said. "As long as she doesn't plan anything we'll loathe, I'm content leaving the preparations to your mother."

"She insists I have to pack up my studio before the wedding, but it's the only thing that calms me right now. Will you mind if I move that into our new home upon our return?"

"Of course not," he whispered. "All I care about is that we have time alone, with no meddling family or friends. Where we don't have to sneak around for a stolen kiss." He kissed her tenderly. He stiffened when he felt her tense. "What's the matter, Zee?"

"It's not that I don't want us to have time away together. I do. It's just that there's a meeting here in Boston in November that I want to attend."

He pushed her up so that she was sitting, and he sat so they were facing each other. "Zee, are you telling me that you want to cut our honeymoon short so that you can return for a meeting?" At her nod, he groaned. "Should we have waited until December for our wedding? When would I have been guaranteed time alone with you?"

"It's not that we can't have time alone, just not as much time as you'd hoped. We'll have one week." She watched him warily.

"Do you want to marry me, Zee?" When she remained silent, he pushed away from her and the sofa and rose, pacing to the fireplace. He gripped the mantel, unable to banish the memory of another argument that had led to their separation. "I should take your silence as your answer, shouldn't I?"

He felt her behind him as she reached for his hand, tugging on it to turn him toward her. She swallowed and shook her head. She spoke in a voice barely above a whisper. "I couldn't speak. I can't speak when I imagine a life without you. The thought of not marrying you is more terrifying than never voting. Than never painting again." She dropped his hand and took a hold of both his cheeks between her palms. "I need you, Teddy. Please, darling, don't doubt my desire for us to wed."

"And I need you, Zee. I need to know I'm as important to you as the cause you've chained yourself to." He met her gaze with impassioned entreaty.

She nodded. "I agree. I'll speak with Sophie, and I know she'll inform me of what happens at the meeting."

His face brightened with delighted surprise. "You mean it? You'll spend the honeymoon as I planned rather than cutting it short?" At her nod, he pulled her close. "Promise me that you won't regret it."

"I promise, for I'll be with you," she murmured, kissing him beneath his ear.

***

Lucas tapped on the door and slipped inside, closing it behind him. Zylphia, curled on the settee, looked toward the door and smiled in welcome. She fought tears as she saw the bouquet of yellow roses he carried, and she reached out a hand to him. "Oh, Lucas, thank you," she murmured.

"How are you, Zee?" He gripped her hand once before releasing it. He placed the bouquet in a clean pot of water she had waiting for a painting project before he pulled over a tufted red chair toward the settee and sat. "You don't look like a blushing bride-to-be."

Zylphia curled up farther on the settee, burying her face into a pillow. "It's terrible enough we lost the referendum two days ago. Now I'm terrified of Saturday."

Lucas leaned forward and traced a soothing hand down her back. "Why terrified, Zee? I'd think you'd be eager to marry your Tedd after all you've been through."

"I know this sounds mean, but I don't know that you can understand all a woman gives up with marriage. I'm petrified I'll no longer know who I am. That it will change us somehow."

Lucas laughed. "It will change you, Zee. It will change your relationship with Tedd. As it should. You'll be as committed to his life as he is to yours, as in a good marriage. And that's the type of marriage I hope for you." His voice became teasing. "Besides, you'll no longer have to skulk around for time alone. You'll no longer have to hide in alcoves ..." He laughed as he dodged the pillow she threw at him.

"We never hid in alcoves!"

"No, you were smart enough to meet at his house."

At his raised eyebrow, Zylphia flushed.

"What else troubles you, Zee?" His brows furrowed as he saw her momentary joy rapidly disappear.

She took the pillow back from him and hugged it to her chest. "I never told you how I'd visited your mother." At his shocked expression, she grimaced. "I wanted to meet your parents and invite them to my show. I thought they would be like an aunt and uncle to me as I consider you my cousin."

"Oh, Zee," Lucas breathed, as he closed his eyes and pinched the bridge of his nose with two fingers.

"I never believed she was as horrid as you'd said."

"I have no doubt she proved herself to be so," Lucas rasped, his eyes lit with fury. "Anything she said to you was meant to hurt and give rise to self-doubt. If she could provoke discord, she would consider it a successful day."

Zylphia flushed, her grip on the pillow tightening.

"Tell me what she said, Zee."

"Oh, Lucas, I should never have mentioned it! I'm causing a greater rift between you and your mother now."

"There could exist no greater rift between my mother and me, unless she were dead," he snapped. He flushed at his harsh words and looked away. "Forgive me."

She reached out to clasp his hand. "Lucas, I'm sorry I wasn't more understanding when you spoke of how difficult things were with your parents. I wish ... I wish you could have known what it was like to have parents who found joy in all you do." A tear leaked from her left eye.

Lucas smiled at her fondly, the anger slowly seeping away. "My father does. Sav does. You do. I take comfort in that." He leaned forward, and his gaze sharpened. "Now tell me what Mother said to you."

Zylphia flushed. "She said I'd fail at obtaining the vote for women and that the women who'd had their hopes raised would come to despise me as they became bitter at their unchanged circumstances. That I'd never succeed."

"You know she only speaks her truth. It's not a universal truth. She's the woman who's become bitter and cynical, despairing of any hope, any change. It's a reflection on her, not you, Zee." He reached forward and swiped away another tear. "Don't allow her voice to tarnish what you know to be true."

"I know. I thought I'd forgotten what she said. Then we lost by such a huge margin, and all I felt was embarrassed. Embarrassed that we couldn't even get 40 percent of the men to agree with us."

"There is no embarrassment in trying to change the world you live in, Zee. I think persuading 20 percent is monumental, never mind almost 40 percent as you did." He smiled fondly at her. "You'll continue to take what you learned from this campaign and use it so that you will be even more successful next time." They shared a smile. "Now tell me what I can do for your wedding."

"Promise you'll be there with Teddy. That you'll ensure he's there," Zylphia entreated.

Lucas threw his head back and laughed. She swatted him on his knee. "Oh, Zee, you have no concerns about him not showing up. He's anxious to wed you. He'd wed you this instant if it were possible."

Zee relaxed onto the couch and flushed. "I know. I hate waiting, and the longer we wait, the more my mind conjures all the things that could prevent us from marrying."

"Nothing will, Zee. Soon you will be Mrs. Goff, and you will be departing on a grand adventure." He winked at her. "And, no, I will not give you a hint." He leaned forward to kiss her on her forehead and then left her contemplating her mysterious honeymoon.

***

Parthena and Rowena sat in Sophie's small back parlor, sipping warm cups of tea and eating too many tea cakes as they awaited the arrival of a few more guests. Sophie sat in disillusioned silence in a seat near the fire, her gaze focused as though on a distant object. She glared at the new arrival. "You're late," she said in her scratchy voice.

Zylphia shook her head. "It couldn't be helped. I had a last-minute fitting with my dressmaker, and then the automobile broke down. I had to walk the last few blocks," she said as she bent to kiss them all on the cheek. "Have I missed anything?" She settled on the settee, running a hand down her plum-colored skirt.

"We waited for you. I assume your mother isn't coming?" Sophie asked as Zylphia accepted a cup of tea from Parthena. Zylphia shook her head. "Now that we are all here, I want to first say that I couldn't be more appreciative of the hard work you did for the ballot measure. I want none of you to believe you could have done more to see it succeed."

Sophronia's aquamarine gaze became piercing as she met their inquisitive gazes. "However, now we must work even harder. I am convinced the only way forward is the constitutional amendment, and I believe the national leaders are also in accord. Alice was right when she pushed for the amendment in '13."

Parthena set down her cup with such force that she cracked the bottom of her saucer on the marble top of the tea table. "I think we should move to Washington, DC, now and join Miss Paul and Miss Burns in the movement. Wouldn't it have been thrilling to drive across country as we've been reading about in the Suffragist? Why should we continue to miss out on the important events because we are here?"

Zylphia arched an amused eyebrow at her friend. "You seem to forget that you are married and that we have participated in important events, the recent march in Boston an illustrious example."

"Are you saying you no longer wish to travel to DC?" Rowena asked.

"I'm marrying Teddy in two days. I can't make any plans for a while," she said. "I know I will eventually join Miss Paul in Washington, but I can't yet."

"I want all of you to sit beside me at the gathering in Faneuil Hall on the sixteenth. It is imperative that we have a show of force and that our opinion about desiring an amendment be heard." Sophie frowned as she saw Zylphia squirm.

"I won't be there, Sophie," Zylphia admitted, earning a gasp of shock from Parthena. "I promised Teddy that I would travel with him on the honeymoon he planned for us. I can't ask him to shorten that trip, not after he's already waited for the vote."

Sophie squinted at Zylphia in displeasure. "Are you saying that you are allowing the dictates of your marriage to already interfere with your commitment to universal suffrage?"

"Not at all. I will always be committed. I know that you will represent me well and that you will inform me of what is discussed. However, I want a good marriage with Teddy, and we need to start well. I can't ask him to always come second. I won't," Zylphia proclaimed with a defiant tilt of her jaw.

Sophie smiled and nodded her approval. "Good. That's how it should be. I will not always approve if you absent yourself from your activities, but I understand. You must start your marriage as you want to go on. With mutual respect."

Rowena smiled at Zylphia. "Even without you, Zee, we'll be a strong force to contend with. We'll keep you informed."

"But not on your honeymoon," Sophie barked. "I believe your young man has been patient with us and our cause, and you both have earned time together, free of interference from family, a war, or any suffragist activities." She shared a warm glance with Zylphia. "However, on your return, you had better be prepared to plunge back into the battle."

Zylphia smiled. "I will. Never doubt my devotion to the cause."

Sophie jabbed Parthena with her cane. "Quit sitting there as though you were at a wake. She's only going on her honeymoon."

Parthena raised luminous eyes to Zylphia and shook her head. "I know. I hope you have a wonderful time, Zee. I couldn't help but feel melancholy as I know that, no matter how much you say it won't change things, it will. You have another allegiance now."

"As do you," Rowena murmured, earning a glower from Parthena and a snicker from Sophie.

"Some choose to acknowledge such an alliance. Others choose to ignore it," Sophie said. She cleared her throat. "I presume we are all in agreement that the only way forward is the constitutional amendment?" At their nods, her mouth firmed. "We will have to find some way to change President Wilson's mind."

Zylphia took a sip of her tea. "I have no doubt that Miss Paul will think of something." She shared a small smile with Parthena and Rowena. "And soon we will be in Washington to help."

CHAPTER NINETEEN

Zylphia stood in front of her mirror, her hands shaking as she smoothed down the long ivory-colored satin skirt of her wedding gown. She stilled her instinctive bristling as the maid fussed with her hair before placing the veil on her head. The thin lace did little to obscure the panic reflected in her gaze.

"Oh, dearest Zee, you look marvelous," Delia breathed. "I can't wait for your father to see you."

Zylphia almost bit her lip, stopping at the last moment to prevent a reprimand from her mother and maid. "Don't you think it's a bit over-done? I would have liked something a bit more simple." She eyed the dress's long train. "I fear I'll trip."

"You'll do fine, darling," Delia said. She nodded for the maid to leave the room and waited until she heard the *click* of the door behind her. "Why are you nervous? I know you love Teddy."

"It's a big step, Mother. I feel like I'm leaving my girlhood behind."

Delia laughed. "You left that behind years ago. With your successful career as a painter and your involvement with the suffragists, you have been a woman grown for some time." Delia gripped Zylphia's hands for a moment. "My mother died before you were born and long before I was reunited with your father. However, she instilled in me a belief that I should be loyal to my husband first. As you should to Teddy."

"I know, Mother. We've already suffered through enough disagreements and misunderstandings for me to understand that I must speak with him when I'm concerned about something or when we've quarreled. Although the counsel of good friends and family is often needed."

"Exactly, my darling." Delia tugged on Zylphia's hands, urging her toward the door. "Let's meet your father and get to the church so your poor man isn't left to wonder if he's being stood up."

"I'd never do that to Teddy," Zylphia said, her pace quickening behind her mother. She looked behind her as her dress's train flowed like a small creek in her wake.

She paused halfway down the velvet-covered staircase to see her father pacing at the base of the stairs. He'd tossed his top hat on the newel post, and he looked dashing in tails. "Father," she whispered.

He looked up at her, and a broad smile burst forth. "Oh, Zee. I knew you'd be a beautiful bride, but I never suspected you'd be this beautiful. You'd better be careful, for some other young man may try to steal you away on the drive to the church."

Zylphia laughed at her father's teasing and walked the rest of the way down the stairs. She leaned in for his kiss against her cheek and then forced herself to straighten.

He took her gently by her shoulders, staring with loving intensity into her gaze. "This is a momentous day for you, my darling daughter. For your mother and me as you leave our home. I want you to know how proud I am to call you my daughter. You are a brave, intelligent, inspiring woman, and I feel so fortunate to have found you." He swiped at her cheek, marring the thin lace veil with her tears.

"Thank you, Father," Zylphia whispered.

He nodded his understanding that she was unable to say more. He smiled at the love shining in her expression. "Let's go meet your young man. I imagine he's anxious to see you," he said, winging his arm out for her. She gripped his arm, walking beside him as they moved outside to the waiting automobile.

***

Teddy paced the alcove off the main nave in the church, the long tails of his formal attire snapping behind him. Lucas Russell sat on one of the uncomfortable wooden chairs with his legs crossed and fingers tapping away on his knees as though he were playing the piano. "She's a bit late, but brides are always late," Teddy muttered to himself.

"Knowing Zee, she made a fuss about the fancy dress Mrs. McLeod bought, and it took extra time to dress her," Lucas said with a chuckle. He watched Teddy with amused interest.

Teddy took a deep breath and nodded before continuing his pacing.

"If you're this nervous, I'm surprised you'd want to marry the girl," a man with a deep voice intoned from the doorway. He stood with shoulders slightly stooped, his gray hair parted to one side and nearly matching his eyes. "I'm sure your mother could have found you a more appropriate girl had you asked for her assistance."

Teddy stiffened at the older man's entrance. "I'm surprised you could rouse yourself from the delights of New York City. And I haven't needed neither your nor Mother's assistance for some time." Teddy shook his head at Lucas in silent entreaty to not leave him alone. Lucas settled into his chair, an air of relaxed ennui about him as he studied the two men.

"I couldn't have my only living son marry without my presence," Mr. Goff said.

Teddy's previous nervous agitation had fled, and he stood stock-still as he faced his father. "I don't see why not. You've approved of little I've done since I was a child. I don't see that your appearance today will make much difference."

The elder Mr. Goff flushed, accenting his gray hair and the sallow color of his complexion. "There's been little to celebrate in a hermitlike son whose one great claim was causing the death of my heir. You can't even go to war and become a hero. You come back a wounded recluse."

Teddy took a step back as though he'd been hit in the chest.

Lucas jumped to his feet and stood between Teddy and his father. "I know you think a fatherly reunion is de rigueur at moments like this, but I have to admit, I find them overrated. At least with regard to my family. Why don't you join your wife and see if she is more desirous of your company than we are?" Lucas asked with a feral smile as he effectively pushed Teddy's father from the alcove.

When the elder Mr. Goff had departed, Lucas spun to face Teddy, who remained frozen in place. "I thought I was the only unfortunate one to have a parent desirous of causing internal bleeding." He slapped Teddy on the shoulder, the action jolting Teddy so that he reentered the moment. "He spoke lies intent to hurt, Tedd. Ignore him."

Teddy raised luminous eyes to meet Lucas's worried gaze. "I wish you could have met my twin, Lawrence. Larry. He was everything I'm not."

"If you even utter what I think you're going to utter, you'll marry with a black eye," Lucas grumbled.

Teddy laughed at Lucas and shook his head. "I can see why Zee is so fond of you." His smile faded. "I know it's not my fault he died. It wouldn't be better had he lived and I'd been the one to die." He took a deep breath. "And I hate my father for making me think about all this minutes before I'm to marry Zee."

"You stopped your infernal pacing," Lucas said as he sat again on his chair. He glanced to the doorway again, this time filled by one of the young men acting as ushers, all from the orphanage Delia used to run, although none of the high society members or businessmen would suspect as much with their fine dress. Lucas smirked. As long as they refrained from speaking. He nodded to the young man in silent understanding and motioned for him to leave. "It's time, Tedd." He shared a smile with him. "Your bride awaits you." He slapped him on the back again as he propelled him from the alcove into the front of the church.

***

Zylphia stood in the receiving line, smiling at the ever-growing number of well-wishers. She shifted as her new shoes dug into her heels and attempted to feign interest in another business associate of her father's. She felt Teddy stiffen and glanced up, meeting a pair of eyes that matched her husband's. Her smile faltered for a moment as she awaited the introduction.

"Zylphia, Mrs. Goff, this is my father, Mr. Goff. He was unable to attend any of the pre-wedding festivities," Teddy intoned in a flat voice.

His lack of all emotion sent a shiver down Zylphia's spine. She conjured a smile for her father-in-law. "Mr. Goff, it is lovely to finally meet you."

"I hope you understand what you've just done, my girl," he said, the crisp British accent unmistakable.

"Yes, I've married the man I love and admire," Zylphia said, her smile fading as she dared him with an intense stare to contradict her. "As should anyone who knows him." She turned her attention from Teddy's father to his mother, her vivacity diminished as she stood next to her husband. "Mrs. Goff, thank you so much for all your kindness and support." She pasted on a smile as her in-laws were pushed into the large ballroom.

Zylphia reached her hand down and gripped Teddy's in solidarity and support. "Ignore his spite, darling," she whispered as she straightened her shoulders.

A few guests later, she smiled broadly and leaned in for a warm embrace when Parthena reached her. "Oh, P.T. Thank you for being here today," Zylphia whispered.

"I wouldn't have missed it. You look radiant, Zee, and I'm delighted for you and Teddy. At last," she murmured, her gaze shining with joy for her friend. "Be happy."

Zylphia hugged her again quickly before shaking Morgan's hand and focusing on enduring the remainder of the receiving line.

When they were free from greeting their guests, Zylphia separated from Teddy to mingle. She snagged a flute of champagne and joined Sophie and Florence for a moment. Parthena was across the room with Rowena, while Morgan was nearby with his business associates. The ballroom—festooned in bouquets of yellow roses, sunflowers, and dahlias—was filled with people she barely knew. "How did they find all these yellow flowers this time of year?" Zylphia asked.

"It's why they have hothouses," Sophie said. "I want to know why a piano is on that dais." She nodded to a corner of the room. At Zylphia's confused stare, Sophie frowned. "I was surprised to see that Russell boy stand up with Teddy today."

"He and Teddy became friends, and Teddy didn't really have anyone else to ask. His English family refused to come over due to the dangers of sea travel."

"There is an agreement that the Germans will no longer sink American merchant ships," Florence said.

"Yes, and I'm thankful for that agreement as that's how Teddy managed to return to me a few months ago. However, I think his English relatives were afraid the truce would end and they'd become marooned in America." Zylphia shared a wry smile with Sophie and Florence.

"Heaven forbid," Sophie said. "It's a pity a train didn't derail and prevent his father from arriving in time to attend the wedding. A singularly uncouth man."

Zylphia bit back a bark of laughter. "I agree." Her face lit with joy as she saw Teddy motioning for her. "I have to go." She leaned forward to embrace Sophie and Florence. "If I don't see you before I leave, thank you for everything."

"Don't for one moment think about meetings or the cause. We'll have plenty of work for you upon your return. Enjoy your time with your young man," Sophie said.

Florence raised her eyebrows. "Yes, enjoy yourself." She giggled as Zylphia blushed.

Zylphia wove her way through the crowd to join Teddy toward the center of the ballroom. He took her hand and raised it, kissing her fingertips. "What is it?" she whispered.

"First, I missed you and wanted a moment with you," he said, his smile reaching his eyes when he saw the pleasure his simple comment evoked. "Second, this is my surprise for you. Dance with me?" he asked.

Zylphia glanced around to realize the majority of the dance floor had been cleared for them. She saw Lucas sitting at the piano but with no music in front of him. Teddy nodded to Lucas, who winked at Zylphia before he raised his hands and began to play.

A soothing, slow lullaby of a song emerged, and Zylphia followed Teddy into a sedate dance akin to a waltz. The sweet, melodious music was filled with yearning, love, and promise. She gazed into Teddy's eyes and battled tears.

"Why the tears, my love?" he murmured as they danced in front of the large crowd. "I had hoped to please you."

"You do please me. Your desire to bring me joy dispels all my nonsensical fears." She leaned forward and laid her head on his shoulder and whispered into his ear, "I love you, Teddy. I wish I had thought of a wedding present for you."

He chuckled. "You are a fine present, my love. I could ask for nothing more." He fought a groan as his father-in-law, Aidan, interrupted his dance with Zylphia, while Teddy found himself dancing with his mother.

The music changed subtly, no longer meant for a newly married husband and wife but for family and friends. The harmony from the song "Suwannee River" echoed throughout the arrangement, and Zylphia beamed at Lucas while others joined them on the dance floor.

"It does me good to see you this happy, Zee," her father said as they danced. "Lucas wrote you a beautiful song."

"Yes, he did. And now he's forcing everyone to dance to one of our songs." At her father's confused expression, she said, "This is a suffragist song, Father."

Aidan threw back his head and laughed. "Oh, I need to learn to never underestimate the cunning of an artist." He shared a smile with his daughter. "He has us dancing to your tune."

"He does," Zee said with pride. "I just wish we could sing the lyrics so everyone understood."

Aidan saw a few disgruntled faces on the dance floor and nodded to them in an approving manner. "Enough of them understand, Zee. And, if they didn't realize we weren't giving up the battle, the fact that every flower and adornment in the room is a variation of white, yellow, and purple should have given them their first indication."

He could sense his time with his daughter was coming to an end, and he held her arms a bit more tightly. "Take your time with your husband, and enjoy it. Don't fret about what needs to be done. Plenty of opportunities await you to further make your mark in the movement." He kissed her head and released her as the music came to an end.

Aidan and Zylphia joined in applauding Lucas, and she blew him a kiss. He nodded his understanding to her, and they shared a smile. He bowed a few times, ignored calls for an encore, and disappeared into the crowd.

***

Lucas pushed through the crowd, intent on finding a space to hide away from peering eyes and preening fans. He pushed into a small room, the family's private parlor, and sighed with relief to find it empty. He moved to a comfortable gentleman's chair and settled into it. He stared into the banked fire, stretching his legs in front of him. At the *click* of the door opening, he groaned. "Please go away and leave me alone," he murmured.

"If you wish," a female whispered. A voice he dreamed about still.

"Parthena, wait," Lucas rasped, rising from his chair and facing her as she made to leave the parlor. "What are you doing here?"

"Same as you, I suspect. I wanted to escape the crush of bilious businessmen." They shared an amused smile. "My husband is in his element."

"He'll be irate if he finds you here with me," he said, settling again into his chair, now angled so he could see her near the doorway.

"He has no reason to doubt my constancy, not after months as a dutiful wife."

"I suspect he fears you have a quota of such months in you and that you'll run through them quickly. His unease comes from the fact he doesn't know how many months you have, so he is left in constant trepidation of your imminent departure," Lucas said with a teasing smile.

"Don't," Parthena snapped. "Don't be nice to me. Not after how I treated you." She entered the room and shut the door to ensure privacy but remained near the exit of the room. She held her hands low over her waist, the sage green of her skirts highlighting her beauty.

"I'm not an idiot, Parthena. I might act like one on occasion, but I'm not a permanent idiot. I came to understand why you acted like you did."

"Why? Why did I act like I did?" she challenged.

"Because you needed to have marital harmony and couldn't have me pressuring you to dishonor your vows. It was wrong of me, and I am sorry." He looked away, toward the fire. "My only excuse is that I thought I'd found in you someone who, ... well, someone who'd understand." He shook his head ruefully. "I found that dream hard to relinquish." He frowned when he saw her battling tears.

"I never meant to hurt you, Lucas. I'm sorry for ... for everything."

He rose, his cheeks limned with an angry flush. "For God's sake, don't be sorry. For, if you're sorry, then it means it was all a mistake. A mistake for me to write you. To find hope in another. I will never regret that."

A tear trickled down her cheek. "I pray you find that hope again, Lucas."

He reached forward, grasping her hand and preventing her from fleeing the room as she had intended after speaking those words. "Have you found your hope, Parthena?" His worried gaze roved over her face. "Does he understand you any better now than before?"

She sniffled. "My marriage is not your concern, Mr. Russell."

He smiled sadly. "Then that is my answer. I'm sorry, Thena—for you will always be Thena to me—that you have martyred yourself for the sake of your family's well-being. I will find another who fills me with joy. And what you and I shared will become nothing more than a wonderful memory." He released her hand and looked toward the door in dismissal. "Good-bye, Mrs. Wheeler."

He returned to his chair and sat, his gaze again focused on the grate. He counted his breaths after the door *clicked* behind her retreating form. He counted to one hundred, then one thousand, and knew that he had lied. He had little hope for finding joy for himself.

***

Aidan stood in a rear parlor with business associates, discussing the war's impact on trade. He excused himself when he saw Delia enter the room. After clasping her hand, he kissed it, frowning as he saw her battling tears. "What's the matter, my love?"

She swiped at her cheek at his gentle inquiry. "Zee is preparing to leave." Her voice broke on the word leave.

"She'll come back to us," Aidan whispered as he kissed his wife's forehead. "Come. Let's be there to send her off."

He and Delia maneuvered their way through the crowd, their arms linked. He smiled and called out his thanks to those who congratulated them but kept moving. They approached the grand staircase as Zylphia descended, sophisticated in an ice-blue traveling suit.

She laughed at something Florence said as she accepted her bouquet from her. Then she spun, flinging it over her shoulder as she giggled. "There, those who were prepared had a fighting chance." She laughed with glee as one of Rowena's cousins caught the elaborate floral display.

Aidan stepped forward to embrace her. "I'm very proud of you, my darling daughter. Today and every day." He swiped at her cheeks as a tear fell. "I hope you have a wonderful journey and that you come home with a multitude of stories for us."

"I will, Father. I'll miss you," she whispered as she first hugged him and then her mother. "I'll write."

"I should hope not too often," Delia said, causing Zylphia to laugh and Aidan to snicker. "Enjoy your time away, my darling Zee."

Zylphia squeezed her mother's arm, her gaze brightening as she beheld Teddy. She moved toward him, and they departed amid cheers and catcalls to the awaiting automobile.

Aidan exhaled deeply, his breath stuttering. "And they're off. The house will seem deserted without her."

Delia leaned into his side, seeking comfort as she comforted him.

***

"Russell," a man called out in a deep voice, and a hand clapped on his shoulder, just as Lucas was about to depart the McLeod mansion. "I need a word with you."

Lucas stilled and studied a very apprehensive-looking Morgan. "Speak."

Morgan shook his head and motioned for him to follow him into Aidan's library. He shut the door behind him, the room softly lit with a desk lamp and a wall sconce near Zylphia's painting. "I asked Aidan if I could use his study, and he agreed."

Lucas remained standing near the door, ignoring Morgan's wave to take a seat in one of the comfortable leather chairs in front of Aidan's desk. He crossed his arms and glowered at Morgan.

"I'll not attack you, so please sit. I have a proposition for you, and I would appreciate it if you would hear me out." Morgan settled into his high-backed chair and crossed his legs, appearing relaxed. Lucas sat and mimicked Morgan's pose.

"I know you've taken quite an interest in Mrs. Wheeler's artistic accomplishments. I also know that you both believe I married her out of spite, which is patently untrue." He took a deep breath. "One of my main reasons for marrying her was to save her from the likes of Mr. Carlisle."

Lucas squinted as he thought through the catalog of influential people he'd met in Boston. "I remain unacquainted with him."

"Consider yourself fortunate. He's older than our fathers and has a cruel streak. He's desirous of a young bride to produce a legitimate son, and he doesn't care if the woman who is his bride is willing or not."

Lucas paled. "Surely her father would have sense to protect his daughters from such a man?"

Morgan arched an eyebrow. "When one is desperate ..."

Lucas stared at Zylphia's painting. "She never explained to me what had been threatened, only that she needed to marry you to help her family."

"If she didn't marry a man wealthy enough to overcompensate what Mr. Carlisle offered, then she, or her next younger sister Genevieve, was to marry him."

Lucas's expression became desolate. "I never understood because I was too caught up in my own sense of betrayal."

Morgan laughed. "An interesting word choice, Russell. It seems her father has little sense of honor as he's promised his next eldest daughter to marry Carlisle on the fourth of December."

Lucas's appalled expression clashed with Morgan's stormy one. "Why? I know you provided a generous settlement. It was the talk of Boston last summer, with most thinking you a fool for paying so dearly for a woman ..." Lucas flushed and bit off the remainder of his words.

"For paying so dearly for a woman who hated me?" Morgan asked, ignoring what else Lucas could have said. "Yes, perhaps I was a fool, but I couldn't allow harm to come to Mrs. Wheeler or her sister."

"For God's sake, call her Parthena," Lucas snapped. He leaned his head against the high back of his chair as he thought through what he'd learned. "I'm sorry for the predicament your extended family finds themselves in, but I don't know what it has to do with me or why you've shared the sordid details with me. A man you must despise."

"If rumors are to be believed, you've done quite well for yourself this past year. You've made a tiny fortune," Morgan murmured. "And, from what I've discovered, you live a modest life in rented rooms barely big enough to hold your cherished piano."

"Not that it's any of your business, but you are correct." Lucas shrugged his shoulders. "I was raised among the elite, and I've learned that there is very little they have that would cause me to want to beggar myself in the obtaining of it."

"I also heard you were left a sizeable amount from your childless aunt." Morgan speared him with an intense look as Lucas flushed with anger.

"How dare you make inquiries into my personal finances," he rasped.

"I needed to learn if my wife had good instincts in trusting you. I believe she was correct. I've already tried once, and failed, to save Genevieve with my money. I won't be so foolish a second time." He paused, nodding as he saw understanding glimmer in Lucas's gaze. "I want someone Mrs. Wheeler and I trust to travel with her sister. To take her far away."

"You can't know what you're asking," Lucas said.

Morgan steepled his fingers. "I do actually. I'm asking you to travel with Genevieve. Whisk her away from Boston and keep her safe from her father and Mr. Carlisle."

Lucas gripped the arms of his chair in panic before he rose and paced around Aidan's office. "I can't travel with a young unmarried woman, unchaperoned." He ran a hand through his hair. "Not unless ..."

"Not unless you're married."

Lucas stilled, staring out the blackened window overlooking the front garden. In the distance, he heard the faint sounds of laughter, of guests taking their leave, of the front door opening and closing. "You ask too much."

"Parthena is lost to you. She always will be." Morgan's voice held no note of triumph in that statement. "She is an honorable woman."

"She cares for you," Lucas murmured. "Yes, she's honorable, but she also cares." He rested his forehead against the cool windowpane, his thoughts racing. "I'll need a few days to consider what you are requesting," he murmured.

"That's more than I thought you'd give," Morgan said. He rose and followed Lucas from the room, nodding once before he melted into the crowd.

Lucas sighed and reentered the office, shutting the door behind him. He slumped into the chair he'd only just vacated, deep in thought as he sat mesmerized, staring at Zylphia's painting. He rubbed a hand over his face, uncertain of his decision.

***

Zylphia roamed around the large suite at the Parker House Hotel. Uncertainty filled her. She remained in her traveling clothes she had changed into from her lavish wedding dress at her parents' house before departing with Teddy. However, they'd traveled barely more than a mile before he'd said they'd reached their first destination. She paced away from her trunk, which contained a lacy peignoir for the evening, and spun toward the window. She stared down at the bright lights of Scollay Square, although they failed to beckon to her.

An adjoining door eased open, and she stiffened.

"I thought I'd given you plenty of time to change," Teddy murmured.

She saw his reflection in the glass, wearing a dressing gown, his chest bare, but still wearing pants. "Why are we here, Teddy? I thought you were taking me away on a grand adventure." She shivered as he caressed a hand down her back.

"And I am. However, I refuse to spend my wedding night on a rocking, uncomfortable train. I want time, alone, with my wife, in a comfortable bed, where no servants or parents will interrupt us."

"A train?" she asked, turning toward him with furrowed brows as she tried to determine where they were traveling to on their secret wedding trip.

"No more clues, my inquisitive darling. For now, let us enjoy being married," he whispered, trailing his fingers through her hair. Although the tips of his right hand were injured and not as nimble as those of his left, he managed to free her hair of the many pins holding it in place. Her raven hair cascaded over her shoulders to her lower back, and he leaned forward, burying his face in it.

"I love your long hair. And the fact that I am the only one who ever sees it down." He shared an amused smile with her. "I know that may make me a chauvinist, but I can't help it." He leaned forward to kiss her, but she pushed him away. He backed away with a hurt frown.

"Teddy, please, wait. I have a special ... special nightgown for tonight. It's selfish of me not to have changed." She pointed vaguely at her trunk as she spoke in agitated bursts.

"Darling, I don't care if you are wearing sackcloth. All I care is freeing you of your clothing." He leaned forward, kissing her deeply. "Save the frippery for a night on the train," he whispered before leading her toward the large bed.

When she stood with her legs backing into the edge of it, he paused, unbuttoning her dress and easing it off her. "I'm glad I didn't know these were under here," Teddy teased as he ran a hand over her lace undergarments.

"I wanted something special for the day," Zylphia said, blushing.

He kissed along the lace chemise strap. "I hope you know how precious you are to me, Zee."

She lifted up as he helped free her from all her finery. She watched with passion-ladened eyes as he worked on the buttons of his pants, biting her lip as she detected his frustration that his fingers were not as nimble as they used to be. "We have all night, darling."

"I can't help but feel desperate for you now," he said with a triumphant laugh as he tossed his pants to the floor. He joined her on the bed, as they became lost in each other's gaze. His laughter faded as he caressed her silky skin and as they found their joy in each other for the first time as husband and wife.

***

He held her in his arms, contentment suffusing him, although not yet ready for sleep. Zylphia snuggled into his side, her arm across his belly and her hand tracing circles on his chest. "Thank you," he whispered.

She raised her head, confusion evident in her expression. "For what? Marrying you? Loving you?" She smiled. "That was easy."

"I think marriage terrified you more than you were willing to admit, especially as you were walking down the aisle." He kissed her on her forehead as she closed her eyes to hide her embarrassment.

"I was scared. Not of you. Not of building a future with you. But of what it means. I fear I'll no longer be me. I'm Mrs. Goff now. Not Zylphia. Not a McLeod. And that terrifies me."

He tilted his head to one side as he studied her. "You'll always be Zylphia. Besides, you've done this once before, when you changed your name from Maidstone to McLeod."

"I know, and I had to battle an intrinsic fear and sense of unworthiness for years," she admitted.

He rolled so that Zylphia was underneath him, his hands clasped on either side of her face. His intense, fervent gaze bore into hers. "Never doubt your worth. Not with me. You are everything." He frowned as she began to cry.

She pulled him down to her for an impassioned kiss. "You are everything to me too. It's why I couldn't stand your father. I'm sorry, Teddy. I know I shouldn't say that about the man who sired you, but I could find no warmth in him." She shook her head mournfully.

"I know. He still mourns Larry." His expression was haunted as he thought about his long-dead twin.

"And fails to find delight in you, his living son," Zylphia said.

Teddy smiled as he leaned forward to kiss her. "I pray I never lose your passionate loyalty, Zee. I'd be adrift without it."

He lay on his side, tugging her into his arms. "I promised myself I'd surprise you tomorrow, but I find that I need to share my plans with you." He met her amused gaze as she rolled so she faced him. "If you want me to wait, I will."

"Half the fun is the anticipation of the journey. Where are we going? What do you have planned, dearest?" she asked, rubbing her foot over his calf and causing a low moan.

"If you keep that up, I will forget my good intentions and not tell you," he teased. He leaned forward and kissed her again. "Do you remember when we met?" At her gentle nod, his gaze became more tender. "Not the dance, although that's technically when I was introduced to you. Instead, that wonderful walk after you'd hurt yourself."

He brushed back a lock of her black hair as he gazed at her with adoration. "You were the antithesis of every woman I'd ever met in those insipid ballrooms. You were vibrant and vital and filled to the brim with your enthusiasm for life. I couldn't believe I'd been fortunate enough to meet you, let alone have time just with you."

Zylphia laughed. "You were cryptic. Barely talking about yourself and me almost baring my greatest secrets." She sobered. "I was fascinated by you from the first, although I didn't have the good sense to realize it."

"On our walk, you spoke of your time in San Francisco. Of how you missed your home there. Of how you loved the journey across country." He traced a thumb over her eyebrow. "I wanted to give you that again. To travel with you, to see the land through your eyes and to go to San Francisco with you."

"Oh, Teddy." Zylphia lunged to embrace him. "I can't believe you remembered what I said more than two years ago."

"I remember everything we've ever discussed, Zee. You are precious to me. And, if I can bring you happiness, I will." He ran a hand over the back of her head and shoulders. "Thank you for not insisting we cut our honeymoon journey short. I don't know what I would have done."

Zylphia shook her head as she burrowed farther into his embrace. "I don't either. It's the perfect wedding trip." She leaned away and clasped his face. "And you planned it for me."

"Of course. I love you," he whispered, capturing her lips in an impassioned kiss.

"What time is our train?" she asked, giggling as he peppered her face with kisses.

"It leaves tomorrow afternoon." He kissed his way down her neck. "That gives us the entire night, and morning, for passion."

She pushed him away, and he frowned in confusion. "Do we have our own private compartment on the train?"

"Of course," he said as they shared a smile.

"Good," Zylphia breathed as she scattered kisses across his chest. "Let's hope we make the train." They shared a laugh before forgetting about everything but their love for each other.

CHAPTER TWENTY

The Tuesday after Zylphia's wedding, Lucas entered his father's linen store, frowning when he saw his mother working behind the counter. Never a heavy woman, she was now thin to the point of appearing emaciated. "I'm surprised to see you here," he said after the customer left and they were alone in the shop.

Matilda adeptly folded a piece of linen the customer hadn't chosen, stuffing it back in its place on the shelf. "I heard the wedding was beautiful." She moved to a stool, her face contorting as she sat.

Lucas frowned as they had never allowed stools behind the counter before now. "You were missed," Lucas said. "They would have welcomed you." He rolled his eyes at his mother's martyred expression. "I'll never understand why you had to ruin Father's chances for an evening out by feigning an illness."

Heavy footsteps heralded his father's approach, and he turned to meet him. "Father." He frowned further when he saw the haggard expression on his father's face.

"Quit badgering your mother," Martin said and motioned for Lucas to follow him into his office. The office, never a testament to order, was in complete chaos. Papers overflowed their files, ledgers piled atop each other appeared on the verge of toppling over, and all available chairs, except Martin's, were covered.

"What's happened?" Lucas asked.

"I'll explain later. First, tell me your news," Martin said as he hefted a pile of papers off a chair for Lucas. He settled into his well-worn chair behind his desk, delight and curiosity alight in his brown eyes, replacing the earlier fatigue and cloak of worry. "How was the wedding?"

"As beautiful as I'd hoped it would be for Zee. She and Teddy looked as though they couldn't believe their good fortune."

"Ah, that's as it should be. How did they like your new piece?"

"Very much. They danced beautifully. I'm told it will become one of the most popular wedding songs of the upcoming year," he said as he flushed with pride.

"Excellent," Martin said. "As long as you keep the majority of the profits." At Lucas's nod, he sighed with contentment. "What bothers you?"

Lucas tapped his fingers on his leg, an action he routinely did whenever nervous. "Morgan Wheeler approached me with an interesting proposition. I'm uncertain what to do and wanted to speak with you as you had a similar experience."

Martin squinted his eyes and waited for his son to continue to speak.

"You know I loved his wife, Parthena. Well, she appears determined to have a committed marriage with her husband. I can't fault her, and I tell myself daily I should admire her for her strength. I learned last night that she married Wheeler because her father was in financial ruin and he would have married her or her younger sister to a letch just to make up for his losses."

"You are wealthy, Lucas. She could have married you," Martin said with a frown.

"From what I gleaned from Morgan, it would have taken my entire savings and maybe a little more to save her father. To save her sister really." He stilled his fingers, clasping them together.

After his prolonged silence, Martin asked, "What is his proposition?"

"To marry Parthena's next younger sister, Genevieve." He shared a bleak look with his father. "It turns out that her father needs more money and is willing to marry her to that horrid man. Wheeler doesn't want to give him any more of his own fortune as he's already gifted him twice more than you and I would use in decades, maybe in our lifetime."

"Why would you marry her?" Martin asked.

"I keep asking myself that question. I don't know her. I can't even remember a vague introduction. And yet the thought of her hurting, when I could have helped her ..."

"She's not Savannah, Lucas," Martin snapped. "You weren't responsible for her then, and you aren't now." He glowered at his son. "I wish you'd lose your guilt over what happened to her." He leaned forward, his elbows on his desk as he watched his son. "I entered a marriage similar to what you are proposing."

"I know, and that's why I'm asking for your advice," Lucas said.

"Lucas, have you even conversed with her? Do you have anything in common? Do you know that she will make you a good wife?" Martin sighed with frustration. "I want you to be as happy as Savannah now is with her Jeremy. You deserve that."

"Why were you willing to accept less when you married Mother?" Lucas speared his father with an intense stare. "I know you say it's because you needed to help save the store, but I believe it had to be more than that."

"It was a combination of many things. I could help the store, save a proud woman from society's censure, and raise the stature of my family with its association to a higher-ranking family." He looked around his cluttered office. "It might not seem like much, but this has been a good life, Lucas. I've had you and Savannah. For many years, your mother and I had a good relationship. I can't ask for more than that."

He remained silent for a moment. "When I think of you and Parthena's sister, I can't help but wonder if you are considering this merely because you want to impress Parthena in some way with your sacrifice. Will you always believe that her sister should be thankful for what you were willing to give up for her? Will you believe, in some small corner of your heart, that she is second best? For, if that is the case, you should run away and never consider undertaking such a marriage. You will both be miserable within the first month."

Lucas sat back in his chair, lost in thought. "That's the problem, Father. I don't know why I would be willing to marry her. I've never truly thought I'd ever marry. Not until Parthena. Then, when she married another, I tucked away that dream again."

"What happens if you do wed this sister and then you meet a woman you truly desire to marry? Would you divorce her? Live a lie? You need to understand that you are committing to providing for her happiness as well as a home and other basic necessities." He shared a long look with his son. "Some believe, if they could just have some such thing occur in their life, then they'd be happy. I don't agree. You can choose to be happy or miserable. It's your decision."

Lucas frowned at his father. "So you are saying any woman would make me happy or bring me joy?"

"No. What I'm saying is that, if you do decide to marry her, commit to the relationship. Don't enter it half-heartedly. Don't compare the might-have-beens to what is. Embrace your moments of joy. For too long you've focused on the next composition, the next concert, never enjoying now."

Lucas flushed at his father's assessment of his life, although he didn't argue with it as it was a fair assessment.

"Would this young woman aid you in appreciating what you've already accomplished? Or would she be dissatisfied and expect more?"

Lucas shrugged. "I have no idea."

"All I can advise is that you don't marry her without meeting her. It's advice I didn't even follow myself," Martin said with a sardonic smile. "I refuse to believe that time is so short that you don't have the opportunity to meet with her a few times before you make your decision. You are an honorable man. No matter what decision you make, it would be an honorable one."

Lucas nodded before focusing on his father. "What's wrong? Your desk is much more disorganized than is usual, and you look awful. Mother appears ..." He paused a moment. "She actually looks ill."

"It's nothing to concern yourself with. You have enough to worry about in coming to your big decision," Martin said.

"No, I'm forty years old. I'm not a child, Father. Tell me."

Martin's broad shoulders stooped, and the haggard look returned. "I've wanted to spare you, and your mother will not be pleased with me. She is ill, and they think it is cancer."

"Why is she working? Why isn't she resting?" Lucas asked. He shared a horrified look with his father.

"It's what she wants. She wants to be among people, not alone with her thoughts. She admitted to me last night that she suspects she doesn't have much time left. I have to respect her final wishes."

Lucas slumped into his chair, his head shaking side to side in denial. "Is there nothing that can be done?"

Martin shook his head, slumping farther into his chair. "I keep telling myself that this is a bad dream, and I'll wake up, and she'll be fine."

Lucas ran his hands through his hair. "Will you work the shop front a few moments? I should speak with her." Martin was about to say no, but Lucas held up his hand in entreaty. "I promise I won't pester her. I need to talk with her. For only a few minutes."

Martin nodded, rose, and placed a hand on Lucas's shoulder. He exited the room, and, after a while, Matilda's heels could be heard on the wooden floors as they approached Martin's office. She entered and came to an abrupt stop when she saw Lucas sitting in shock in a chair.

She shut the door behind her and headed to the rocking chair. After moving the precariously piled papers to the floor, she sat. "I don't want your pity."

"I'd never pity you," Lucas said. "That preposterous story last spring about lunacy. That was all a ploy to have me remain in Boston to prove I was sane. Because you wanted me here." At Matilda's emotionless gaze, Lucas flushed with anger. "Even as you face your own mortality, do you remain unable to ask my forgiveness? Have you written Savannah?" When Matilda merely stared at him blankly, he shook his head with a mixture of disappointment and resignation. "Why couldn't you have simply asked me to stay?"

"As though you would ever have done anything that would have pleased me," she snapped. "You've lived the past ten years rejoicing in your ability to bring shame and notoriety onto our family name. When I pleaded with you to cease such activities, you strived to become even more infamous. Nothing I could have said would have induced you to change your ways or to remain in Boston."

"Nothing but the need to repair my name and reputation," he said.

She nodded. "You like to believe we are so different. You proved we aren't." He flinched at her words. "The important point is you stayed."

"How long do you have, Mother?" he whispered.

"A few weeks, maybe a month." Her lip trembled before she stiffened her spine and gripped her hands together on her lap. "I've known this moment was coming for some time. There's no need to be sad."

Lucas lowered his head, his long hair flopping over his forehead. "You're my mother. No matter what you've done, how much I've railed against you, you will be missed."

"Why?" She watched him with a curious expression. "You've acted as though you haven't had a mother for over ten years."

He watched her in silence before he spoke in a soft voice. "I remember you tucking me into bed every night. You read me a bedtime story and ensured my stuffed puppy was by my side. You came when I had nightmares, soothing me and promising me how I would be safe. You had joy in you then." His brown eyes clouded with grief. "I'll mourn the woman you were and the dream of what you could have been to me. To Savannah."

They shared a long look as they both battled tears.

"Will you remain here until the end?" she asked.

"I don't know if I'll be able to. I've been asked to perform a favor, for a friend, and it might force me to leave." He studied his mother. "If you had to do it again, would you marry Father, a man you didn't even meet until your wedding day?" At his mother's prolonged silence, he prompted, "Would you do it?"

"Yes. He's a good, honorable, decent man who provides well for me. He gave me wonderful children and never thought less of me for my past transgressions." Her smile was rueful. "I haven't always treated him well, but he has never failed to treat me with respect. The question is whether or not he'd do it again." She rose, lifted a hand to place it on Lucas's head as she passed but lowered her arm without touching him. She departed, leaving Lucas deep in thought.

***

Parthena covered the hand of her next youngest sister Genevieve. "I don't want you to panic, Viv. Morgan has promised he'll find a way out of this for you."

Genevieve sat next to her elegantly dressed sister. "How can he? No man will want to be burdened with an unattractive bride. There is no incentive for any man to marry me." She picked at the seams of her modestly styled sage-green dress, her dull brown hair pulled up in a stylish chignon. She met her sister's vibrant hazel eyes with her plain brown ones.

"You aren't unattractive. You've decided to dress in clothes as appealing as sackcloth, for reasons I'll never understand." Parthena looked at her sister expectantly as though trying to coax a confidence from her.

"I can't help but feel like ..."

Parthena patted her sister on the hand as the door opened. Her eyes widened a fraction in surprise before she smoothed on an impersonal smile. "I didn't expect you," Parthena said.

"I should think you never would have imagined me to be welcomed here," Lucas said with a laugh. He shared a smile with Morgan and sat in one of the chairs facing the couch and the two women.

Genevieve nudged her sister, and Parthena waved to Lucas. "Excuse me, this is Mr. Russell. He has been my piano mentor. This is my sister, Miss Tyler."

Genevieve's mouth formed a shocked O before she smiled at him. "It's nice to meet you."

Lucas fought a smile at how he was introduced while Morgan frowned. "How are you, Miss Tyler?" Lucas asked.

She smiled inanely. "I'm fine. I'm enjoying my visit with my sister."

"I imagine you'd want to as you'll be separated soon." At their confused stare, he said, "I've been told congratulations are in order." His offhand comment provoked instant tension in the room as Parthena stiffened and glared at Morgan, and Genevieve slouched in her chair. "Mr. Wheeler told me of your father's plans."

"He had no right," Parthena hissed.

"No need to act as you are, Hennie," Morgan said, ignoring Lucas's snicker at his nickname for her. "You asked for my help, and I think he can help us."

"Hennie?" Lucas said as he fought a smile while Parthena glared at him.

"It's an old childhood nickname," Morgan said absently.

The reminder that he'd known her since his youth sobered Lucas.

Genevieve crumpled farther into her chair as though she were hoping to disappear. "I don't know why you believe this man could help me, Morgan." She tapped her fingers on her knees but then moved them under her legs as she noted Lucas's interest.

"He has influence, wealth, and family far outside Boston." Morgan shared a quelling glance with Parthena, although it also contained an entreaty with her not to argue with him.

"Do you desire to marry Mr. Carlisle?" Lucas asked. "For, if you do, I'd hate to pose any interference, no matter what your brother-in-law has informed me."

Genevieve's head shot up as she glared at Lucas. "Of course not! He's old enough to be my grandfather, and he's ... he's ... he's a pervert."

Lucas's gaze became contrite as he watched her fuss under his stare. "What's he done?" he asked.

"Yes, Viv, how do you know he's such a man?" Parthena demanded. "We are determined to help you, so please tell us what he's done."

Genevieve closed her eyes and spoke in such a soft voice that Lucas and Morgan canted forward to hear her. "He considers me his already. He traps me in ballroom corners and speaks of lewd things. He peers down my ball gown, comments on my endowments, and talks of how much I please him." Her voice trembled as she fisted her hands, now on her lap.

"Bastard," Lucas hissed. "I beg your pardon," he muttered as Morgan hit him on the leg. "You know you were thinking it too." Parthena nodded as did Morgan.

"You can't marry him," Parthena said, her voice choked with panic and tears. "She can't." She faced her husband and then Lucas, her expression filled with entreaty.

"Which is why you've altered your normal elegant form of dress into one better suited to a millworker," Morgan commented.

Parthena bit her lip to forestall crying as her sister nodded her agreement. "I should have noticed sooner. I should have paid more attention. Forgive me, Viv."

"I think we know what it is you and Morgan desire, Mrs. Wheeler. Why don't we ascertain what your sister wants?" Lucas turned to an ashen Genevieve. "Miss Tyler?" he asked in a softly coaxing voice. "What is it that you desire?"

"I want to be free to play the violin. I want to not fear my husband," she said in a rush. "I don't want to have to leave Boston."

"You play the violin?" Lucas asked. At her nod, he smiled. "How fascinating to have two artists among sisters."

"Ironic," Morgan said, "considering their father detests music."

Parthena snorted. "I think we started playing just to annoy him. And then we realized how much we loved it."

"And to gain some attention from him, even if it wasn't always positive," Genevieve said, sharing a secret smile with her eldest sister. She clasped hands with Parthena for a moment before looking up to see Lucas's curious gaze and flushed.

Lucas crossed his legs as he studied the sisters. "I can't promise that I will be able to come to your aid in the manner you hope. I've received troubling news in the past few days." He shook his head to silence any inquiries to extrapolate further. "However, I want you to know that I am considering all that can be done to help you, Miss Tyler. Including what my part in that might be." He shared an intense stare with Parthena before breaking eye contact and watching Genevieve.

CHAPTER TWENTY-ONE

Two weeks after the disastrous Massachusetts vote, where 64.5 percent of the men of Massachusetts voted NO to universal enfranchisement, the women of the movement met. They decided to meet at historic Faneuil Hall. Many of the movement liked the symbolism of using the hall to signal they were far from defeated. The upstairs meeting area was packed with women and men supportive of the movement, the wooden floor filled with wooden folding chairs. A large painting of the American forefathers hung behind the platform at one end of the room where a lectern stood. Anemic light filtered in through the high windows along the galley, with little sunlight passing through the thick gray clouds outside.

Sophie found a seat next to Parthena, Rowena, and Delia. She exchanged nods with others present but refrained from mingling as she settled onto the hard, uncomfortable chair. Most remained standing as they engaged each other, and so the four women had privacy for their conversation as no one sat near them. They spoke in hushed tones to ensure their conversation remained private. "Delia, any news from Zylphia?" Sophie asked.

"I just received word from her in this morning's post. She and Teddy are enjoying their time in San Francisco." Delia smiled as she thought of her daughter. "I know she was disappointed to miss today's meeting. However, they will attend the Pan Pacific Exposition, and there will be much to engage her."

"Do you think they will extend their journey by traveling to Montana?" Parthena asked.

"I'm uncertain. I think Zee would like Teddy to visit Montana, but winters are quite dreary there. Besides, I'd like her home for Christmas," Delia admitted.

"I received a letter from her last week, describing the beauty of the first part of the trip. I never thought a frozen cornfield could be beautiful until she drew a small picture of it for me in her letter," Rowena said with a laugh. "She admitted being concerned that we were upset with her for missing today's meeting."

"She should spend time with her husband. They're newly married, and they won't have this time again," Florence said. "Besides, we'll be able to inform her later of any momentous decisions."

"I'd think the momentous decision will be what that young Russell boy decides to do," Sophie said with an imperious arch of her brow as she stared pointedly at Parthena.

"I fear he won't save my sister," Parthena whispered. "He doesn't want to marry where there isn't affection."

Sophie proffered a small noise but failed at her full-throated *harrumph.* "I wouldn't lose hope yet. If my sources are correct, his mother will be dead within the next day or two. I imagine he'll feel freer to act, and leave Boston if necessary, once he's stood beside his father as they bury her." She met Parthena's stunned gaze. "He may seem open and without a care in the world, but he's a deep river."

Parthena nodded. "I can't go to him. Not now. Not if he's to be my brother-in-law," she rasped.

"No, you can't," Delia said with a scowl. "Nor would he want you to. And it would be horrifically unfair to your sister, if they are to marry."

Rowena shook her head at Parthena. "You acted like you let him go months ago, P.T. You have to do it now. You can't continue to pine for a man you'll never have. It's not fair to him or to your husband."

Parthena nodded. "He would be a good husband to Viv." She closed her eyes. "I hate imagining holiday dinners." She fought a smile as Sophie snorted and Delia laughed.

"Yes, they would be awkward. But, by that point, you'd have your own children, your own family, and your memories would have faded," Sophie said with a pointed stare.

"What does your sister think of him?" Delia asked.

"She isn't convinced she wants to marry, but she knows that he is a much better option than the man my father has chosen for her. I think she worries that Lucas will dither too long and she will be forced to flee on her own or succumb to my father's will."

"You must reassure her and inform her of what you just learned about Lucas," Sophie said.

"Yes, but does she like him?" Rowena asked. "If she at least likes him, it's a good beginning for a marriage."

"I think she does. She likes that he's a musician and won't resent her disappearing to play the violin. She likes that he is wealthy but not snob-by about it. She likes how he talks about his sister." Parthena shrugged.

"We know he's an honorable man. If your sister is too witless to discover that for herself, there is little hope for her, with or without your aid," Sophie said, her hands gripping the handle of her cane.

Parthena nodded.

More women moved to the chairs, and the foursome was soon surrounded by fellow suffragists who had fought hard for the referendum. Parthena spoke in a carrying voice, changing the topic. "I can't imagine what they could plan that would be momentous, considering that all four ballot measures in four different states failed two weeks ago. I'd think Mrs. Catt and Mrs. Shaw would be panicking right now with their chosen course."

Sophie *harrumphed.* "Anyone with sense would know what we need to do. However, I will be patient and listen to our esteemed leaders to see if they have come to the same conclusion I have."

They turned toward the front of the convention hall as the chairwoman rose to stand in front of the lectern. After a few moments the hall silenced, and the speeches began. Within a few minutes, it was apparent to all present.

The course was set.

The next fight would be for a national constitutional amendment.

The battle had just begun.

Historical Notes

When I thought about my Banished Saga, I never planned on writing this book. However, I learned about the struggle for the vote in Massachusetts when I visited a friend and saw a piece of propaganda that was used in 1915. You will recognize it as the metal bird that Zee designs and is given out at her art show. Thus, when I decided to write this, I thought I'd write a short novella. However, as you probably know by now, I don't write short stories often, and it evolved into a full-length novel. (And I had a lot of fun writing it!)

The drawing for The Suffragist by Nina Allender was in a March edition of the Suffragist, but I thought it was a wonderful drawing and used it in June in my novel.

The Remonstrance Against Women's Suffrage cited in the novel was released in July 1915, but it worked for late June in my novel.

Author's Notes

Thank you for reading *Unrelenting Love*. Never fear, dear reader, I'm already busy at work on the next two books in the series. I hope you will continue to join me on this journey.

Would you like to know more about behind the scenes, insider scoop of my writing process? Would you like to receive special bonuses not available to everyone? Would you like to know first when my next book is available? You can sign up for my new release e-mail list, where you'll be the first to know of updates and special giveaways at http://www.ramonaflightner.com/newsletter/

Or, you can like my Facebook page for frequent updates: http://facebook.com/authorramonaflightner

Reviews help other readers find books. I appreciate all reviews. Please consider reviewing on the retailer you purchased the book, at Goodreads or both.

Most people learn about books by recommendations from their friends. Please, share *Unrelenting Love* with a friend!

Made in the USA
Columbia, SC
26 April 2017